The
House by
the Creek

Elizabeth
BROMKE
The
House by
the Creek

bookouture

Published by Bookouture in 2022

An imprint of Storyfire Ltd.
Carmelite House
50 Victoria Embankment
London EC4Y 0DZ

www.bookouture.com

ISBN: 978-1-83790-162-3
eBook ISBN: 978-1-80314-648-5

Previously published as *Home to Brambleberry Creek* (978-1-80314-649-2)

For Dorothy Rita Flanagan, the best storyteller west of the Mississippi.

PROLOGUE
1958

Essie

If there was one thing Esther Nelson loved to do, it was picking blackberries. Raspberries, too. Well, any kind of berry, so long as it grew on a vine and sat plump and ripe and sweet and ready to be eaten.

She plucked a purple-black, dimpled blackberry now. Studying it, she swung her braid back off her shoulder, then popped the precious wild fruit in her mouth. A blast of tart succulence cleared her sinuses and puckered her lips. She squeezed her eyes shut, her nostrils flared, and an involuntary shudder coursed through her slender body.

Billy Coyle, who watched her, clicked his tongue and scowled. "You're gonna get good 'n' sick from picking wild berries and eatin' 'em."

She gave him a look. "You didn't grow up eating fruit right off of the earth?"

"Naw." He kicked at a rock, and together they continued along the back fence of Esther's daddy's farm. They were different, Esther and Billy. Different, but also the same. Their parents worked hard to make ends meet, and they'd grown up just a stone's throw one from th'other. But whereas Esther shared her life with twelve siblings brung up on a sprawling family farm, Billy Coyle was an only child brung up down in a holler just north of Brambleberry. And whereas Esther's daddy raised tobacco and bootlegged moonshine, Billy's daddy dug graves. That's how Billy had come to take up a job in the morgue at Louisville City Hospital. The mortician and groundskeeper at the local cemetery were ol' pals.

Anyway, it was the hospital where the young lovebirds had met. Esther, a candy striper, took her smoke break at the exact same time as Billy, the mortician's assistant.

Now, here they were, on their third date. Supper in the big house with Daddy and Mom and a walk around the farm after. If everything went well, Billy was going to take her for a drive in his brand-new, cherry-red Ford pickup truck.

Esther hadn't been nervous about introducing Billy to her folks. They'd met the boys she went out with here and there. In a family as big as hers, friends and secret boyfriends came and went more often than the train that ran down the tracks that split the town in two. And, what, with Esther as the youngest of the bunch, she'd been given extra leeway, anyhow. Well, *technically* the youngest. She was made the youngest after the death of her twin, Dottie, who passed when the pair were just ten. But that was another story.

"What'd you grow up eating?" she asked Billy, half teasing and half serious.

He gave her a sidelong look then shrugged. "Regular food my mother prepares."

"Well, I eat that, too. But for a snack, wild berries hit the spot." She grabbed another off the vine as they strode by a hanging spur chock-full of ripe berries. Popping that one in her mouth, she added, "Anyway, why would anybody get sick from them?"

"You never know. Some berries are poisonous."

Billy's nervousness was a new thing in Esther's world. A world in which children rolled down hills and got all cut up, and in which adults worked from sunup to sundown and didn't have time to worry about things like poison.

Esther and Billy's walk ended at the far side of the tobacco hangar, where sheaths of leaves hung drying. The heavy, earthen musk of the plant blew out of the wood-sided building and knocked them hard.

"Woo-wee!" Billy cried. "Smells like pure heaven." He grinned ear to ear, and Esther's heart settled, her mind, too, now that their spat about berries had resolved. They'd moved on to safer topics, like the good smell of drying tobacco. Or 'baccy, as Daddy called it.

Esther smiled back and turned to face him, her braid slipping over her shoulder again, and her whole rail-thin body facing Billy Coyle and away from the big house and the rest of the expanse that was the Moonshine Creek Farm.

"Now, Esther Nelson." Billy's smile fell away and he gave her a stern look, like he might be aggravated with her all over again. "Now, I want to talk serious about somethin'."

"All right." Esther couldn't imagine what serious thing he might want to talk about. Maybe his daddy was real sick. Maybe Billy was sick. Or moving. Sometimes that happened. People who made their way out of the holler and into big cities got the bug sometimes. And they just kept running. Maybe that was Billy. He might be a runner. She steeled herself for such an admission.

Instead, though, he grabbed her shoulders real firm and stared into her eyes real deep, and said, "You got a choice to make, Esther."

"A choice?" Esther didn't know much about choices. She'd been brung up as the baby of the family, and rarely did she ever have to choose between two things. "What choice?"

His lips worked themselves in and out of a straight line. "Now, you been running around with other boys, too. I know. So you got to choose, see. You can keep running around or," he swallowed and his lips worked in and out again, "or else ya marry me."

Esther's stomach flipped. *Marriage.* She did want to get married. And Billy could sure be a great lot of fun. But a nagging question wedged its way up into her throat and came out her mouth. "Are you gonna let me eat wild berries?"

He seemed to think soberly for a moment, but after just a couple of beats, he gave her an earnest nod. "So long as you're careful. I don't want to marry someone who's liable to go off and do something stupid."

His harsh words ought to have been a slap in the face.

They weren't.

Excitement or thrill, or maybe just pure love, took over, and Esther gave right in. "I'll be careful."

But she lied.

Not on purpose. Not to hurt Billy.

She lied, because she wasn't a careful person. She wasn't raised to be.

She was raised by her daddy and mamaw and older sisters and brothers. And if they'd taught her anything, it was that life wasn't about being careful. That in this world, you took risks. You rolled down grassy hills in your Sunday dress, and you ran around with boys until one of them asked you to marry him, and you picked wild berries. And you ate them, too.

And call her stupid if you want to, but that's just how Essie Nelson's marriage began there along the vine-covered fences of her family's farm in Brambleberry Creek.

CHAPTER ONE
PRESENT DAY

Morgan Jo

Red-orange sunlight sank below the mountains, casting a warm glow across the patio. The color soaked through the floor-to-ceiling windows of that mid-century ranch-style house in which Morgan Jo Coyle now stood.

It did not belong to her, though. Not the view. Not the house.

Morgan found herself entranced by the waning light, as if the sunset itself was tugging her with it, pulling her through the desert, beyond the mountain, and clear down to the far side of the earth. Pulling her away from the house and her clients and back to Brambleberry Creek, her hometown. It was as though she didn't belong in Arizona.

Of course, that sensation was decidedly wrong, because Morgan *wanted* to be there, in a house for sale in Arizona. She wanted to be the realtor selling the house. She wanted to go home after, to her three-bedroom townhouse on the fairway of one of Tucson's nicest golf courses. She didn't own it, not yet, but that was coming. According to Morgan's boyfriend of a year,

Nick, fall in the Old Pueblo was just the start of the busy season for real estate. Snowbirds flew in and locals itched for a change, since in the desert, they didn't exactly get the seasonal overhaul that other places enjoyed.

She hadn't originally set out from her tiny hometown in Kentucky for the dry riverbeds of the southwest, but it wasn't too far a cry from her initial goal, which was the West Coast. Arizona came close, sharing the sunlight and the vistas with her Californian neighbor, and there were jobs. Jobs and good places to rent.

And there was Nick.

One of Morgan's clients came into the great room, rediscovering that succulent sunset all over again after her third walkthrough. "It's breathtaking," the impeccably dressed woman confirmed. She moved a sheet of her long, salon-blonde hair over her shoulder. Morgan spotted a diamond ring the size of a whiskey barrel on the woman's ring finger. In a bizarre way, the jewel matched her fingernails, French tips that weren't too long or too short but had to be *too expensive*. For someone like Morgan, at least. Then, the glamorous woman lifted her voice toward the bedrooms on the south side of the house, where her husband had been lingering. "Babe!"

The husband appeared instantly, swaggering over in a fitted blue suit. With each step, it sheened in the creases. If they were back in Kentucky, he'd be headed for the Derby. Well, assuming that he spent most of his days in an outskirts town like Brambleberry Creek or Bardstown. Men who dressed in suits there were attorneys or accountants, and they itched to get home and pull on a pair of jeans and boots and head out on the Gator for a ride in the woods.

Morgan's client, the man in the blue suit, was a restauranteur with a chain of high-end restaurants in Catalina Foothills. He probably wore that suit to bed.

Then again, even Morgan's boyfriend, Nick, wore dapper

tailored suits, too. He was every bit the bespoke gentleman that Morgan had never in her life known before. It was equally alluring and off-putting, actually. Which was why Morgan appreciated spending time with Nick after hours, when he wore his running digs instead. Morgan wished Nick had come along to deal with this particular couple. He'd wow them more than she could. He'd speak their language. Without him, she'd be nothing more than her Greater-Louisville-area twang. Oh, well. It'd have to do.

The husband cupped his wife's elbow and lowered his eyebrows at Morgan. "It *is* beautiful. But market comps are well below the asking for this house."

Morgan had practiced her response. "Everything's negotiable." Had she been too quick to say that? She backtracked smoothly. "But this property is on a full acre and offers both an Olympic-sized swimming pool and a hot tub. That's not to mention the many upgrades we've already discussed." She gave them a winning grin. Maybe it was working, Morgan's approach. She looked at the wife and pointed out, "We've got four more properties to look at tomorrow. Each of those is *juuuust* south of your preferred school district, but not to worry —Arizona has open enrollment!"

Schools were critical to people like these. Morgan could not relate. Formal schooling was tangential to her upbringing. All she needed to know in life, she'd learned living on her grandparents' farm. It was there that Memaw had taught Morgan to balance a checkbook. There, Granddad had taught her to change a tire and check the oil and change that, too. Then there were the animals. In Brambleberry Creek, sex ed happened right there on the farm in the spring, when you inseminated a heifer.

In Morgan's childhood world, there were no fancy school uniforms or skiing trips, but she wouldn't change it for anything.

Her remark about the school district had its desired effect

because Morgan noted a quick flash of panic streaking across the wife's face.

Morgan sucked in a quick breath. She was out of tactics, and though applying friendly pressure was okay, she refused to take it farther. She wanted her clients, above all else, to make choices they were comfortable with and would later be happy about.

Choices were everything in life. Morgan knew this all too well. She'd made a slew of them, good and bad. She'd chosen to go to college. She'd chosen to break up with her high school sweetheart and roam the Midwest looking for something that would make her happy.

When that failed, she'd chosen to go back home to Brambleberry Creek.

Then, she made the choice to interfere in a family matter.

And that choice had gotten her here: to Arizona. Thousands of miles away from home with a good job and a good boyfriend and a good life. Good enough, at least.

Morgan clapped her hands together, smiled at her clients, and then opened her mouth to speak again, until she was cut off.

From the front door came the loud and distinctive voice of none other than Morgan's boyfriend and real estate colleague, Nick Martinez. Morgan followed her clients' worried stares to see Nick, who was speaking loudly on his phone and generally ignoring their presence. "Tonight, yes! We've got a showing going on now, but—" He looked up, his phone still stuck to his ear. Then, he pressed a hand over the receiver. "Oh, Ms. Coyle —I am *so* sorry. I should have knocked louder." He gave a regretful grimace and indicated the door behind him.

Morgan, confused by his very presence and even more so by his showy phone call, glanced quickly at the couple, offering a meek apology before moving with care over the Santa Fe–style area rug and toward Nick, her eyes locked on his in a *what's going on?* glare.

Nick kept his voice louder than it had to be as he continued his phone call. "I'll see you here at the property in half an hour." Then he lowered the phone, making a show of hitting the red end-call button. "Morgan, again, I am *so* sorry," he boomed, but the lascivious look in his eye told Morgan he was not sorry at all. He was delightful about this little game he seemed to be playing. Nick leaned into Morgan, gripped her elbow, and said low but not quietly, "We have an offer." But his touch was cold and his words slick. Morgan felt her skin crawl. She wanted to tell her boyfriend that she'd rather do this the *right* way, but by the time she mustered the courage to whisper such an affront to him, Nick had turned away and fiddled on his phone, putting his back to his ear for another conversation. Apparently.

Morgan turned slowly and went back to her clients. "I'm so sorry about this."

The woman asked, "What's going on? Who is that?"

Morgan took a breath and balanced herself before replying. "This is, um, this is Nick Martinez. He's another agent at Casas Adobes Realty. We work together, and—"

"I'll see what their situation is and get right back to you!" Nick was there now, ending his "phone call." He pocketed his device and lifted his hand in supplication to the couple. "I am *genuinely* sorry. I didn't realize Morgan was still here. I have a showing—well, a *second* showing." He slapped the heel of his hand to his head. "I mean I have clients coming to look at this home a second time. I don't want to overstep." He moved his hand to his heart. "So, I'll head out. You take your time." He looked at Morgan meaningfully and squeezed her shoulder, another ingratiating performance. "If you need me, give me a ring."

Once he was out the door, the husband and wife gave each

other one last look. The husband said, "I guess we *will* make an offer."

Morgan let out the breath she'd been holding. "Okay. We'll get the paperwork going back at the office."

Nick had already disappeared, and the couple left next, eager to sink their claws into the hot piece of real estate, made hotter by Nick's cool act. Technically, what he'd done was fine. Morgan knew this house *was* generating a ton of attention and there were at least three more showings later in the day. So, it wasn't that Nick pointed all that out. It was how he did it. But she had to shake her frustration with him, because he was helping her, and she needed his help.

Morgan had to do a quick walk through and lock up. As she moved through the house, it occurred to Morgan just how much easier it was for her, physically, considering her hip injury. It was an old wound, from years before, but a serious one that sometimes affected her comfort and mobility.

Whereas here, in this foothills ranch-style house, the tiles spread smoothly from room to room and the area rugs were clean and low pile, back home, at Brambleberry, wood flooring gave way to rumpled knotted rugs and the first floor led up to the second floor, then the attic. Don't forget about the basement down below. Or the barn out back. Or the other houses with the cobbled walkways. Everything in Brambleberry Creek was tiered, leveled, up and down and never a straight line.

But here, in this sunset-kissed cowboy home that cost more than Morgan was ever likely to see in her life, she could move about just fine. It was *easy*. It was the path she'd chosen and now trod. Maybe Morgan would never need therapy if she stayed here and kept doing this. Maybe the limp from her injury would go away and with it, her troublesome past in Brambleberry Creek, Kentucky.

CHAPTER TWO
PRESENT DAY

Morgan Jo

That night, after finalizing the paperwork, submitting it, and returning home, Morgan settled at the table with a microwavable dinner—cauliflower mac 'n' cheese. Her people back in Kentucky would die to know what Morgan had succumbed to, especially her friends. A memory of high school floated into her brain.

Emmett Dawson, Morgan's first boyfriend, first *love*, had come over to the big house. He'd had grand plans to fix supper for the whole family. The menu included fried pork chops, mashed potatoes, collard greens, and fresh-baked rolls. He'd gotten all gussied up in Wranglers and a button-down, tucked in and stiff. His hair was gelled. He smelled like his daddy's aftershave. Cooking dinner had taken longer than he'd planned, and Morgan had felt all awkward about it. Her family, though, had loved it. They were the reason it took forever. Her mother kept trying to add butter and Memaw kept trying to add sugar, and even Grandad Bill kept interrupting the process to tell a story or two. By the time the night was over, Morgan was certain she'd have to end the relationship. She couldn't see herself spending five hours cooking pork chops and letting Grandad Bill carry on and on about this and that while the women micromanaged her boyfriend's cooking.

She didn't break up with Emmett. Not that night, at least. The food was too damn good.

No. Morgan had broken up with him on another night. One that had been more important. The summer before they each left for college, Morgan and Emmett had gotten permission to go up to Bardstown for a date night. It was meant to be special, and indeed, all concerned parties had trumped the affair up to something much bigger than a teenage night out. Morgan's mom had paid for her to get highlights and a haircut. Emmett had worn a button-down shirt. He never wore a button-down shirt. He'd smelled different, too. Not a bad different. Probably a *good* different, but Morgan's mind had been a million miles away. It had been focused on college and leaving Brambleberry Creek, and the farm and then the show. The show had stirred something in her.

They'd gotten tickets to see *My Old Kentucky Home* performed on a riverboat on the Ohio. The songs, the actors— Morgan was seeing and feeling the world anew for the first time in her life. She'd seen boys who were a little older and a little cuter. But the sights couldn't hold a candle to how she'd felt. *What was it, that feeling?* Memaw probably would have called it an *itch*.

When the play was over, they were supposed to have rushed through dinner and then lingered off onto some backroad for kissing and fooling around. In fact, dinner had gone fast. Morgan hardly touched her food. Her mind was still on Stephen Foster's characters and the cute lead with his skin-tingling voice. Emmett, too, had acted differently. He'd gobbled up his food, betraying all the gentlemanliness he'd usually abided by. He'd asked for the check and barely made eye contact with Morgan.

The drive home had been quiet. When they'd pulled up to the farm, a good hour ahead of curfew, Emmett hadn't even moved to get out and open her door. Morgan, angry with him for not trying hard and angry with herself for not caring if he did, had crossed her arms and pouted. "Aren't you gon' come in and say good night to everyone?" she'd asked.

"Morgan Jo," he'd replied, quiet like a church mouse. Calm. Eerily so. "Are we going to stay together?"

She'd been shocked. Breaking up with Emmett had never once been an option. Now here he'd been, *suggesting* it. Morgan hadn't stopped to ask him why he'd asked that or what he had wanted. Instead, being an eighteen-year-old with a newfound interest in theater (an interest that hadn't lasted), Morgan scoffed, indignant and self-righteous. "I guess not." Then, she'd let herself out of his truck and never looked back.

Morgan shook her head free of thoughts from the past and stabbed a cauliflower noodle and popped it in her mouth. Living alone in a new city presented different obstacles entirely. Only a year in, and Morgan had come to learn that cooking what she was used to made little sense. A pitcher of sweet tea would go bad over the week it took to finish off. Fried chicken took too long to make and ended up too greasy, anyway. Collard greens lost their flavor altogether.

On the plus side, Morgan had lost five of the pesky fifteen pounds she'd gained and sustained over the course of her twenties. Maybe another month or two and she'd be down to her precollege weight. A girl could dream, couldn't she?

Finishing the last of the uninspired (at best) and bland (at worst) dish, Morgan turned her cell phone in her hands, debating whether to call Nick or let it go. She'd spent the better half of the evening musing on his interruption at the property. Yes, his scheme had helped her move the house. Her commission would lend wonderfully to the down payment she needed. But it wasn't Morgan's style. And the fact that it was apparently *Nick's* style? Well, it made him a little less attractive.

But just as she was clearing her microwave dinner from the table and running over the faux-stone top with a Clorox wipe, a knock came at the door.

Morgan stilled herself before bracing against the table, then the chair, then the breakfast bar on her way to the door. She peered through the peephole to confirm. *Nick.* Looking more handsome in his running shirt and shorts. His hair a little mussed. More normal. Less salesy. His attractiveness returned, and her heart did miniature leaps in her chest. There was no mistaking infatuation, even in the face of questionable ethics.

"Hi." She smiled at him, holding on to the doorknob as he stepped in.

Nick looped a hand around her waist, dipping her back and planting a swoony kiss on her mouth, before scooping her up—those extra ten pounds be damned—and whisking her to the sofa, where he set her gently.

The thing about Nick, apart from his good looks, was his protectiveness. He didn't mind that Morgan had a mild limp from an old injury. He didn't mind, not one bit. If anything, it endeared her to him. He treated her with kid gloves, and it was sort of nice. To be tended to and cared for. She hadn't gotten that treatment back home on the family farm. There, she was expected to be normal. Even when the old injury flared up. Act normal. Do normal things like mow and weed-whack and clear the garden in the spring and—

"Congratulations." He kissed her tenderly on her cheek and eased into his corner of the sofa. "That was a hell of a sale, Morgan." She watched him, almost removed from her own body, as he patted her thigh. Here it was again, the to and fro. The here and there of her affections for Nick. Hot. Cold.

"I didn't do it alone," she said cryptically, but he turned his face to the kitchen, stood for a moment, and then walked towards it.

"Tonight we celebrate. What kind of wine do you have on hand?" He lifted an eyebrow back at her. "Or champagne?"

"Um..." She faltered and frowned, thinking. "Nothing fancy." But she *did* like the idea of celebrating. "What if we go to the hot tub instead? Maybe slip in under the cover of darkness? Let the water and the jets loosen us up?" If it weren't a community hot tub, she'd suggest to Nick that they skinny-dip, but it was a public space, and Nick didn't really like the water.

In fact, he ignored her idea entirely. "What kind of realtor doesn't keep a top-shelf bottle of Merlot on hand?"

Morgan felt the twist of an argument corkscrew its way up from her guts, through her chest, crawl out of her throat, and there it was. She picked a fight. "What kind of realtor lies?"

He froze, the fridge door open; cool air escaping every moment. Swiveling her way, he flashed a grin. "Huh?"

"You pretended you had another offer on the line," she replied bluntly.

He closed the fridge and opened the cabinet above it, still looking hard for that bottle of wine she did have on hand but hadn't pointed out quite yet. "Morgan, that's part of the game. And, anyway, I *did* have a client in mind for that house. No doubt he'd have snapped it right up, if I'd expanded his criteria just a tad."

"You lied," she repeated. "It was kind of scammy, Nick."

He let out a sigh and closed the cabinet doors. "You've never lied before?"

"Not professionally, no."

"So, personally, then?"

Morgan set her jaw, blinking thoughtfully. "I mean, obviously I've probably told small lies. But not to con someone."

"Morgan, were they planning to buy a house or not?"

"They were."

"And were they interested in that particular house or not?"

"Well, yeah."

"All we did was apply the right amount of pressure to help them *decide*." He leaned against her counter, a grin curling his lips mischievously. "We made someone's dream come true."

Morgan pushed up from the sofa and ambled towards Nick, returning his grin with a coy one of her own, until she arrived beside him at the sink and reached teasingly across his body. She pulled open the breadbox, and rolled out an unopened bottle of blackberry wine, a gift from her grandad's waning stock back home. "Then I guess a toast is in order." She held the bottle by the neck, lifting it with one hand and scooching in front of Nick to grab a pair of wine glasses with the other.

"That's my girl," Nick coaxed, taking the bottle from her and inspecting the label-less glass. "What is this?"

She nudged him to pour her a glass. "It's from my papaw. He used to make wine. A bottle here or there."

"Cool," Nick responded, pouring two glasses, then hesitating as he lifted his goblet for a toast. "Does he run a vineyard, or—?"

"Nope." She closed her eyes, clinked her glass against Nick's, and said, "To making dreams come true."

They both swigged, and Morgan recoiled at the sharp taste. Nick seemed unfazed, though. He swished the drink in his mouth before swallowing. "He's good."

"*Was* good," Morgan corrected, wincing at the bitter aftertaste. The recipe was fine, she thought. It tasted like wine. But it lacked the smoothness she was used to in store-bought stuff.

"Your grandfather passed?" He looked alarmed at first, but it passed and his face twisted into some version of sympathy. "Oh. Right. I knew that."

She nodded slowly, engrossed for the moment in the final memory she had of her grandad. A bitter one, to be sure. Not quite as bitter as the wine, though. "Throat cancer. Remember?"

"Yeah. Crazy. I suppose that's what happens when you smoke and chew." Nick offered, shaking his head and studying the glass more intently. "Should we be drinking this, then? I mean—do you have more? Other bottles?"

Morgan frowned, as if she had to think about it. But she didn't, of course. She had the answer right there, on the tip of her tongue, at the front of her brain, in the center of her heart. "I don't. But my grandmother does, I think."

"Are you sure?"

She glanced up at Nick, her mind swimming in recollections. "I don't know." She let out a sigh and downed the rest of the drink. "I haven't talked to her since his funeral."

He knew this, of course. Morgan had already told Nick all about the *incident*. Further proof that no matter how far she ran, Morgan would never be far enough away from Brambleberry Creek.

CHAPTER THREE

PRESENT DAY

Essie

Essie Coyle was beating rugs on the back porch when the phone rang inside. She cursed and set the broom down, moving elegantly into the kitchen and scooping up the receiver from its cradle but not before glancing at the caller ID. "Hey, girl," she cooed to her eldest daughter.

"Mom," CarlaMay started in on her, rattling off a list of gripes as she always did when she set about calling her mom. "Amber's bathtub is clogged from here to the Mississippi. Travis says his furnace won't kick on, and I know—*I know*, it's *July*, but we may as well get ahead of that, too. Now I've already snaked the tub, but as for the heater, I checked the pilot light, and it's on, so I have no idea what to do."

Essie replied, "If Billy were here, he'd know what to do. He was so good at plumbing." Her voice turned dreamy with thoughts of her husband. Bill Coyle had died just about four years ago. After that, life had changed for Essie. Well, it had changed before his death, when things were going downhill in the family and especially with ol' Bill. But neither time nor hard memories would suck away the heartache Essie felt when she conjured up his name. "Billy was so good at *ever'thing*." The dream snapped shut like the heavy lid of a wooden jewelry box. "But I can't do it, CarlaMay."

Sometimes Essie wondered if CarlaMay remembered her mama was in her eighties, because she sure acted like Essie was still thirty-six and held the world in her hands.

Of course, Essie felt like she was still thirty-six. She'd felt like she was thirty-six since she *was* thirty-six. Like time stood still at that perfect number. Maybe it was because she'd had her last baby at thirty-six. Maybe it was because she'd turned the corner financially at thirty-six. It was a big age for her, that was no doubt. Nowadays, though, Essie figured she looked good for her age.

However, a good diet and physical activity (mostly in the way of cleaning and working) could only carry a female form so far. They couldn't change the slight stoop in her walk or her skinny legs and knobby knees. All the bathtub scrubbing in the world couldn't lift her sagging boobs—although a great bra did help. As for her face, well, the wrinkles that had come with years of working the farm put up a good fight against makeup. Even so, Essie liked doing herself up. Creamy foundation helped to smooth out even the deepest lines. Blossoms of blush brought back her high cheekbones. Only a few strokes of mascara and her blue eyes went from watery to piercing. Lastly, a heavy application of her favorite red lipstick took ten years off her mouth. When Essie put her face on, she looked real pretty. People at church had told her as much. And she got even *more* compliments when she had her white hair dyed back to its original black color and set in rollers for a good coupla hours. The only thing was that she'd usually needed help with all that, which was why she liked having at least one of her daughters at home. Daughters were good for that sort of thing, helping bring out their mama's innate beauty.

"And that's not all," CarlaMay added with a huff. "This morning—where *were* you?"

Essie missed the questions, because she was busy thinking about how she was getting sick of making repairs for her grandchildren who doubled as tenants at the farm. They were lazy and good-for-nothin' and old enough to make their own repairs. Now that Billy was dead and gone and the others had moved away and moved on, shouldn't the ones left behind step up a little more? Essie thought so. It would help with her worry if the three grandchildren who *did* live there at the farm, in the back houses, stepped up and took on some of the work.

"Well?" CarlaMay said, moving Essie to action.

"Well, what?" Essie asked.

"Where *were* you this morning? You missed your appointment."

Essie frowned. "Oh, *that*." Sure enough, she was supposed to have been at the lawyer's office at nine. She squinted at the grandfather clock in the hall that led out from the kitchen to the front rooms. It was quarter after ten. Essie wasn't a forgetful woman. And truth be told, she hadn't forgotten that appointment, either. But CarlaMay didn't know any better. Best thing was for her to think Essie was slipping. If CarlaMay and the other kids figured Mom was slipping, it could only work in Essie's favor. More sympathy. More concern. More *attention*. "I done forgot, CarlaMay."

"Oh, Mom." It came out like a whisper on the phone line. "It's okay. The lawyer'll meet us this afternoon."

Hell. "I've got a hair appointment, CarlaMay." It wasn't that Essie didn't want to settle her affairs. In fact, she'd settled and resettled her affairs at least a dozen times in as many years. But it was that she was waiting on someone.

CarlaMay must have sensed this. She said, "We'll reschedule your hair appointment, Mom. You've got to come to the lawyer's office. What if—*you know*. I mean, nothing *will* happen, but you never know. You know?" CarlaMay was in a right tizzy, and Essie couldn't blame her. Especially if she figured her mama was slipping.

"It's just I need to talk to her first."

CarlaMay didn't have to ask who. She knew. She knew that Essie was holding out for her eldest granddaughter. Her favorite. The apple of her cataract-ridden eye.

CarlaMay's own daughter.

Morgan Jo.

CHAPTER FOUR

PRESENT DAY

Morgan Jo

The whipping storms of monsoon season carried Morgan from July into August like a sailboat tumbling through rough seas.

She toiled away that summer, trying to move houses in a blistering heat unlike any she'd encountered back home. Fall couldn't come soon enough, and not only for its promise of cooler mornings and chilly nights, but because Nick assured her that the market would heat up.

It was on one such muggy night—and *muggy* was an unusual state for the city of Tucson to be in—that Morgan got the phone call.

She and Nick were at her house, where she'd fixed up a southern dinner. Fried pork chops, a buttery casserole, home-made yeast rolls, and a store-bought apple pie—for shame. She'd kept her phone on silent and plugged into her charger on the breakfast bar. It was any wonder she heard the faint buzzing.

And she probably wouldn't have, either, if it weren't for the quietness of their supper. Nick had been talking shop, mostly, discussing a fixer-upper down near the university. It sounded like Morgan's dream project. An older home with original cherry-wood floors and crumbling adobe bricks; the small property was hidden away from the college scene by a thicket fence made purely of ocotillos. Morgan didn't much care for desert landscape or design, but she relished the history—and the chance at a remodel. There was something about fixing history that had embedded itself in Morgan's heart long ago. Probably because she'd grown up in a house that was always a work in progress. Farms, unless they were the so-called "modern farmhouse," were always work. Morgan liked that. It meant she always had something to do, and getting stuff done was a source of pride for Coyle women.

Also, though, Morgan dreamed of having a home of her own, something she could make *hers*. After years of living with family, the desire to build one's life from the ground up sprouted like a weed. Morgan could pinpoint her dream to this very fact—that she'd always been a hanger-on. Never quite the mistress of her own world.

The fixer-upper was where their conversation had gotten hung up, though, with Nick forgetting that Morgan's dream had been crushed the day she'd suffered her injury. That she couldn't very well complete a grand-scale remodel, even on a smaller home, without substantial help. It wasn't so much the work itself that Morgan couldn't do but rather the moving around to get the work done. Ladders were almost impossible. And her range of movement, or lack thereof, made it difficult to pull weeds with efficiency, load and unload materials or appliances. All of those tasks were very likely a part of Morgan's past. While a different person might rejoice in having a built-in excuse to avoid heavy labor, Morgan regretted it. She liked to work with her hands and make something out of nothing, just like Grandad.

Plus, Nick really wasn't one for the job. He preferred to move turnkey homes. This was a major point of divergence for the couple—Morgan sometimes wondered at how she could respect a man without calluses on his hands. But, to his credit, he had to admit this particular home had great potential for serious profit. Maybe he'd change. Maybe he'd find that he enjoyed stripping paint, sanding floors, and replacing toilets.

Morgan had her doubts. And she had her limitations. "I wish I could just take it on all by myself. It'd be a dream project, like when I helped renovate one of the bunkhouses on the farm when I was a kid."

"Morgan," Nick said in a low voice. "Selling real estate is easier than flipping houses, anyway." He moved his hand to the top of hers and gave it a squeeze. "I know you thought you'd get in there and do the nitty-gritty, but..." His voice trailed off and his gaze fell dramatically, as if he was reliving *her* tragedy. The shattering of her left hip, the shredding of the surrounding tissue, and the whole event sending irreparable shock waves through the rest of her body—it was an experience that Nick would never understand. Especially if he preferred the easy ways in life. Morgan held back her opinion on that and rubbed the metal implant made to function as her hip.

Even though it happened five years prior, it felt fresh, that wound. Not the physical one, no. But the emotional one. Morgan was sensitive about the whole thing. Defiantly sensitive and defensive. She'd only ever told Nick the whole story because she'd had one glass of wine too many on their third date. A time when his newness and differentness felt so safe to her. Like a brand-new fleece blanket, fresh from the package.

The newness had worn off, and the differentness had lost its feel of safety, but she'd learned that there was a lot to love about Nick, and they shared a lot in common. Like Morgan, he was ambitious. He came from a big boisterous family and spent as much or more time with them on the weekends as he did with Morgan. Nick's adoration for his family was one of the things

Morgan loved the most about him. She only wished that it sometimes extended to at least an *interest* in her family, too.

She cleared her throat and shifted in her seat.

"Real estate is a natural place for me to be right now. But in the future, I hope to do something different." Surely, there was more to working within the housing industry than just *selling* homes. What Morgan really wanted was to take a house and bring it back to life. It went back to her deep-seated dream, the urge that lived down inside of her like it was the marrow in her bones, the blood in her veins. And really, what Morgan hoped to do wasn't something different per se. She wanted to do something *more*.

His jaw fell open. "Different?" Then he gave his head a firm shake. "You're *meant* for real estate. You're pretty, for starters. But not, like..." He searched for the right phrasing, but every moment that lapsed, Morgan grew edgier. "You're not obnoxiously hot, you're like a more girl-next-door attractive." He leaned in and pushed his fingers up beneath her hair, and she braced for a passionate kiss, but instead, Nick tugged her long chestnut strands outward and said, "See? I don't even think I've *met* a girl who doesn't bleach her roots every week. It's the Kentucky in you that's really going to succeed, babe."

"The Kentucky in me?" She raised an eyebrow. "You know, there are women in Kentucky who dye their hair. I'm just not one of them."

Nick laughed obnoxiously. "That is what I *love* about you, babe. You're *real*."

When Morgan didn't reply with anything more than a half-smile, Nick reached across and squeezed her shoulder, giving her a gentle shake. "Listen, people's dreams can change. You can decide to change your life goals, you know? Maybe when you were in Kentucky, you figured your life would look one way. And now that you're here, out in the Wild West, reality hits a little differently. Right?" Again he glanced down her body toward her bad hip. "Circumstances being what they are, how can you *not* see that?"

What she didn't say was that she was taught to know better than to settle.

But she didn't need to say anything because her phone rang.

CHAPTER FIVE

1990

Essie

For Essie's fiftieth birthday, there was a party. Oh, boy, was there *ever* a party. It was a true golden age, not only in the matriarch's personal life, but for the greater Coyle family. The birthday girl herself opted for a great big celebration at home on the farm.

What with the tobacco industry roaring, and since the Coyle place was one of Kentucky's leading production hubs, planning the shindig had to be real, real detailed. They couldn't well do it in July, Essie's birthday month proper, because every weekend was all booked up with tobacco tours *this* or harvest festivals *that*. So, they waited until late August, once the hubbub had died down but before all the kids were back to school.

Essie had all three daughters in the big house with her, helping her get all fancied up. CarlaMay steamed Essie's outfit, a pleated maroon skirt that hit just below the knees, a white button-down blouse with lace at the wrists and neck, and a gauzy chiffon vest the same color as the skirt. Essie had her hose laid out by her pumps.

BarbaraJean debated whether to do Essie's hair before or after makeup.

DanaSue argued that makeup ought to go on first, on account of the curlers getting in the way.

"How in the hell are the curlers gon' get in the way of my painting on Mom's face?" Barbara asked, hands on hips and full lips pursed. Though Barbara's predilection for sweets grated on Essie, the old woman understood there was something to be said for a woman with curves. That's what Essie read in *Ladies' Home Journal*, anyway. Whether she was big-boned or curvy, Essie loved her daughter no matter what. Period.

"Because I need Mom to lie down on the table so I can get a good angle on her brows."

"On my brows? Ain't nothing to do on my eyebrows," Essie complained.

"Fine—hair can go last." Barbara threw up her hands and swept the fruit bowl from the center of the kitchen table, though not before stealing an apple and crunching down on it harder than Essie knew was ladylike.

With DanaSue's help, Essie mounted the long farmhouse table, lying on her back and staring up at the ceiling fan. It needed dusting, and this was sure to bother Essie for time eternal if she didn't do something about it right now. "Carla-May!" she barked as DanaSue arranged jars of tinctures and brushes and paints around Essie's head. "Go get a rag and some wood oil and climb up there and clean that, honey, would you?"

CarlaMay barked back, "Mom, I'm working on your outfit. We can clean later."

Essie pointed straight above her. "That's going to drive me to drink if we don't handle it now." Then she rose up, as if to go grab the rag and oil herself, but DanaSue pulled her back down.

"Mom. Later. It's your birthday, remember? Fun? We're having *fun*?"

Essie took in a breath and let it out before smiling. DanaSue was right. She was a sweetheart, and she was right. How often did Essie get to let loose? Never, that's how often. She closed her eyes and let her youngest set about fixing up her face. It'd give her a real tickle to see what Billy thought when she emerged into the party a made-over woman. He didn't often get to see that side of her. Save for church on Sundays, but even then, Essie preferred to go with just lipstick and a fresh hairdo.

"Okay, Mom. Just close your eyes and I'll do the rest." Essie could feel her daughter work, painting her eyebrows into clean black arches to match the natural ebony hue of Essie's hair. Well, formerly natural. Lately, she'd had to take up appointments with Rita at the Cutting Edge Salon on Main Street, where black dye was carefully applied to Essie's roots. "One day," Rita had said, "you'll be the sort to let it go."

"Let it go, how?" Essie had wondered aloud.

"You know," Rita had replied. "You've got that perfect face and the perfect frame to carry off wild gray curls, like a witch."

Essie didn't mind the comparison, and even the image she held in her brain, like an important reminder for the future. *One day*, Essie sometimes told herself, *you'll turn into a witch.* But then, she didn't write her present self off as *not* a witch. She liked the idea of it. The cackling laugh and the cruel gaze she might cast when it was warranted. And sometimes such a glare *was* warranted.

DanaSue was working steadily down, pleasant as a pea and unfazed by Essie's bossing here and there. "Keep the rouge in my cheek hollers. That's what I read in *Ladies' Home Journal*. The cheek hollers."

"I know, Mom."

"And the lip liner is key," Essie said as she kept her mouth in a taut O for her daughter.

It was during the workup of the lips that Essie heard the distinct sound of one of her daughters crying.

Essie blinked and rolled her eyes left, searching for Barbara in her periphery. "Who in the hell is crying?"

No one answered her, and DanaSue suspended the cranberry-red lip liner in the air before looking over her shoulder. Essie remained prone on the table. "Is it Barbara?"

"No," Barbara replied. "It's CarlaMay. CarlaMay, why are you crying? What's wrong?"

Essie could see the edges of her daughters' bodies close in, but DanaSue remained there, at the tableside, just watching.

CarlaMay came into a better view, and Essie echoed Barbara's question. "What in the world is wrong? Did you burn my skirt?" That girl had better be crying if she burned the skirt. All of them would be.

"No," CarlaMay sobbed. "It's not the damn skirt, it's..." She flapped a hand toward Essie, let it fall, and then leaned back into Barbara. "Look at you."

"Well, shit, DanaSue, what have you done? Do I look that bad?" Essie started up, but Dana gently pressed her back down.

CarlaMay sobbed anew. "She looks like she's dead!"

"Like I'm dead? What in the Sam Hill are you talking about?"

CarlaMay joined Dana at the table and gripped Essie's hand hard. "I'm just imagining you on an undertaker's slab. Dead. Getting ready for your funeral."

Dana snorted. "I'm not doing her funeral makeup. No siree."

"It's just upsetting is all. Mom's getting old."

"I'm *fifty*, for hog's sake!" Essie couldn't take this. "What is the matter with you, CarlaMay? I'm fifty years old, getting my makeup and hair done for a party."

CHAPTER SIX

PRESENT DAY

Morgan Jo

Morgan's phone started buzzing itself clear across the breakfast bar, nearly off the tiled top and onto the Saltillo floor. She scooped it up. It was her mom.

"Hey," she answered, frowning at her wristwatch. It was seven o'clock in Tucson, which meant it was bedtime for CarlaMay out east. "Everything okay?"

Her mother's voice was low and calm, and that was the second red flag. "Morgan, Memaw had a stroke."

At first, Morgan didn't react. Maybe she was frozen from the hit of the words. *Memaw had a stroke.* Memaw had had health matters before. She'd broken things. She'd had heart scares and Morgan was fairly sure the woman had had TIAs, too.

A stroke, though? Full-blown?

Yes, Morgan's heart had hardened against the woman years back. And now her heart, well, it was nearly a vault. But maybe the vault had a crack. She swallowed, measuring her own tone and turning from Nick, who busied himself on his own cell phone. "Is she okay?" Morgan asked, almost perfunctorily.

Her mother replied, "Yes and no. She's alive. The right side of her face and body is slack; she's like a ghost, almost. She's hardly talking at all. She doesn't recognize me and seems confused about the medical people. But we got her in fast. They gave her the clot buster, and they think it'll work."

The details stirred up something deep inside of Morgan. "Wow," she managed, running her tongue over her lips and swallowing again. "Are *you* okay?" she asked her mother. Surely CarlaMay was a mess. "Are you there with her?"

"I'm here at the hospital. Right here in the room. I'm okay. A little stressed, I guess. We're up in Louisville."

"Is anyone else there with you?" Morgan was referring distinctly to her aunts and uncles, her cousins. In all, there were close to twenty kin who had stuck close to home. Sure, they might have stumbled their ways into Indiana and down south into Tennessee, but without question, they were closer than Morgan. They could get there in a jiff. Morgan gave her head a clearing shake. How quickly she fell into the state of mind that she'd be traveling back to Kentucky because Essie Coyle had had a medical incident.

But no. Morgan was not traveling back to Kentucky. Not for Essie Coyle. Not after everything that had happened.

Her mother confirmed her suspicions. "I haven't called anyone else yet."

"Mom," Morgan scolded. "Call your sisters. Call your brothers. They need to know, right?" She stole a glance over her shoulder at Nick. He hadn't yet tuned in. His head was still ducked down, his thumb was still swiping up and down and left and right over a seven-hundred-dollar phone screen.

"I'll call them in the morning. No sense in waking them. There's nothing that can be done. Not now. She's resting."

Morgan nodded. "You need to rest, too, Mom. Go home.

You can return to the hospital in the morning." Worry gnawed at Morgan's insides. Without Morgan around to absorb some of CarlaMay's anxiety and concern, it was certain that the poor woman was taking on mountains of stress beneath the veneer of composure. Morgan's mother might be a monument to handling pressure, but that didn't mean the pressure would stay at bay.

Not only that, but it sounded like Memaw wasn't doing well. Morgan forced herself to push her fears aside and remain calm.

Sure enough, CarlaMay replied, "No, no. I'm staying here. I'll want to talk to her first thing. You know how hospitals can be." But Morgan was miles away, and there was no controlling either one of the matriarchs in her life. Least of all when the other one wasn't well.

"Okay, well. Just, *please* take care of yourself too, Mom." Morgan paused and looked again at Nick, who was now watching her with doleful eyes. She pressed her mouth in a line and held up a finger at him. Then said into the phone, "Is there anything... I can *do*?" She stilled herself for the answer.

Her mother waited a beat. Then two. "Um, let's just talk in the morning. See how things are then. All right?"

"All right. Love you, Mama." Morgan let out a breath she hadn't realized she'd been holding. Her dinner sat waiting at the table, but her appetite had been gobbled up by the news of Memaw.

CHAPTER SEVEN

PRESENT DAY

Morgan Jo

"Hospital?" Nick gave Morgan a look that fell somewhere between concerned and suspicious. He knew too much about her family. He'd picked over his food. Nick was strict about his diet and comfort food didn't exactly fit into his balance of micros and macros or whatever.

Morgan cleared their plates, scooping full servings into Tupperware to have for lunch another day.

She then scraped the remnants from the plates into the trash as the sink filled with hot bubbles. Nick's eyes were on her as Morgan put together the right order of words to convey what she'd learned.

"My grandmother had a stroke. She's in the hospital." She glanced up at him, and he raised both eyebrows.

"Is this the infamous Memaw we're talking about?"

"The one and only." Morgan started scrubbing their plates.

"Why don't you use the dishwasher? I read in an article that it saves water."

Morgan frowned and shrugged. "I guess I sort of like to do it this way."

"Even when you were back there? Washing dishes for a dinner party of ten?"

A grin broke out on her mouth. "I liked doing it even more back home. 'Cause I never did it alone. There'd always be a group of us in the kitchen, gossiping and washing up after supper." She remembered little moments like that with great fondness. Even moments that included Memaw. They were the bits of cinnamon and sugar, as she liked to think of it. Her whole world there, her whole upbringing, was comprised of a pinch of cinnamon here, a spoonful of sugar there. And, anyway, it was her grandmother's cooking motto, too. Regardless of what Memaw whipped up in the kitchen, she added sugar to it. Like a bad habit—or maybe a good one.

It occurred to Morgan that Nick was staring at her, and when she looked up, she saw his arms were crossed over his chest. "That was a little passive-aggressive."

"Huh?" She worked the sponge in and out of his water glass, then rinsed it and set it on the drying towel. "What are you talking about?"

"I offered to help. When you got off the phone, I said I'd load the dishwasher. But you said no."

"Oh," Morgan laughed, "no, I didn't mean I wanted your help. I just mean that it was one of those things I liked about home. I guess it's something I miss." She must have looked guilty because Nick let out a scoff. "What?" She dried the last plate, set it on the towel, and collected her wine glass, downing the last of Grandad's wine. It tasted even more bitter now. Maybe she'd got the dregs. Maybe he didn't let the sediments settle, and she was tasting bits of berry pulp.

"What did your mom say? On the phone, I mean."

"Oh." Morgan turned and set about washing her wine glass, ruing the fact she was clear out of the good stuff. She'd have to hit the farmer's market that weekend for a new bottle, because store-bought wine was basically out of the question. Not that Morgan preferred anything fancy. She just preferred... well... not store-bought. "She said she's lost her speech so far. Half her face is drooping. Her body, too. I suppose that's the typical stroke scenario." The coldness in her voice and demeanor didn't quite match the rumblings in her chest.

"I'm really sorry to hear that. Good thing your mom is with her." He said this with an edge, and it compounded on the hollow feeling building up inside of Morgan.

"Thank you." She knitted her eyebrows together. Technically, their date was over. She hadn't planned for a nightcap or a movie or anything. Just the supper she'd made. Normally, of course, he'd stay and they'd cuddle and kiss on the sofa, and things would even progress a bit. And he'd leave her, lips swollen and eyes lazy, only to promise to see her bright and early in the morning, at the office. It was their game of cat and mouse. He knew she planned to buy her house. She knew he already owned his. They were content like this. Keeping their spaces separate.

And that's why she should have had no reason to defend what she said next.

"I might consider going back home."

"What?" Nick nearly choked on the last of his wine, but maybe that was because he'd got a swish of sediment, too. "Like, *now*?"

"Well, not *right this minute*, but I mean... maybe I'll look at flights. Maybe I can get something for this week. Even a red-eye."

"But, *why*?"

"Why? She's my grandmother. She's had a stroke. And my mom, she's alone there..." Morgan's voice drifted off, allowing Nick to cut in.

"I thought you were estranged. You told me earlier you haven't even spoken to her in years. And after what happened back then—?"

Morgan set her jaw. "Nick, she's family."

"Family doesn't do that."

"Family is complicated." And she knew it was. No matter what Memaw had ever done, she was still Morgan's memaw. She was still responsible for throwing pinches of cinnamon and spoonfuls of sugar into Morgan's little cloth sack. The one with all those sweet, happy memories. They were all she had. No matter what had happened before.

"Morgan, *tell* me you're not going home. Not after what she did."

"She had a stroke, Nick."

His hands flew up in surrender, but she knew he was right. To run home now would be foolish. She had to see through this sale. It could amount to a quarter of her annual income. Maybe even more if she didn't score anything else the rest of the year.

"You're right," he said at last. "You should go. I can cover the sale for you." Nick said this with valiance. Like he knew it was the right thing to say and to do, and so he would say it. He would do it. He was a good person that way, Nick Martinez.

But she couldn't let him. Memaw would be okay. She was strong. She'd had the clot buster. At the very least, Morgan could wait to see how she improved over the next day. "You know what? I'm not going to rush into it. This is an important sale, and I can't just make you do the work for me."

"I would do it for you, of course I would, Morgan."

She let herself ease into his arms, a careful embrace. Tentative. "But you're right, Nick. Things are weird between my grandma and me. There is so much unsaid between us." She blinked and looked up at him. "Let's just wait and see what happens. Maybe she'll do a one-eighty by the morning. Maybe this is just one more of her episodes."

Nick pressed his mouth in a line and shook his head, looking beyond Morgan thoughtfully. "I didn't want to say that. Jinx it, or anything. I mean I know she's had health issues before—"

"But it's true."

And it was. Essie Coyle wasn't *just* a pistol. It wasn't *just* that she had a mean streak. There was more to her.

Much, *much* more.

CHAPTER EIGHT

1990

Essie

When her daughters dropped the bombshell on Essie—that her eldest, smartest daughter had gotten herself knocked up—it just about ruined Essie's birthday. How could she face everyone with that new burdensome knowledge that her daughter was a trollop?

And it wasn't just that CarlaMay wasn't married. It was far worse than that. CarlaMay didn't even have a boyfriend to speak of. Or if she did, he was too awful for anyone to know about.

Essie sat up from her position on the table. Only half her face was done. "Is this true, CarlaMay?"

CarlaMay nodded miserably. Barbara moved behind her, holding her older sister about the waist and tugging her close.

Essie narrowed her gaze upon her daughter's belly. It didn't look all that pregnant. Or was that just wishful thinking on Essie's part? Of course, she loved babies and would welcome a grandchild. But CarlaMay wasn't married. This was all best ignored. Or, at the very least, downplayed. She lowered herself back onto the table and pointed to the right side of her face. "Well?" she asked DanaSue. "Aren't you going to finish?"

* * *

The party turned out wonderfully, and CarlaMay's news was just a blip on the radar. Essie and Billy danced into the night, with their friends and family clapping and cheering them on. Drinks were flying, and by the time Essie and Billy fell into their bed in the wee hours of the morning, he smelled like a bottle of bourbon and she smelled like a mint julep.

They made love, giggling over their foibles and missteps and enjoying each other so much that by the time the morning light poured in through Chantilly lace curtains, all was right in the world. So much so, that the first thing Essie did was march from their bedroom upstairs in the big house down to the guest wing, where CarlaMay lived.

She rapped on the door and softened up her voice until it was melted butter. "CarlaMay, girl?"

A muffled response emerged on the other side.

"You up, honey?"

The door whipped open, and CarlaMay's red face appeared. White splotches around her eyes and a rat's nest for a head of hair proved she'd probably cried herself to sleep. She looked almost beat up, Essie thought.

"I want to take you out to breakfast. After, we're gonna go shopping."

"Huh?" CarlaMay scratched her tangled brown hair and rubbed at her raw eyes.

"Get dressed. Meet me at the truck in fifteen minutes. Your daddy's gonna drive us in the Ford. It was his idea, even."

* * *

They began at the Dewdrop Diner, a 1950s-style café that Essie loved, and that Essie knew CarlaMay loved. Bill dropped them there then headed into town to meet up with his cousin.

Essie and CarlaMay ordered the exact same thing: Betsy's famous half-pounder cinnamon roll. They ought to have shared one between the two of them—especially after such an indulgent night before—but Essie prodded her daughter on. "Go on. I don't believe what they say—that expecting ladies are 'eating for two,' but I *do* believe you've earned it." She winked at her daughter, who glowed back. That was all Essie wanted to say about the subject of CarlaMay's pregnancy. At least for now, anyway. She knew it was enough by the way her daughter scarfed the delicious sweet. CarlaMay had always been like her mother in that respect—her appetite only existed when she was feeling like herself, comfortable. Content.

CarlaMay slugged down a medium glass of milk, and Essie worked on her black coffee. Once they were full and liable to roll out of the diner, Essie paid the bill and led her daughter directly out and up Main Street.

Brambleberry had the best Main Street that America had ever seen. The Dewdrop sat on the southwest corner, the perfect starting point for a pair of long-game shoppers such as Essie and CarlaMay were that day. If you'd happened there for lunch instead of breakfast, you could expect an all-beef hot dog with a great tall milkshake. Or a hamburger if you were hankerin' for a patty rather than a tube steak. As she'd aged, though, Essie preferred to keep both her budget and her diet in tight check, which precluded luxuries like huge tall milkshakes with maraschino cherries on top, especially when they came in at six dollars a pop.

Originally founded in the height of the mid-century drive-through craze, the Dewdrop had once deployed roller-skate-wearing carhops to dispense with its fatty goods. Those days were over, but not gone were the red vinyl booths and the jukebox in the corner that, miracle of miracles, still hummed like a bird.

Beyond the Dewdrop and up along the west side of Main were over a dozen other shops, cafés, and boutiques. They passed Fullton's All Occasion Florals and Antiques Attic, stopping first in Clancy's, a women's wear boutique. Essie's daughters often complained that Clancy's was stuck in the seventies. *The seventies were only eleven years ago!* Essie would cackle.

But CarlaMay conveyed no such complaint right now. She swept into the store easily, admiring the window-box outfits with what Essie figured had to be a new appreciation for all things *modern woman*. All things *modern mother*. A modern mother liked the modesty of a knee-length skirt. A modern mother liked turtlenecks and drapey vests and pleated denim and baby-doll dresses and flattering denim jumpers. Such garments tastefully hid a little tummy, even after the baby had long since been born.

But what Essie wanted to show CarlaMay was in the back of the store. A small section of the little square shop with a discreet sign hovering above two circular racks and one narrow box of intimates.

When CarlaMay arrived there at her mother's elbow, she gasped. "I didn't even think about getting *maternity* clothes."

"Oh, don't be silly. Sure, you did. Every girl thinks about muumuus when she gets that positive test result. I read about them in the *Ladies' Home Journal*. Can you imagine wearing denim jeans when your belly starts to pop out?" She clicked her tongue, but it was meant to be playful. "It's time you wear dresses again, CarlaMay."

CarlaMay gave her a sidelong glance. "Every girl thinks about wearing muumuus? Did you hear what you just said, Essie Coyle?"

Essie brushed her off and plucked a floral empire-waist number from the rack. She inspected the size, unsure what to expect. Did maternity sizes mirror normal sizes? Essie, without the benefit of ever shopping for her older sisters when they were pregnant or ever having shopped for herself when she was— Billy and Essie were too poor to buy special pregnancy clothing —hadn't the slightest idea. "This is a size eight. Might not fit." She eyed her daughter, who, though slight through her waist, was on the tall side.

CarlaMay wandered to the rack over, which was filled with denim pieces. Truth be told, Essie hated denim. It wasn't lady-like, she figured, and this was coming from a farm girl who'd known more denim than the average Joe. Essie hated that part of her past. The denim days. The long pants and short pants days that separated her and her sisters from the rest of the free women of the world. Essie and other ragtag kids would run around barefoot in nothing but their older brothers' washed-out denim overalls, like real backwoods hicks. To Essie, if a lady didn't *have* to wear denim, then she oughtn't.

Still, CarlaMay presented a wide-shaped denim overall jumper. It was everything Essie stood against. She gave her head a quick, sharp shake, and then they carried on, leaving the store an hour later with maternity pantyhose, a cornflower-blue nightgown that could fit any overweight woman, regardless of pregnancy status, and a nursing bra, which Essie found to be indulgent at the very least.

The pair moved on.

Strolling past the beauty shop and the coffee place, they stopped next at the Puppet Show, Brambleberry's own little toy shop. "It's a little early for toys, Mom," CarlaMay complained.

"This place has more than toys. Just you wait."

They swung into the little boxy store, and Essie could see CarlaMay was surprised. "You don't remember this place from your childhood, do you?"

Her daughter gave her a funny look. "I've never been in here in my life."

"What're you talking about? This place has been open since Stephen Foster spent the night at the farm." Whenever Essie needed to reference a time before her children—and, indeed, a time before *her*—she used the family legend that not only had the famous American composer visited family on Federal Hill up in Bardstown, but on his way back east, he got lost and found himself at the Nelson farm. Once there, he realized he wasn't only lost, but famished, too. So, he stopped and picked berries from the northern fence.

"I can tell you I have never, in my life, been in this place." CarlaMay didn't say it with amazement or anything. She said it, Essie thought, with a bit of a bad taste in her mouth.

Essie set her mouth in a line. She could read perfectly well where her daughter was taking this. The accusation was cutting and rough. But today was to be a good day. Essie had already decided as much. And so she forced a smile and plowed onward, toward the back of the store, where the baby items were kept. "Well, today that changes. Your daddy told me to spoil you, and that's just what we're gon' do."

CHAPTER NINE
PRESENT DAY

Morgan Jo

Morgan slept fitfully that night. What little sleep she did manage was riddled with confusing dreams featuring Memaw, a younger Memaw. The one from Morgan's early youth, all dark hair and eyebrows, red lips and charm. But she was doing strange things in the dreams. She was holding hands with other men, not Grandad. In one episode, she was dying, choking on something. Morgan was the only other person there and was trying in vain to remove something stuck in the old woman's throat, but all she could pull out were, oddly, letters. Each letter she dislodged she lay out on a table until the alphabet was represented several times over. Then Nick came into the room and swept the letters from the table, and they fell in clumps to the floor, forming words. But for the life of Morgan, she couldn't read the words, as if she were illiterate. She knew they *made* words, but the words were like gibberish to her dreaming brain.

Morgan awoke the next morning with a jolting start, and it sent spasms down her right side, all along her outer thigh. Her flesh buzzed with something between throbbing pain and a bizarre, aching numbness. Reaching for her phone, Morgan braced herself. Maybe she'd already missed the call. Or maybe her mother had texted her. Maybe things were going downhill and Morgan would be forced to admit that *no*, she wasn't coming home. Sorry. Not after what happened. Not after all the pain her grandmother had caused the family at large and Morgan specifically.

Morgan was reeling.

She slid a finger boldly across her phone screen, waking up the device. No messages or missed calls. A quick swipe to the call log and a tap on her mom's contact forced Morgan forward.

"Hey, baby girl."

Morgan loved it when her mom called her pet names. It was a rarity, but a softness Morgan sometimes longed for. "Hi, Mama."

"What ya been doin'?" Her twang was heavier than usual, cluing Morgan in to the fact that she hadn't slept.

"How is she?" Morgan asked, rolling out of her bed and stumbling to the coffee maker. It was a cheapie machine, and if Morgan let it sit for a minute too long, *bam*, the coffee was burnt. She longed for the slow-drip machine at the farm. And talking to her mom in the early morning like this stabbed at her heart and at her stomach a little. But then again Morgan's mom wasn't even at the farm herself. Twenty bucks said she was sitting right there in the hospital room, next to Memaw.

"She woke up a while ago. The doctors just left, in fact. Everything is stable, I guess."

"Is she talking any better?"

Her mother spoke away from the phone before coming back on the line. "It's hard to say. She's so tired, sweetheart. She didn't get a lick of sleep herself. They ran the MRI late last night, then blood work. Or maybe the other way around. Would you like to speak with her?"

"No, no. Let her rest. We can talk later." Morgan hoped.

"Morgan." CarlaMay's voice turned more somber. "I talked to Dana and Barb. They're coming in after they get off work today. Amber and Travis, too. And Tiffany. I think Rachel, even. They're all going to come by at some point today."

In total, her mother had listed off the majority of Memaw's children and grandchildren who were nearest. There was another bunch down in Tennessee: Billy and his family, and then Chuck and his family out in the eastern part of the state. Uncle Garold was somewhere, no one knew exactly where. But his son, Geddy, stuck close by in Bardstown. But Morgan's three uncles and their wives and kids weren't as close-knit as Morgan's two aunts and their children.

Morgan knew what her mom was hinting at, and so she quickly changed the conversation. "It looks like I'm going to make my first big sale out here."

"Oh, honey. That's so great. Tell me about it."

"Are you sure?"

"I'm walking to the cafeteria for a coffee. Pray for me. You know I can't stand any other coffee than the percolator."

Morgan had to smile. She felt the same way. "Well, it's a gorgeous house in the foothills of the Catalina Mountains. Lots of adobe brick, these big vista windows. Ranch-style, so you just walk right out onto the back patio. The couple does well, and they've made a great offer." Morgan hesitated. Should she admit that Nick had something to do with it? She cleared her throat. "Nick sort of helped me."

"Nick, huh? And how's *that* going?"

"It's fine. We're casual, you know. I mean, it's awkward, since we work together." Morgan popped an English muffin into her toaster oven then made for the bathroom to brush out her hair and slather on sunscreen. Word had it Arizona was nearly as bad as Australia when it came to skin cancer. It was one of the things she didn't quite love about the "Grand Canyon State": the blistering sun.

"And he helped you make the sale? Did he bring you clients, or...? I guess I'm not sure how real estate works." CarlaMay had never bought a house in her life. She'd lived on at the farm since she was a girl, never moving away. Never starting fresh or trying something new. She worked as a 9-1-1 dispatcher in town, and that was enough excitement for her, she'd often reminded everyone.

"It was kind of weird. He says sometimes potential buyers need a little pressure to help them commit or not. It's," Morgan swallowed, "*complicated.*"

"Oh. Right." CarlaMay made a shuffling noise on her end, thanked someone, and returned to Morgan. "Well, that's great, Mo. I'm glad it's going so well."

"It is." Morgan returned to the kitchen and coated her English muffin in margarine. It wasn't the same as butter from home, churned fresh and salted just so. But it'd do. She set about eating her breakfast as her mom dangled on the line.

"Right. Of course it is. Anything you do seems to go well."

This struck Morgan as a jab, but it wasn't like her mother to make digs at her. Something was decidedly *up*. "What's going on, Mom?"

"Nothing. What do you mean?"

"You're acting strange. Like you want to say something but you can't."

"If I had something to say to you, I'd say it, Morgan Jo."

"Right." Morgan rolled her eyes. "Well, if that's the case, then I'd better let you go. I hope to get this sale underway fast."

"Fast?" Her mother was clinging to the word, Morgan knew.

"Well, sure. Sooner we can close, the sooner the money hits the bank. The closer I am to making a down payment."

"Right." Now it was CarlaMay who was being short.

"Mom, I know you don't think I should be here." Morgan's acknowledgment of this fact was unending. Her apologies to her mother stretched on and on. The funny thing was, CarlaMay didn't want Morgan to stay on at the farm, either. What she wanted of her only daughter was a life far bigger than either of them could have imagined. CarlaMay had wanted Morgan to get all the way to California. She wanted her to go to wine country, find a fixer-upper, and *really* follow her dreams of rehabbing old homes and turning them into vineyards.

In fact, it was Memaw's idea that Morgan lower her standards. It was Memaw who offered to pay Morgan's way to Tucson, Arizona, and her first and last month's rent on a nice little house on a nice little country club in a nice little suburb where there were realtor job openings.

It was all Memaw. Memaw who wanted something else than Morgan had. Or CarlaMay had. She wanted something else for everyone in her life.

Maybe even for herself.

"I just don't want you to settle, Mo."

"Tucson isn't settling. It's a stepping stone."

"It's easy to get stuck, is all I'm saying."

"Memaw said it was a good idea."

Her mom huffed. "Memaw says a lot of things."

They both fell silent at the irony.

"Morgan," CarlaMay started after a moment, "there's no reason for you to worry about her, you know. She'll be fine."

Morgan knew better than this. Memaw was never fine. Or when she was fine, she was about to be *un*fine. But there was little sense in arguing. Anyway, Morgan had decided now, she had no intention of going to Kentucky. She couldn't possibly face the heartache of all that would be wrapped up in such a move. The heartache of seeing her mom, aunts, and cousins. Of seeing the farm. Mostly, though, Morgan couldn't stand the heartache of facing Memaw.

CHAPTER TEN

PRESENT DAY

Morgan Jo

Morgan felt herself moving through the motions that day. But after she'd gotten paperwork on the sale rolled out, signatures requested, and inspections scheduled, she was ready for a lunch break.

Nick had to work through lunch, and there was no one else to join her, so Morgan opted for a Mexican café in Oro Valley, near home.

There, she video-called her best friend in the whole wide world, Julia Miles.

The screen revealed a familiar image. Julia's sea-blue eyes and bouncing blonde waves, cut shorter now, in a bob, flashed to life. Her angular jaw and perky nose still gave her a pixie effect. Julia Miles looked like a movie star, but maybe not the lead actress. The lead actress's cute best friend with a bubbly personality and fun ideas about how they ought to spend the weekend. Little had changed about Julia since Morgan had last seen her. *Maybe she was a shade tanner? Was her hair woven through in honey lowlights?* She looked great. Morgan would have said as much if Julia's face hadn't broken immediately into a dark expression.

"Morgan, I heard." Julia rushed into an overview of *how* she'd heard about Essie Coyle, and from whom, and where she was when she heard. It felt a little soap-operatic to Morgan, but she didn't half mind the account. "I was getting my hair done at the shop, and Terry McFly came in, and was she in a tizzy. Did you know Terry was going to Mass with Miss Essie?"

"At least someone was," Morgan replied.

"Well, Terry mostly talked about how sudden it all was and how the parish'll be praying for that woman and that's when Sheila—she does my hair now, ever since Jenny moved to Bard-stown—realized she'd let the foils set for too damn long. Morgan, she burned my hair to kingdom come. What were supposed to be highlights are now curly fries."

"Wow," Morgan replied. "That's a sin. Are you gonna go back to her? Get it fixed?"

"Well, Mo, who cares about my *hair*?" Julia screeched. "Miss Essie! Aren't you just worried sick? When my Mimi had her stroke, it took her six months to walk normal again. And, no offense, Mo, but Miss Essie is a lot older than Mimi was. And I hate to worry you even sicker, but that stroke, it was the *end*."

"Well, sure I'm worried," Morgan acknowledged. "It's just, well, *you* know. It's Memaw. She can be dramatic. And even if she's not being dramatic, she's like a jockey. Her horse might buck and toss, but Memaw isn't going anywhere."

"Have you spoken with her?" Julia wasn't about to pull any punches.

"I talked to my mom." The reply fell flatly. Lamely. Morgan rushed to explain. "Memaw was resting this morning. I'll call back in a bit and check on her." Julia didn't answer immediately, so Morgan went on ahead. "How've you been? Any word on booking that trip out here?"

"What, me? Go to Arizona? I don't think my hair would do

well in Arizona. It's dry enough as it is." She belted out a laugh, and Morgan relaxed. She missed Julia something awful but talking on the phone with her best friend soothed her somewhat. "And, anyway," Julia went on, "I mean, aren't you coming out here soon?"

"What, to Brambleberry?"

"Well, yeah, girl. What with Memaw laid up and your mama in it up to her eyeballs."

Morgan pursed her lips and stretched her neck back and forth. Her order was up at the counter—a burrito, big and fat and bursting at the seams with spices and cheese, lettuce, and *carne asada*. But her appetite was quelled by the whole overhanging conversation with her BFF. Not only that. *CarlaMay wasn't any busier than usual, was she?* What did Julia know that Morgan didn't?

"In what up to her eyeballs?" Morgan delayed answering the *real* question with a *real* question of her own.

"Well, you know. The farm, generally. Keeping up at her own job. And now her mama. It's a lot. Plus, I don't see your aunts swooping into town and saving the day. And even Amber and Tiffany and Travis. They're around, but what in the hell are they doing? Do they even work?"

"Sure, they work. I think Travis is a clerk at Western Drugs. And Tiffany was doling out samples at Sally's Groceries and Sundries. Or was it the Amish market? I can't recall which. Amber and Rachel aren't mooches. They have rent to pay, all of them." It was beyond Morgan why she ought to be defending her cousins. "Do you keep in touch with them still?" The relationship carved out between Julia and Morgan's cousins wasn't much more than that between acquaintances.

"I've seen Travis at Western, that's right. But I go to at least one of the markets once a week, and I can't remember the last time I saw Tiffany around. Then again, I can't quite remember the Amish market ever passing out samples. If you taste it you buy it with them."

"Hmm. Well. They work, sure enough. Pay their rent. That's about it, though."

"Well, that's something, at least. Anyway, when are you coming back?"

Morgan chewed her lower lip then sank her teeth into the corner of her burrito. Maybe she could force an appetite on herself and delay Julia in one fell swoop.

After a moment of chewing but still with a full mouth, Morgan managed, "I'm not."

Julia didn't answer for a beat. Morgan swallowed her food and washed it down with a swig of fountain iced tea—which tasted bitter and horrible and not sweet at all. But when Julia did answer, it wasn't the passive-aggressive monosyllabic response Morgan might have gotten from her mom or anyone else. Oh, no. Julia gave her a mouthful.

"You might hate your memaw, Morgan Jo Coyle. Hell, even worse, you might not care about her one iota. But you know who does care? Your mama. And you know who else cares?" She snorted. "God."

"Julia, *please*," Morgan tried but was immediately cut off.

"And you know what else? You might not be going to church every Sunday and you might not be as religious as you once were, but God is more than just that white-bearded old man upstairs. He's in your heart. And he's in your soul. He's in you, Mo. In everything you do and in everything you don't do. Are you going to regret this in five years? When Memaw is faking a broken hip or swindling some tow truck driver out of a hundred bucks by pretending she's worse off than she is? No, you won't. But what about in ten years? When Memaw is dead and gone? Or twenty, when you're back here digging through files and you find an old birthday card your memaw gave you back when you were five years old? Will you regret it then? If you're not going to come back and see to things for Memaw, *fine*. If you're not going to come back and see to things for your mama, *fine*. But do it for yourself, Morgan."

Morgan returned her burrito to her plate, disgusted with herself for taking so much as a single bite. She let her eyes close then responded to Julia. "You don't understand. Memaw is *fine*." As she said this out loud, Morgan realized that she was trying to convince herself as well as Julia.

Because for the first time in a long time Morgan really hoped Memaw was okay.

CHAPTER ELEVEN

2000

Essie

Essie was sixty the first time it happened.

Her grown-up daughters were all off on their own family vacations. Her eldest, CarlaMay, and her girl, Morgan, had gone to Lexington to shop for back-to-school clothes at the outlet mall.

Her second child, Barbara, and her daughters, Tiffany and Amber, and her son, Travis, took the RV down to Sarasota.

And her youngest girl, DanaSue, was spending the summer with Dana's husband's family in Hickory Grove, along with their daughter, Rachel. This was a while before DanaSue and Bridge would divorce.

Her husband, Billy, was still alive then. And it seemed he wa'n't ever gonna die. They got into it, Bill and Essie. He'd just finished hanging a batch of tobacco when she called him in for lunch. She'd made tuna sandwiches and poured two tall glasses of milk. She'd set the table, put a record on, and applied a fresh coat of red lipstick. Bill didn't come in when she called for him, by way of the supper bell that'd hung out front of the big house for so long it was any wonder it hadn't rusted clear off its hook.

Fifteen minutes had passed. Then thirty. Essie picked her way through the grass and up to the hangar. He was there, all right. Hangin' his tobacco. Right in that spot. That spot that no tobacco was supposed to go.

You see, the tobacco hangar was a whole big hall of a barn. Four times what you'd think, with rafters and lofts and old dry hay poking out of corners from those days back when Essie's daddy used it to keep horses, too.

When Essie and her brothers and sisters were little, when Dottie was still alive even, they'd play in the hangar. The girls would claim one loft and the boys th'other. They'd wage wars and hoard sweetbread. They'd play house and every other thing a kid could think to play back then, which was a lot, since those were the times when it was upon the children to entertain themselves. There weren't no movie theaters in Brambleberry. And there weren't no televisions in any houses. Nor computers and cell phones, ha!

But those days were long gone, and since then, Essie had often thought about tearing the whole damn thing down. Maybe Essie's daddy had the same idea, too, because he'd boarded up the back half of the hangar and made everybody swear never to go back there again.

Of course, once Essie'd convinced Billy to live on her family farm and take up the growing of tobacco, they needed use of the hangar, so her idea about taking it to the ground was dead in the water. It was good enough that the soft parts of the hangar, the sore parts, were boarded up and hidden away, like a secret.

But now, that day back in 2000 when Essie went out to fetch her husband and tell him the milk was gonna turn, she saw he wasn't just hanging up leaves. He was pulling off boards from the back of the hangar. He was undoing everything Essie's daddy had done. He was doing the one thing he wasn't allowed to. He was opening up a wound the size of her lost twin sister Dottie and everything that had happened.

He still hadn't heard her when she screamed at him to "Stop it right there, Bill Coyle!"

He still hadn't cared when she ran over, her linen pants soaking up the warm smell of 'baccy leaves, and tore him away from the splintered wood. He worked at it with a need that she couldn't fathom. What did he need to see? What did she have to prove?

Why couldn't he just let it *be* and let her keep her heart closed on this very matter? Why couldn't he let this thing just stay here, this tomb, frozen in time? Let her keep her sister's memory alive behind the boards? After all, if he wasn't going to let Essie tear the hangar to the ground and bury Dottie for once and for all, then he could at least let her memory rest privately.

But Bill didn't do that.

Because Bill didn't care.

But he *had* started to care when Essie froze in the middle of their argument, her face a blank sheet, her mouth bumbling through words that didn't make sentences and sentences that sounded like riddles.

When Essie had her very first mini-stroke and couldn't find the words to tell him to leave the damn hangar be, Billy cared.

Yes. Billy had cared then. Whether it was over his pride or her health, though, no one could be sure.

CHAPTER TWELVE

PRESENT DAY

Morgan Jo

September first hit Morgan like a load of bricks. The air in Tucson dried out as if monsoon season was nothing more than a fever dream. With her sale in the bag, and a hefty commission simmering in her bank account, she felt good.

But it was just a couple of weeks after Memaw's stroke, and there hadn't been progress on that front. It was this that kept Morgan from celebrating with Nick to his fullest measure.

The date of the closing on the ranch-style home at the base of the Catalinas was the two-week mark of Memaw's hospital stay. Nick had planned for them to go out to an extravagant dinner. Morgan had agreed, though reluctantly. Things simply weren't sitting well with her. Not lately. Not with the absence of a nip in the air. With the absence of a windy, rainy day that she'd immediately begun to miss once the Arizona forecast had cleared itself right up. And not with the lingering guilt trip she'd been enduring from Julia and her mom—Memaw wasn't going to Mass. She still wasn't saying hardly anything. She didn't know who her own daughter was, much less her grandchildren who *had* finally paid her visits. She could scarcely walk. Not only that, but she now had home health nurses taking rounds. By all accounts, Memaw had not fabricated this particular health scare. Although she was always whipping up a drama around her health, this one wasn't a fake.

It was very obviously real.

Even so, Morgan still couldn't face the idea of going back to Brambleberry, so she went through the motions, meeting the new homeowners with a bottle of wine and their matching sets of keys, paired with a keychain emblazoned over with *Casas Adobes Realty Executives*.

Afterwards, she returned home for the day. There, she soaked in the tub, giving in to using those special bath products she saved for occasions like that night—a fancy dinner date with her boyfriend. That's what Nick officially was these days. Her boyfriend. Somehow, slowly and carefully, the uncertainty of what Morgan and Nick *were* had slipped away just like those wet, stormy afternoons of the southwest.

She exfoliated with both the sugar scrub and a sea-sponge loofah that was nearly going crusty from lack of use. Then, Morgan shaved with a fresh razor and a bottle of shave cream. Lastly, she let a hair mask sit for the recommended five minutes, timed perfectly with a charcoal face mask of the same time limit. After washing all those good smells and suds down the drain, Morgan set about primping. Not one to blow out her hair or do makeup, she figured *why not*? They'd be going to North, which was both uppity and trendy—or at least, uppity and trendy in relation to Morgan's usual fare of Mi Nidito and Eegee's, two Tucson staples.

After dolling herself up, hair and makeup, Morgan went to her closet. Along the folding door hung a black dress she'd found on clearance at White House Black Market. A satin slip lay silkily beneath a lacy chiffon draping and was altogether the fanciest thing she'd worn since her first communion in the second grade. She put it on, and then slid each foot into black lace-trimmed ballet flats.

Studying herself in the mirror, Morgan saw a woman who was far removed from the girl she'd known. It was a cliché in every sense, but the dress, makeup, and hair transformed her. That much was clear. What was less clear, however, was whether Morgan liked herself this way.

Of course, when Nick arrived in his lime-green Prius to pick her up, he made his opinion crystal clear.

"I love when you dress up," he whispered into her ear, sliding his lips across her neck until he finished at her collarbone. Morgan pushed him away playfully.

"Let's go. I'm starving."

"My farm girl," he joked, but she didn't think it was funny.

They sat at a window overlooking the city. The lights of businesses and homes twinkled against the evening desertscape. The view was unlike anything Morgan had seen back home. It was beautiful. But a different beautiful. Not the undulating green hills. The orchards and farms and white picket fences of her childhood that rolled on across rural land so vivid it could become a jigsaw puzzle. Not the images that she dreamt of at night.

Morgan focused on Nick and their table setting. A charcuterie board spread between them. Morgan dug in. She was an appetizer girl. A bread girl. A dessert girl. An everything girl. But as a *girl*, generally, she had come to particularly appreciate the more artisanal and delicate of foods. They were still delish but sometimes even a bit healthy.

The server brought a bottle of Chardonnay, uncorking it with little fanfare, and the couple ordered.

Nick chose the beet salad with arugula.

Morgan flushed when it was her turn and she chose the

margherita pizza, but she was beginning to set aside Nick's perception of her in favor of her preferences. This felt good.

The server left, and Nick lifted his freshly poured glass. "To Ms. Morgan Coyle, on her first *big* sale."

He always left out her middle name, and it always felt weird to her. Never in her life had anyone called her by her full name without adding in the *Jo*. But that's what Morgan liked about Nick. He was cosmopolitan, and everything he did followed that suit. It was as though he knew who he was and he didn't deviate from that. Morgan could learn a thing or two from Nick.

"To me." She beamed back, clinking his glass before taking a swill of the dry drink. She felt the liquid run over her tongue and down her throat. "Mmm." She picked up the bottle. "This is good. Familiar, even."

"Well, it's wine. You drink it regularly." Nick pulled out his phone and begged off to reply to a text from a client.

Morgan read on aloud. "Newton Vineyard. Sonoma." She took another drink, this one slower. "It's... *buttery*. I bet you five bucks the grapes were aged in oak barrels. There's a hint of vanilla, I think." She took one more drink then gave the bottle an assured nod. "Yes. Oak barrel."

Nick glanced up. "For someone who orders pizza for dinner, you're pretty up on your wine."

"I wanted to go to the Napa Valley. That's where I started out for, originally. Thought I'd rebuild an old winery there or renovate one. Maybe one day, I'd go to Tuscany for research and bring home special fruits. Can you bring fruit on an airplane?"

Nick furrowed his brow line. "Morgan," he started, pocketing his phone and moving his wine glass out of the way and then hers. Lastly, he reached for her hands. She offered them, titillated by the experience of the night in general and by Nick's renewed attention particularly. "I want to talk to you about something serious."

Morgan tensed. "Serious?" What could be serious for them to discuss? It couldn't be her job performance if they were right there, right now *celebrating* it. Unless he was ready to apologize for infringing on her sale, in which case, well, she agreed. That was serious. And it would definitely take the wind out of her sails.

"I know you want to buy your townhome. And now you're one big step closer to that," he went on.

Morgan nodded uneasily. It did seem to be real-estate related. So far. She nibbled her lower lip until she remembered she was wearing lipstick, then got extra nervous and pulled one hand away to shield her mouth as she ran her tongue over her teeth.

"I see us going in a different direction, though."

Morgan snorted a laugh. "What do you mean, us going in a different direction?"

"Well, not Tuscany, to be clear." He laughed—*nervously?*—and his bright white smile hung crookedly for a moment.

"What?" She shook her head, thoroughly confused.

"Morgan, we've been together a few months, and I see this going somewhere. Do you?"

"Oh." She blinked. "Right. Um. Maybe. Yeah." She licked her lips and blinked again. "You're talking about *us* us."

Nick flashed a grin anew and reached again for her hands, squeezing them. "Of course I'm talking about *us* us. What did you think I was talking about, silly girl?"

She melted. "Right. Well, to answer your question, yes. I like you." But as she was saying the words, she wasn't exactly believing them. Nick was a great co-worker and supervisor. He was hot. And he was that "different" that Morgan had so needed when she set up shop in Tucson. *But... things were good as they were. Right?*

"What if I helped you with getting the house?"

"Helped me with getting *my* house? What do you mean?"

"I mean I can grease the loan qualification wheels. Talk to the bank about interest rates. You know, get a bit of an inside deal for you."

All of these were things Morgan could do for herself, she'd figured. She was a realtor. She had quick access to the broker and bank and anyone who might be able to help. But she wasn't about to be rude to her boyfriend. "Well, thank you," she gushed.

"And maybe I can even contribute." His smile slipped away, and in its place, a lip that quivered with anticipation.

Morgan felt her stomach clench. "Contribute?" Her blinking was getting out of control now.

"I really care about you, and I want you to see Tucson as your home. I want to be a part of your home, even."

"Are you asking to move in with me?" she blurted.

"No!" He turned red at his own raised voice and glanced around awkwardly. "Sorry." He tweaked his tie. "No, I'm not asking that. I mean, come on. I love my place. The yard. The community. It's *ideal*. But yours could be a great property investment one day. A rental, if that's really what you see for yourself."

"If I rent it out, then where will I live?" she asked this dumbly, but she knew his answer before the smile curled back across his mouth.

"I'm just saying, I want to be part of your present and your future, Morgan. And that starts with financial support, in my opinion."

It was all shades of confusion for Morgan. Financial support sounded like something a pyramid schemer would schlep. Or a college tuition loan agency would pitch.

Or even something her own grandmother might scheme up as a way to hold Morgan to something.

And *yet*.

If Nick helped her with the down payment, she'd get the house. No questions asked. It'd be a done deal, and her future would be set. And that was a nice thought. Almost as nice as renovating a sleepy little vineyard somewhere. But the truth was she wanted it to be her own...

Before she could come up with an answer, her purse buzzed on the chair beside her. Morgan wasn't one to answer after hours, despite the demand to do so. And she certainly wasn't one to answer a call or text on a date. But she needed a break from wherever the conversation was going, and *besides*, she really, really, really, really thought she was about to say yes. And then everything would change.

"I have to take this." She waved her phone at him. "I'm sorry."

She left the table. Nick, who wasn't so used to rejection or even delays in such grand gestures, didn't even go for his phone right away.

Safely outside in front the restaurant, Morgan held the phone to her ear. "Mom? Everything okay?"

"Yes, *yes*," her mother replied, breathless and excited. "She's talking more. We're here in her bedroom, and she woke up and hollered for the nurse. Then they called me up. And she's talking more. She made a whole sentence, Mo!"

"That's great. Does she recognize you now?" Morgan let her heart leap a little at the uptick in her grandmother's health.

But a sigh came in response. "No, no. Not yet."

"Oh. Well, what did she say?" Morgan figured she'd make Nick sweat. Heck, she'd make herself sweat, too. His proposition hung heavily in her chest. Maybe she'd mention it to her mom just then. Maybe her mom would give her the green light. *Do it, Mo. You only live once. Take his offer, turn it into a rental. Move in with Nick and marry him and live happily ever after in the Sonoran desert, far away from this mess here at home.*

But her mama's answer wasn't anything Morgan could have expected.

"Mo, honey. She doesn't recognize me or Amber or Travis. We called Barb and DanaSue on video. She doesn't know her rear from a cow's, but she's... Morgan Jo, baby, she's asking for *you*."

CHAPTER THIRTEEN

PRESENT DAY

Morgan Jo

Morgan took her carry-on from Nick, who'd hefted it begrudgingly from the trunk of his Prius.

After the phone call and bombshell revelation from her mother, their dinner dried up. To hear that Memaw was better was great. But to know that she wanted to talk to only one person on earth—no, wait. To know that Memaw only *recalled and requested* one person on earth, and that person was Morgan... it would be comical if it weren't so heart-wrenching. From that morsel of news, Morgan's decision had been made.

She'd go home. Only briefly, but she'd go. Do what she could. Come back to Tucson. That was the plan.

And though Nick was irritated to see her off, Morgan was perhaps even angrier. She didn't want to go home. She didn't want to leave the life she was creating in Tucson, not now. Not at the very beginning of the hot real-estate season.

But most of all, the truth was that she did not want to see her grandmother.

No.

She didn't want to see the grandmother who was now asking to see Morgan. Who could only say Morgan's name, of the dozens—maybe even hundreds or thousands—of names that ought to have arrived more quickly on the old woman's addled tongue.

There was so much hurt dwelling between them, Morgan and Memaw. And yet, the old woman had somehow trudged up the seed of a critical memory, and that memory was Morgan. Morgan was the memory, so Morgan *had* to go home. She didn't want to go and open herself up to it, but there was no choice.

"Morgan, you don't *have* to do this." Nick didn't take his hand from the handle. Morgan's eyes fell to its raw corners and scuffed edges. She didn't know luggage could become threadbare.

"Don't have to go see my grandmother who's had a stroke and can't recall any information other than *my* name? I think I have to." She said it with a sour taste on her tongue, and her lips worked together as if that taste were so palpable she might throw it up, right there at the curb of the bizarrely quaint Tucson International Airport.

"Right. Well." Nick passed the bag over and slid an arm around her waist, pulling her close and kissing her neck. He then waved toward the nearest concierge desk, one of the curb-side stations. She pulled up the handle on her bag and spun around to see an attendant coming.

"Oh, no, no. I'm fine. I don't need help." She mounted the sidewalk, and Nick lifted her bag the short distance up, awkwardly interfering with the fact that she really could manage a small rolling carry-on. But Nick passed the kind man a folded bill, and he grabbed up the little suitcase and held out a hand to take her shoulder bag, too.

"I got it, really." She gave both men a thankful look, holding her bag against herself and leaning in to give Nick one last peck on the cheek. "I'll see you soon."

"Not soon enough," he whispered, and kept his hand on her lower back until they parted at the automatic doors.

Morgan followed the attendant pitiably as he rolled her lightweight bag toward the check-in area. The pull to look back for Nick, to search for that final, desperate wave set against the lazy, hazy morning sun, didn't come. By the time she was stationed neatly in front of a computer kiosk, printing her boarding pass and waiving the baggage check-in, she'd forgotten all about Tucson.

And all about Nick.

Instead, her mind filled with all things *home*. She could already picture the gently rolling green hills of Brambleberry. She could smell the kitchen of the farm and Memaw there, cooking at the stove, stooped slightly over a pot of boiling potatoes and gesturing Morgan to come taste to see if it needed more sugar. *Potatoes don't take sugar, Memaw.*

There was one more thing that she envisioned, too. Well, not a *thing*. A someone. Someone with dirty blond hair and blue eyes the color of those gently rolling green hills and who smelled like home cooking and whiskey and woods.

Morgan couldn't think about Brambleberry and *not* think of Emmett Dawson.

CHAPTER FOURTEEN

2004

Morgan Jo

Growing up as a farm girl, Morgan Jo had had her share of run-ins with nature. There'd been poison sumac and a tumble off a horse before she was even five. At age six, she'd stepped on a rusty nail, incurring a tetanus shot so painful it ought to have ensured the girl didn't touch rust ever again in her life. But on a farm, there was a lot that could go to rust, of course, and Morgan Jo was too curious, too playful, and too determined to let a thing like a big fat shot get her down. And so, she'd had another one at the age of eight.

Of course, she'd bumped into—and sometimes purposefully grabbed on to—electric fences no fewer than half a dozen times in her twelve years. Morgan's mom was sure she'd have a heart attack before the age of twenty. Those were all the bigger deals. The ones that warranted at least a phone call to the doctor, if not a full-blown hospital visit.

Not even the horse incident, however, had done much in the way of affecting Morgan. She still ran in shorts through the woods and poison shrubs. She still rode horses. And she still played near rusted metal and electric fences. She was unfazed by those blips on the radar of a rambunctious, rural childhood.

But on her thirteenth birthday that was about to change.

Her mom planned a special party, citing the fact that Morgan Jo had never had a formal birthday party to date.

Thrilled to pieces, Morgan Jo had wanted it to be an all-girls party, but the problem with being a member of the Coyle clan was that there were boy cousins. Travis, for one. Ryan and Geddy and Hank, too. Then the little ones like Tim and Baby Billy. It just wasn't possible *not* to invite the boy cousins if the girl cousins were coming, which naturally they were.

Morgan and her girl cousins were best friends. Not in the same way that she was best friends with Julia, who knew her grades and her secrets and which cousin annoyed her the most, but they were as close as cousins could be.

Anyway, one thing led to another, and what was supposed to be Morgan Jo's first ever *real* birthday party had turned into something else altogether. It became at once a kids' party and also a town tour of the farm. Turned out that local interest in what exactly went on at a tobacco farm was greater than Morgan Jo's family's interest in attending to her party.

This was fine, though, because it gave the kids free rein. And it was fine because it meant more than just Julia and Morgan Jo's cousins would come. Kids from school would be there who wouldn't have even been invited, and even some from other townships. The boy cousins—Ryan, Hank, and Geddy—even brought their friends.

At first, upon sight of the crew of boys who spilled out the back of a Ford pickup, Morgan Jo, Julia, Amber, and Tiffany all cried, "Ew!"

But soon enough, introductions were made, crude though they were.

Travis grunted and pushed his red-haired pal forward. "Jimmy."

Then went Ryan. "David." David, with a brown mop of a head and freckles splayed across his nose, looked a bit like Ryan. And since he looked a bit like Ryan, he looked a bit like Morgan. She lifted her eyebrows at him. "What's your last name?"

"Filcher."

"I don't know any Filchers. Never mind."

It was then Geddy's turn. The boy he'd brung along was slightly taller and skinnier than the others. Not skinny in a poor way, like a lot of the kids who ran around the greater Brambleberry area. Skinny in a lithe, bony way. The way a boy ought to be skinny, Morgan figured. His hair was blond, and his eyes were a piercing blue, and those two things set against a deep Kentucky suntan made him look something like a celebrity to Morgan. A movie star. She felt a little funny inside but figured it had more to do with not eating breakfast on account of her excitement.

Geddy shouldered the boy forward, but it wasn't Geddy who introduced him. No. The blond boy stuck out his hand at Morgan. "Happy birthday, Miss Morgan Jo. I'm Emmett."

Morgan jutted her chin forward and crossed her arms over her chest protectively, though what she might be protecting was anybody's guess. "You can call me Morgan. Just plain Morgan." But before he could pull his outstretched, long-fingered hand back into his personal space, Morgan shoved her own hand into his. "Anyway, my birthday isn't until Monday. I'll be thirteen." Why she felt the need to add that last part—who could tell? Morgan, simply put, just wasn't quite feeling like herself. Not since Geddy introduced this out-of-towner. Which begged a question all its own. "You from Bramble?" she said, using the kids' way of referring to their little hillbilly town.

"I'm a Bardstown boy," he said proudly. It was a goofy way to reply, and the others laughed at him, but Emmett was unfazed. He gave a shrug but kept his smiling blue eyes on

Morgan Jo. She frowned and glared at him as seriously as she could.

"Right, well. Let's go."

From that point, it was accepted that they'd march through the farm together, going from one birthday party game to the next as a big happy bunch.

Before the boys had arrived, Morgan Jo was excited to pin the tail on the donkey and whack the piñata but now those sounded like baby games.

They kicked their way through the grass, and Morgan stole a glance across the farm toward where the tables were set up. Her mom wasn't there. Morgan knew they were taking in the grounds with Memaw at the helm. The aunts and uncles sat at the tables, though, picking at chips and dips, and carrot sticks, and swigging on soda pop and beer. Morgan's mom would be crushed if the partygoers didn't want to do the only two party games she'd planned.

"Julia," Morgan Jo whispered once they'd moved ahead of the back of adolescents who kicked their way aimlessly through the grass, talking about this, that, or th'other.

"Huh?"

"What other game do we play? We can't do the piñata now."

"Why not? I was excited for the piñata," Julia whined. This made sense, seeing as Julia was the star homerun-hitter of the little league softball team for which she played very seriously.

Morgan considered the question. Why *not*? Why not do the piñata and pin the tail? "Just, *because*," Morgan replied. "It's dumb. And there are too many of us now." She indicated the others with a nod over her shoulder.

Her cousins caught up. "What you all talkin' about?" Tiffany asked, a twinge of irritation in her voice.

"I just think the games we were going to play are dumb is

all," Morgan answered honestly. "Should have planned other games."

"What about tag?" Amber offered.

"Tag?" Morgan rolled her eyes. But Julia, as fast as she was strong, piped up quickly.

"Yeah!" But before Julia could reach across and tag Morgan, Morgan grabbed her hand.

"No."

"What's the plan, you all?" Geddy hollered up from the back where the boys walked.

"Are those cherry trees yon over there?" This came from Emmett, and Morgan felt herself heat up like a rocket. She'd seen *Apollo 13* and watched how that space shuttle shimmied and sweated its way up, up, up, and that's just *exactly* how she felt right about then.

"Oh, yeah," Tiffany replied on everyone else's behalf. "We got everything here. Cherry trees, blackberries, raspberries, grape vines. Just about everything you could think of. Why? You hungry?" Tiffany hooked a thumb back toward the folding tables laid out with plastic ruby-red tablecloths blowing up and down across them.

The boys had now caught up to the girls, and Morgan found herself separated from Emmett by Geddy. A safe distance. But even so, his voice—which seemed to crack here and there at sharp turns—carried over to her. He leaned forward, and Morgan caught his eye as he said, "Morgan Jo, you ever spit cherry pits?"

She gave him a belligerent frown. "A'course I have. We do it every summer."

"Then let's have a competition." Emmett was a bold one, all right. Morgan didn't like that about him. He raised his voice so the whole of the group could hear, and it cracked in two, but no one laughed at him, and he didn't even bother to flinch or clear it. "Whoever spits the cherry pit the farthest gets to pick the next party game."

The group whooped and hollered and pounced off toward the trees, and Morgan Jo found herself left behind, but that just wasn't right. She was the birthday girl. If she pouted now, she'd look like more of a baby than if she pinned the tail on the donkey. So she dashed after Julia and grabbed a fistful of cherries, joining Amber and Ryan and the others where they drew an invisible line. The girls went first. Tiffany and Amber sprayed cherry spittle through the air, disqualifying themselves off the bat on account of the gross factor. Julia hocked a good one far.

Morgan Jo took her time, swallowing all the pulp down and smoothing the pit across her tongue and behind her teeth, as clean as she could get it. She forced herself to ignore the boys, and especially Emmett, before moving that little pebble of a pit to the center of her tongue, where she rolled it like a burrito, rocked back and forward and popped that sucker so far that every last one of them almost missed where it had landed.

"Here it is!" Emmett announced with an odd beam of pride, pointing with his foot—a long foot in a white sneaker that gave way to tan calves that looked sort of like a man's calves, Morgan was forced to realize. "You're good." He winked at her as he jogged past and joined the boys on their invisible line.

Morgan sidled next to Julia, who gave her a playful shove. "He's flirtin' with you, Morgan." Julia snickered behind her hands. Morgan gave her a death stare.

"Gross. We're probably related."

"No you aren't. All your kin is accounted for. And besides, he's from Bardstown. I don't know a single Brambleberrian who has connections to Bardstown. We're like dueling banjos—they keep up there, we keep down here. And you," she poked Morgan hard in the ribs, "*know* it."

Morgan decided to ignore that particularly convenient truth

as she watched her gross cousins spit their gross cherry pits across the grass. But when it was Emmett's turn, Morgan's stomach flipped inside of her body. He didn't look like any of the boys at school, who smelled like burps and pulled girls' hair and chased them round at recess. He didn't look like her cousins who liked to hug her so tight she thought she'd pop. Maybe it was the blond hair and blue eyes, although Morgan had seen that particular combination on any number of thirteen- and fourteen-year-olds. Maybe it was that he was a stranger, never seen before. Maybe it was something else. The *it* factor. The X factor. The *hot* factor? Morgan tried to shake her observations of him in time for Emmett to win the boys' match.

"All right, you all!" Travis hollered. "It's Emmett versus the birthday girl! Winner picks the next game!"

The pair lined up, each sucking down the pulp of a fresh cherry and eyeing the other with great suspicion, although Morgan couldn't help but notice Emmett wasn't taking this near as serious as she was. Was *Morgan* even taking this seriously? Or was she about to belt out a laugh? It was hard to say. Julia gave the countdown, and they spit their pits at the same time, but Emmett's fell pathetically short.

"Birthday girl wins!" Julia declared, clapping and cheering. "Morgan picks the next game! What'll it be, Morgan? Piñata? Or pin the tail?"

Morgan glared at her best friend with a stare so poisonous it was any wonder Julia didn't drop to the ground right then. But Julia just grinned and kept on clapping.

Meanwhile, Emmett jutted out his hand. "Good game," he said, "*birthday girl.*"

Instead of shaking his hand, though, Morgan slapped it. "Tag!" she cried out through a fit of girlish giggles. "You're it!"

From then on, whenever Morgan thought about Emmett, she saw them in that moment, her running ahead of him with her wild brown hair flying behind her. Him with a boyish grin of determination as he glided easily over the gentle green hills of the farm. Them, together, running from one thing just as much as they were running to something else altogether.

Morgan Jo and all her party guests spread out fast. Julia sprinted off into the orchard, away from Emmett, who gave everyone a chance to escape his clutches. The boys sprinted toward the tables—an excuse to grab a plateful of food. Tiffany, Amber, and Rachel jogged half-heartedly to the nearest structure, the tobacco hangar.

Morgan, meanwhile, raced to the far north edge of the property, where the fence line opened to a fishing pond. She turned as she crossed through the opening and a thicket of ripe wild berries. Emmett had followed her. Didn't he know that when it came to tag you were supposed to mix it up a little? If someone first tagged *you*, you didn't tag back, you went after fresh blood. But there he was, jogging easily and gaining on her. She let out a shriek and squeezed past a scratchy bramble and through the fence opening toward the west side of the pond, which she planned to skirt.

But just as Morgan made it to the edge of the water, Emmett was right on her tail. She stole a look back at him, and as she did that, her foot sank into muck that ran in rings around the pond.

Before Morgan knew what was happening, her leg got sucked down in, and she was sinking fast into the murky water. Before the top of her right thigh submerged down, she felt a yank on her opposite arm.

Emmett was there by her side, pulling her with one swift jerk from the clutches of the fishing pond.

"I got you," he said, pulling her the last few inches away from the pond and against him, but by then, Morgan was mortified and humiliated and enraged and lots of bubbling, fiery emotions she couldn't even name.

"I'm fine," she snapped. Pulling her body away from his and

stomping the soaked leg hard as she made her way back toward the opening in the fence, through the scratchy brambles, and up toward the big house, where her bedroom was.

For all she knew, Emmett had trailed after her or even just stayed back at the pond, skipping stones or some other boyish thing.

But Morgan didn't care what Emmett did. She slammed her bedroom door behind her, but it popped right back open. Julia stood in the doorway, hands on hips, concern bulging out her eyeballs. "What happened?"

Morgan threw her jean shorts down her legs and grabbed a used towel from her clothes hamper, using it both to dry her leg and foot and shield her unclothed bottom half from Julia. Julia had seen Morgan in her undies, sure, but they were getting older now, and stuff was happening to their bodies that neither one was necessarily ready to expose to the other. "I almost fell in the fishing pond."

Julia closed the door behind her then held her hand up to her mouth, hiding shock or amusement or both, probably.

Morgan pursed her lips at her. "Emmett pulled me out."

Julia's eyes grew wide as a pair of half-dollar coins. "What were you two doing at the pond together?"

"What do you mean? We were playing tag. You were, too. I ran up that way, and he followed me."

Julia simply nodded then went to Morgan's wardrobe, where she pulled out a fresh pair of jeans. "Yeah."

"Yeah? What does *yeah* mean?" Morgan looked down at herself. "I need to change my shirt, too. The bottom is wet."

Julia returned to the wardrobe and thumbed through. "How about this?" She presented a tank top with flowers embroidered along the edges.

"No." Morgan pulled on the clean jeans and went to the wardrobe, selecting a Jordache top with a logo emblazoned over the bosom.

"Morgan, *no*. That's so boyish."

"Who cares?" Morgan scoffed, indignant, then spun around, facing away from her friend to pull off the soiled shirt and tug on the new one.

Behind Morgan, Julia gasped. "You're not wearing a bra!"

Morgan tugged her shirt down real quick and slinked toward her full-length mirror on the back of the bedroom door, inspecting herself. Satisfied but not exactly over the moon, she shrugged. "I fibbed."

"We don't fib to each other, Morgan." Morgan caught sight of her friend in the mirror, and Julia had folded her arms over her chest.

"So you're really wearing one?"

"We made a pact, didn't we?" Julia pulled up her shirt shamelessly, revealing a white training bra that looked like half an undershirt rather than anything lacey that they'd spotted in the Victoria's Secret catalog Julia's mom got each month.

Morgan let loose a long, irritable sigh. "It's so awkward." She shuddered, too. "Ew."

"Just have your mom get you one at Save-Mart. No big whoop."

"Save-Mart? Bleh. No thanks."

"Oh, so you're gonna ask sweet ol' CarlaMay to walk you into the ling-er-y section in Mervyn's and wait while you rifle through racks of *thongs*."

"Thongs?" Morgan made a face. "You mean tongs? They don't sell those in underwear. That's a kitchen thing."

Julia cackled and fell backward on Morgan's bed, splaying her arms out. "Now that you're thirteen, and now that you have a crush, you have to wear a bra, Morgan Jo." Her voice was like a mother's, and that made the whole thing ten times worse.

"I don't have a crush."

"Okay, well, Emmett sure likes you. He even saved you." Julia shot up. "He's your *hero*."

Morgan groaned. "If I promise I'll buy a bra—and *wear* it—will you shut up about Emmett?"

Julia crossed herself. "Swear to God."

There was only one problem, though. The main reason that Morgan hadn't gotten or worn a bra yet wasn't because, well, she was flat as a pancake. Rather, it was because she had no one to take her. With her own mom, it'd be weird as sin. Things like bras and sex were complicated between Morgan Jo and Carla-May. Mainly, Morgan figured, this was because she didn't know who her dad was. Her mom sometimes acted like the whole thing was some virginal miracle.

The only problem with that theory was that Morgan Jo was no savior. Not for her mother, not for nobody. Least of all for herself.

Morgan Jo went to her bedroom window and looked out at the party. What was meant to be her birthday had devolved into a free-for-all. Adults drinking Grandad Bill's "Moonshine Wine," as he called it. Her cousins Tiffany, Amber, and Rachel gossiping, probably about Morgan. The boys fighting in the back field, a hair too close to a perfectly balanced cow, if you asked Morgan. She looked closer. Emmett wasn't with them. He was standing near the tobacco hangar, she saw, talking to Father David, of all people.

Morgan did a double take. She didn't know her mom had invited the priest. Then again, it probably wasn't CarlaMay who invited Father David. Her mother seemed almost scared of that man. At least, she acted cold around him. In fact, Father David was the very reason CarlaMay had been so weird about going to church since Morgan could remember, but it was strange. The priest loved Morgan, she felt this. And she loved him.

More likely it was Memaw who'd invited him.

"So, you'll ask your mom to take you, then?" Julia prompted, solidifying their latest promise.

"To get a bra?" Morgan asked back, turning from the window and accepting the fact that it was getting high time to blow out candles and cut the cake. "No. It'd be weird."

"Yeah." Julia understood. "Why don't you ask..." But before Julia could finish her thought, a knock came at the door, gentle and respectful.

Morgan went to open it, cracking it to peek through. "Memaw," she said.

"There's my girl." Memaw came into the room, greeting Julia warmly. Her hands were behind her back, holding something and stretching the older woman's bony shoulders gracefully back. She sometimes reminded Morgan of a bird. A swan. A black swan, maybe, with that shiny black hair and those apple-red lips. The poise and elegance, belying a life of hard manual labor and farm work. Belying everything that she ought to have been.

"I didn't want to embarrass you in front of all of your guests, Morgan Jo," she said, sweet as sugar. "I got you something for your special day that's private." She gave Julia a circumspect look.

"It's okay, Memaw. Julia's my best friend."

"I know." Memaw's face relaxed into a smile, and she set a wrapped gift box on the bed. Julia stood up, all too aware of one of many of the older woman's rules. Beds weren't for casual sitting. It wasn't proper.

Morgan moved to the box, taking in its professional wrapping. Heavy pink paper, pinched into sharp edges and corners and tied up with a big fat velvet bow. It was the prettiest gift Morgan had ever seen in her life. She couldn't imagine anything inside being more beautiful than that box. That paper. That bow.

"Go on. Open it." Memaw inched toward Julia, excited to watch.

Carefully, Morgan did as she was told, untying the bow

with the precision of a surgeon, peeling back the triangle corners of the wrapping paper until she slid out a pristine white box, thick as a hatbox. She lifted the lid. Inside, padded in soft, supple pink tissue paper to match the wrapping paper, a thick envelope.

Morgan slid a finger beneath the seal and worked it open. Inside was a birthday card different from any she'd ever seen. Absent were the balloons or bright colors or cartoon characters of her youth. Instead, on the front was a chic pink birthday cake with tall candles, almost glowing. She opened it.

Happy birthday, Morgan Jo. And a gift certificate to Donovan's department store.

"Donovan's?" Morgan's eyes bulged as she gaped at her grandmother. She gave a guilty look to Julia, but Julia wasn't the jealous sort, and anyway, her parents had more money than Morgan could dream of.

Julia beamed back at Morgan and together they screamed, danced, hugged. *Donovan's.* The fanciest store they knew. Julia had been there before—her mother, a fashionista who did marketing for the Kentucky Derby, took Julia to all sorts of expensive locales from Donovan's to Nordstrom to Saks Fifth Avenue (but the one in Louisville, not in New York). Word had it that Mrs. Miles was planning a blowout vacation for Julia's thirteenth birthday wherein the pair would fly to the Big Apple for a shopping spree.

After her little celebration with Julia, Morgan turned on Memaw, hugging the woman with a careful but earnest might. "Thank you, Memaw. *Wow.* It's the best birthday gift in the whole world! Thank you!"

"Well, you wouldn't have said so a year ago," Memaw replied, holding Morgan's shoulders and studying her. "It's for a very special birthday. Thirteen years old? My Lord, Morgan Jo, you're a woman now. So you need to think very carefully about what you want to spend that on." Memaw tapped the card in Morgan's hand with a red-painted fingernail.

Julia gave Morgan the *look*, and Morgan held back an eye roll. She gripped the card in both hands, setting her mouth in a line. If God was working in His mysterious ways right now, then who was she to thwart Him?

"Memaw," she started, her eyes on the card, burning a hole through it out of mortification and glee and any other number of unpindownable emotions. "Will you take me to buy a..."—she cleared her throat—"*you* know. Could we maybe use some of this money to buy my first—"

Julia stepped up right next to Morgan and placed a calming hand on her shoulder. "Memaw Coyle, Morgan wants you to help her buy her first bra."

CHAPTER FIFTEEN

2004

Essie

Essie had over twenty grandchildren now, and to keep track of each of their birthdays was, plainly put, unreasonable.

But, of course, CarlaMay was taking Morgan Jo's thirteenth birthday very seriously. Essie questioned this. Wasn't the sweet sixteen supposed to be the special birthday? Or even better, why not wait for the girl's confirmation? They could have a big ol' bash then, when she joined Jesus's army and proved her worth.

CarlaMay wouldn't take no for an answer, however. Once she mentioned she'd host it at Black Pond Park, Essie had to step in. If anyone in town knew that a Coyle or a Nelson were hosting a birthday party in the public park, humiliation would rain down on Essie.

That was when she figured she may as well open up Moonshine Creek Farm. It never had been open to the public in all its time. Not when Mom Nelson and Dad Nelson were alive. Not when they were sick and Essie was the one to stay on and look after them. Not when tobacco was in danger of dying on account of the medical people. Not even in the late eighties and early nineties, when Essie and Bill brought it back from the brink and transformed it into a thriving agricultural operation that not only saw great profits but also beautiful landscapes.

It was a private tobacco farm, and the public was probably very curious. At least, in Essie's mind they were.

Little Morgan Jo's party would be the perfect opportunity to show the world what the Nelson-Coyles had done. And besides, thirteen *was* a big age. Essie recalled when she was thirteen. Back in those days, before girls got their first monthly bills so young, thirteen meant you could quit school for good. You could work full-time—of course, Essie and her siblings had worked full-time from the age of five on up. But it also meant you could drive the family truck to town and smoke a pack. You could do anything at the age of thirteen.

These days, though, children didn't get to do just anything. So it was up to Essie to figure out what rite of passage would best fit a modern teenager such as her eldest granddaughter, Morgan Jo.

In the end, a shopping spree was the answer. Essie budgeted out the maximum of what she could—which was quite a lot—and she went down to Donovan's department store and loaded it all on to an embossed gift certificate.

Then, she bestowed the neatly packaged present to Morgan, with her friend Julia watching. Morgan had nearly dropped dead over the whole thing, but it was Julia with the good idea.

A bra! Of all things. Essie should have thought of that. But now the plans were laid, and Morgan and Essie were buckled into the T-Bird—Bill's first wife, in truth—and on the road north to the famously hoity-toity department store just outside of Louisville.

"I think we ought to shop first, then go out to lunch after," Essie suggested as they turned off into the parking lot. Bill hadn't let her take the old red Ford. He was doing repairs on it. The glovebox had broken, and Bill liked to keep his registration in there together with an emergency flashlight, and even a small pistol—for personal defense. So, instead, they took the T-Bird. This was just as well because Essie was good at driving the T-Bird. She'd be comfortable, and with a delicate outing such as this, it was important that Essie be comfortable. And Morgan Jo, too.

"Lunch? Okay, sure." Morgan sat rigid in her seat, her hands tucked between her thighs as she watched out the window.

They parked and got out, making their way with an air of anticipation and excitement toward the glowing double doors of Donovan's.

"Here we go," Essie announced, swinging the door open.

A friendly attendant greeted them. "Good morning and welcome to Donovan's. Is there something I can help you find today?"

Morgan Jo looked up at Essie, who returned the look down her nose and gave her elbow a meaningful squeeze. "Morgan Jo?"

Morgan Jo flushed and then searched the great expanse beyond the woman. Escalators crisscrossed the center of it. Signs pointed this way and that. *Shoes. Women's World. Menswear. Children.* The second floor held the unmentionables, Essie knew. Along with purses and perfumes and jewelry.

Morgan Jo pointed toward the middle of the store. "Ling-er-ee," she fumbled.

The attendant followed the girl's stubby-nailed finger then returned her look to Essie. "Pardon me?" A smile danced in her eyes, mockery at the expense of this newbie shopper.

Essie didn't laugh. She set her jaw and cleared her throat. "Lingerie," she said plain and proper, as though it was the attendant who had bad ears and not Morgan Jo who didn't know the word was French for linen and American English for sexy stuff. Essie wouldn't have known it either if it weren't for their fortieth wedding anniversary spent abroad. She'd correct Morgan Jo later, in private. Essie leveled her chin again at the woman who looked a bit dumbstruck, then said, "My granddaughter and I are having a special girls' day out." And with that, Essie led Morgan Jo toward the escalator going up to the lingerie section. But, in fact, it felt a lot more like they were riding up into heaven together.

CHAPTER SIXTEEN

PRESENT DAY

Morgan Jo

Morgan rolled her bag through the jetway and out into the open area beyond the arrival gate. Louisville Airport felt immediately like home.

She could enjoy a significant shopping spree there, picking up souvenirs ranging from anything Derby-related to shirts that read *Gettin' Lucky in Kentucky*. Nick popped back up in her mind but she shook the thought away. He wouldn't wear a shirt like that. And he wasn't much interested in horse racing. Not that she knew.

Making her way through the airport and out to the curb, Morgan took careful, intentional steps so as not to trip and fall and embarrass other people. She avoided the moving sidewalk and kept her pace slow and deliberate.

That was the thing about Morgan's hip injury, her limp had become second nature. Falling had become second nature. And though she hadn't gotten used to stares or well-meaning offers of help, Morgan was no longer ashamed of her condition. It was other people who seemed to be. More likely than not, uptight-looking middle-aged women would glance at Morgan then quickly look away. Younger women, too. Attractive men often did this. Like they were embarrassed for Morgan. Or embarrassed for themselves that they didn't have a limp or a *difference* about them.

Once outside, she spotted Julia's Christmas-tree-green truck right away, idling directly in front of the terminal, while the wild-haired woman inside thumbed through a tatty paperback. Julia had probably arrived an hour ago, swooping loops through the area until that particular pickup spot had opened up. Even then, she'd probably been hassled by security to "Move along!" Only to swing around and do it over and again until they left her well enough alone. Morgan loved her best friend. And she'd missed her badly.

She rapped her knuckles on the passenger window and gave a broad smile and a little wave. Julia chucked the book onto the dash and pumped the age-old window down with the manual crank. "Get in!" she hollered, and Morgan did, crunching her carry-on between her legs and her shoulder bag on the seat between them. Julia grabbed her into a hug and planted a wet kiss on Morgan's cheek.

Morgan wiped it away. "Gross. You never change, do you?"

"Sorry. I was reading a hot romance. Gotta get a little action *somewhere*. Woo!" She fanned herself dramatically and put the truck in gear. "Let's get you to the farm."

"Oh." Morgan held on to the handle and winced. "I was thinking we could grab a bite first? So I could take a little break and—"

"Nuh-uh," Julia replied without a glance. "I have direct orders from CarlaMay herself. Plus, your aunts are there. Everyone is waiting for you." At that point, Julia did hazard a look at Morgan, whose face was no doubt streaked with apprehension. "Mo, this is a pretty big deal."

Morgan sighed and settled into her seat, resigned to the

plan.

"She hasn't said two sensical words since it happened. How long ago was that? She's been getting intensive speech therapy. She receives physical therapy in the home, too, Mo. Except on Sundays, because Trina doesn't do Sunday calls."

"So, you're not doing the physical therapy?" Morgan had assumed that Memaw would request Julia to be her therapist. Julia was not only the best physical therapist in the greater Louisville area but also a close friend of the family.

"She didn't have the words to request me," Julia answered soberly. "And your mom was more preoccupied with the speech thing, so PT got kicked over to Trina. But I come anyway, so it doesn't matter much. We both work with her." Julia was nothing short of an angel. Working for free *and* traveling out to the Nelson farm just to help a mean old lady. Memaw didn't deserve it.

"She still can't walk?" Morgan asked.

"It's a struggle."

"But she's home now. On home health and therapy services. If she's in such a bad condition, why isn't she still in the hospital? How come they've greenlit in-home services?"

"I pulled some strings." Julia took the bends in the highway until they came upon their exit. In what felt like no time at all, they were getting off of I-65 and onto Rolling Fork East toward Brambleberry. After one more turn south onto Bourbon Boulevard they hit the town limits.

Welcome to Brambleberry, Home of the Moonshine Creek Farm.

Morgan cringed at the ubiquitous and relatively new town sign. She squeezed her eyes shut. "Are we past it yet?"

"Yeah." Julia understood how she felt. The sign had been erected by a kiss-ass mayor who'd attended Morgan Jo's thirteenth birthday party. He was so taken with Essie and Bill and their operations on the northeast side of town, that he put together an effort to rebrand the whole place around the only claim to fame he could think of: the fact that little ol' Brambleberry might resurrect the tobacco industry yet.

It never did.

Yes, the Nelson family farm did well for itself, and for the community. Yes, Memaw and Grandad Bill pumped donations into the township, supporting that mayor for as many terms as were legal, but no. Tobacco was as much a trend as a Pet Rock. The general surgeon saw to that. As did the death of Grandad Bill from throat cancer only a few years earlier.

"It looks exactly the same," Morgan admired as they turned onto First Street and down tree-lined sidewalks.

"You've been gone a year. What could possibly change in a year?" But even with her cynical attitude, Julia put her foot on the brakes, slowing the truck for Morgan's benefit. They crossed over Hickory Lane, which ran down to the courthouse at the south edge of town. Then past Derby Drive, one of several streets named in honor of one of the jockeys who'd ridden in the very first Kentucky Derby, way back when. He'd been the grandson of a founder, Forrest Tuelle, and despite the fact that neither Forrest's grandson nor any horse he'd ever raced had ever won, Forrest realized he'd better capitalize on Kentucky's best-known sport. The town hall building would be named for the jockey grandson—Douglas Tuelle Town Hall—and the streets that sliced north/south through the middle part of town were all coded accordingly. Churchill Downs Drive came up next, but after that they hit Main Street. Up north on Twelfth Street, Morgan didn't have a great view of the town square and the five streets that raced through the heart of Brambleberry.

"Anyone go out of business down there?" Morgan asked, indicating the quaint business district.

"Yep. Sadly the sewing shop shut down."

"The sewing shop?" Morgan asked as they crossed Main

and headed toward Triple Crown Court.

"Thread Bare. Remember? My mom and yours learned to crochet there one year, and we were forced to wear matching scarves that looked like they'd been rung out in the Ohio?" Julia snorted to herself, but Morgan was dismayed that no, she didn't remember.

"What happened to the shop owner?"

"She died. Her daughter didn't want to keep the place going, but I think her *granddaughter* did. It was a big drama, actually. Articles ran in the paper about it. The Ingle family, I think it was. Or... no. That can't be right. They had a daughter our age. Remember the girl? She was a little behind us in school, maybe. Minnie or Millie, I think?"

Then, the memory smacked Morgan so hard in the head she felt like she had whiplash. "Midge. Midge Millbank. She moved up north. I saw it on Facebook. We're friends online."

"Midge, that's right. She was a sweetie."

"Yeah." Morgan closed her eyes and when she opened them again they were rolling past Rose Avenue. Sidewalks gave way to winding white fences and farmland as they left town and moved out east into the countryside. Brambleberry turned from a small cross-section of Americana into rolling hills and expansive plantations. Some upgraded into heartland mansions, like Julia's family's place down south off Smoking Pipe Street. Some of the properties had been demolished, save for a dilapidated barn here or an old silo there. Almost all of them, however, were entirely defunct of any true farming operations.

Except for one.

Julia passed Smoking Pipe and carried on along Twelfth Street until it turned into Railroad Route then took the last left onto Brambleberry Lane.

Brambleberry was something of a misnomer for the mile-long fence that led up to the family farm. No one Morgan knew called any of the vines that ran wild across her family's land brambles. And berry and grape vines were more rampant just here, at this northeast crook of the town. They were everywhere, to be sure. But there was still some truth in the name of the lane at the end of which sat her childhood home. It was there, along those acres that the vines grew twisted and thick and riddled with wild fruit of any flavor and color. It was almost endless. There were raspberries and blueberries and strawberries, and all of them wild as a boar.

Julia's tires crunched over slate-colored gravel for some while until they hit the brick drive that would carry them to the big house, a towering white colonial with gables that soared to the sky and columns that looked as if they rooted the whole structure so deep down into the Kentucky soil that they popped into China.

"Home sweet home." Julia threw the truck into park and unbuckled herself.

But Morgan sat for a second. She stared up at the place. Nothing had changed but everything had changed. The grass was just as green as ever, even now, at the break of autumn. Had it been a dry summer, that green grass would have gone yellow and brown.

"It rained a lot?"

"We've had the usual amount." Julia studied her but remained quiet.

The big house looked bigger than Morgan recalled. Was this an effect of having spent so much time in the desert dwellings of Tucson? Homes there were so different. For starters, multi-level homes were rare and existed mostly within tract developments. It was too hot in Sonoran Arizona for a second floor to be of any practicality. But here in Kentucky, two-story homes were as commonplace as whiskey barrel planters. Sure, ranch-style homes existed, too, but the nice thing about the second floor, Morgan had learned in college and even at a training course or two, was that it saved on construction costs.

She'd never thought about the farm as being a cheap alternative to a more rambling estate. The farm itself was every bit the rambling country estate one could dream of—what with the big white house like a feudalist manor cemented squarely to the front and center of the property. Behind the big house spanned various back buildings. A handful of small homestead-style cabins, a barn, an old brick silo, and a tobacco hangar off in the far distance.

The property was framed by split-rail fencing grown over in vines and creepers, all meant to keep cows in.

Morgan stared out her window at the wood fence that faced the orchards on the east side of the property. She remembered scaling the fence to slip into the orchards and pluck down ripe fruit—plums and peaches. She remembered sitting beneath a peach tree one summer with Emmett. They were fifteen, which felt like the perfect age to be sitting beneath peach trees and nibbling the soft pink skin of the fruit with a cute boy. Emmett and Morgan filled their bellies up with peaches, then lay back and stared up at the sky together.

Morgan could remember kissing him after that. Or rather, Emmett kissing her. But they were found out by Grandad Bill, and the ensuing blow-up was so humiliating that she never thought she'd kiss another boy again. Now, years later, she regretted that she *had* ended up kissing other boys.

Morgan looked away from the orchard and back at the wide front porch of the house. She fought off so many other memories—good ones and bad—that she was just about frozen to the seat. Sometimes, Morgan figured, you could choose which memories to dwell on. You could pick 'em, like a lucid dream.

So, as Morgan Jo Coyle sat in her best friend's green truck in front of her family's big white house in Brambleberry Creek, Kentucky, that's just what she did.

She thought about a good memory.

CHAPTER SEVENTEEN

2008

Essie

After the big opening party for her granddaughter's thirteenth birthday four years before, Essie realized exactly what she had in the farm. Something special.

From that day on, Essie and Bill hosted a great many events at the property. From birthday parties to fish fries, they got good at these hootenannies. So good that Essie was ready to move past the little parties into bigger ones. At first, she wanted to have DanaSue's wedding on the farm, but Bill didn't know about that.

"Just the reception," Essie promised early one summer morning. DanaSue and Bobby had made their engagement official just the night before and were planning fast nuptials. Bobby being her second husband, DanaSue didn't want anything too fussy. "Obviously it'll just be the reception, I mean. They're gettin' married in the church, so it'll just be the after-party."

"The after-party is the worst part," Bill huffed, cranky as all get-out. By this time of year, of course, morning frost had long since turned to dew. Breath had lost its whiteness in the air, but

Bill still wore his usual get-up, heavy though it was. Denim overalls and a light flannel jacket and an ol' red cap. He hesitated at the door, working the cap up and down his forehead like he had a bad itch. "Anyway, crops is rotted, Essie, and what are we gon' do about that? It's the pr'ority!" he raged, and spittle formed at the edges of his mouth over the mispronounced word and bad grammar. Redness flamed over his face and just about fogged up his eyeglasses.

But he was right, Essie knew. They'd had a bad year. Too much rain, maybe. The crops had turned, and they'd lose the lot of it. But wasn't that more of a reason to give themselves a distraction? "Ain't nothin' to do about that now, Billy," Essie said softly, her voice sweet as honey and her hand rubbing small circles on his back.

The red left Bill's face and he gave his head a slow shake. "We got t'clear the fields. That's the pr'ority."

"Billy, it's your DanaSue. It'll be *fine*. We can afford one bad year."

"What about two bad years, Essie?" he roared again. "What if soil's turned!"

"Soil hasn't turned. It's good as ever. Look at them grapevines and berries out there." She pointed a crooked finger out along the fence.

But Bill wasn't convinced, and he was angrier than ever. "That's not a crop. It's a weed!"

He left, and Essie chewed her lip 'til it just about bled. Their livelihood was wrapped up in that damn tobacco. If they didn't have a year to show for, then who knew what reputation could befall the Coyles? Townsfolk'd blame the Coyle name, Essie could hear it now. *Soil was good so long as June and Garold Nelson were alive.* And: *It's that bastard, Bill Coyle. Ol' grump couldn't grow a booger in his nose if he had a head cold.*

She set about breakfast, cracking eggs one-handed into a glass bowl while watching Bill through the kitchen window. His gait had slowed lately, his back twisting to the right like her fingers had started to do. Years of farm work were taking their toll on Bill just as years of housework and cooking and sewing were taking theirs on Essie. But she didn't mind a crooked finger or two. Or a husband with a crooked back. She did, though, mind a husband with a crooked mood. It aggravated her.

She whipped the eggs with a fury until a voice startled her from behind.

"Memaw." It was Morgan Jo, sleepy-eyed and precious, standing in her white nightie at the base of the stairs. "Can I help with breakfast?"

"You sure can, honey pie." Essie squeezed Morgan Jo into her bosom and planted a fat kiss on the girl's freckled cheek. Morgan was graduating from high school in a week, and though she had the brain to prove it, to Essie, she was still a little girl. Always a little girl.

Of all of Essie's grandchildren, it was Morgan Jo she was closest to, mainly out of proximity. The others lived off the farm in town or even out of town, up in Bardstown and Louisville, down in Tennessee. But it was Morgan Jo who lived right there in the farmhouse with her mama and with Essie and Billy.

They set about peeling bacon from wax paper and lining it along the biggest cast-iron pan, which sat heated up on the stove. Essie wasn't one to dwell in history or appreciate antiques like some women and men her age. She liked newfangled. She liked to flaunt her money where she may, and if that meant a stainless-steel stove, then so be it.

But down in the cellar, you can bet Billy kept the Nelsons' original stove, a cast-iron beast of a thing with rust and ash and soot and the memories of Essie's youth—the hard days of living on a working farm that was big and bustling but that produced tobacco in a time when just about everyone was producing tobacco. It was a hard childhood, Essie had. Made much harder by the loss of her twin way back when. Among other things.

"What you up to today, girl?" Essie asked Morgan Jo.

Morgan Jo let out a wide yawn and poured herself a glass of cold milk before falling into the nearest kitchen chair. "Applications."

"Applications? What, for college? You already got in to the University of Kentucky."

"I have to apply to the *school* within the college. You know, declare my area of study." Morgan Jo pushed her glass away and splayed herself across the table. "Julia already knows she wants to be a physical therapist. Like, that's it. It's all she's wanted to be since she was five or something." Morgan Jo sat up quick. "Have you ever heard of a five-year-old who wants to be a physical therapist when she grows up? What happened to princesses and fairies?"

"You never wanted to be a princess or a fairy," Essie pointed out with a wooden ladle covered in partly cooked egg.

"No, that's true." Morgan Jo seemed to give it a think. Then, she said, "What did you want to be when you grew up, Memaw?"

"Me?" Essie withdrew back to the stove. Now it was *her* turn to give it a think. "It wasn't like that when we was growing up, Morgan Jo."

"It wasn't like what?"

"We didn't talk about what we were gon' be. We already knew what we'd do. We'd work on the farm and start our own families. That was that."

"Okay, well, if you were growing up right now, what would you want to be, Memaw?"

Essie smiled absently then slid the skillet of scrambled-up eggs onto a platter, carrying it to the table with a dishrag. Essie loved her dishrags. She really did. She bought up cheesecloths and plain white fabric and embroidered every last one with hens and roosters, and pigs, too. Some had barns and farmhouses. To some she added little sayings. It was her favorite one that she now used as a potholder.

The cross-stitching read *If Mama Ain't Happy, Ain't Nobody Happy*.

It wasn't necessarily true, but it sure did make ol' Essie laugh.

"If I were growing up in this day and age, I'd want to run a vineyard."

Morgan Jo looked with a shade of shock at her grandmother. "A vineyard? Like, for wine?"

"Oh, yes. And I tell you what, Morgan Jo, I wouldn't do any of the farm work, either. I'd wear a fancy outfit and stay cool and comfortable inside a pretty little office—or no, a *tasting* room! I've read about them. My second cousin once removed, Anna, runs a vineyard in Indiana, and she has one of those. People just come and taste little glasses of wine and buy it all up. Makes a fortune." She winked at Morgan Jo then joined her to take a few bites of egg. "Plus, when we went to Rome last year, your grandaddy and me did a wine tasting at a real vineyard—an Italian one. He wanted to take me somewhere romantic. It was so magical, Morgan Jo, I tell you h'what. You've got a good grandaddy."

"Sounds fancy, all right."

"What about you, honey? What are you thinking?"

"I want to work on houses. Like do real work."

"Like a handywoman? A construction person?"

"No." Morgan Jo took up a forkful of egg and shoveled it into her mouth, chewing thoughtfully awhile. After she swallowed and took a fresh swig of milk, she replied, "Like, I want to remodel houses. Like not really a decorator, but you know—restore them."

Essie laughed only because it wasn't a surprise that Morgan Jo was so interested in the homestead. All growing up, Morgan Jo led her cousins down to the cellar to play house at that old-timey stove. Billy was always hollering at them not to touch things. Once, even, Essie found a heavy old iron in Morgan Jo's room, on a makeshift ironing board on the ground, set out like a little housewife was busy getting her husband's clothes all set for the next day.

"What's so funny?"

"Nothin' at all. In fact, it makes perfect sense. What about becoming an architect, then? You could even build houses."

"I want the old stuff," Morgan Jo replied stubbornly. "Old houses that need *work*." Morgan Jo was nothing if not a hard worker, that was for sure.

"And where do you see yourself doing this old-house work?" Essie raised an eyebrow at Morgan Jo, a hopeful eyebrow.

Morgan Jo, however, slid her gaze away and to the bacon, sizzling in its oversized skillet.

"I'll get that." Essie rose and set about moving the fatty strips onto a fresh dish towel—this one with a pair of pigs oinking in their pen on it.

Morgan Jo hemmed and hawed at the table in her response. "I don't know *where*. I'd sort of like to stick around here, but my mom thinks I should see the world first."

"That's good advice. You should see the world. If you settle down one day, you might not get the chance. You're young now. Go to school, then head out. Find an old house somewhere. When you've fixed it up, you can come on home."

"Yeah." Morgan Jo accepted two slices of bacon and chomped into them with a ravenous hunger. "Maybe I could even get into real estate."

"Even better," Essie agreed. "You could buy old places and have 'em fixed up. Great way to turn a fast profit. You'll need capital, though. And you have to hire out, because that's dangerous work."

"That's why I think she needs a *real* job to start." The admonition came from the doorway. CarlaMay was dressed for the day in dark-wash jeans and a simple white T-shirt. She'd be heading out to work shortly.

"A real job, what? Like *you*? Somewhere indoors working for someone else?" Essie was quick to put her daughter back in her place. It wasn't that Essie wasn't proud of CarlaMay or happy with her. It was just that CarlaMay couldn't rightly say she was altogether happy with or proud of herself.

"I'm just saying," CarlaMay indeed did say as she plucked a slice of bacon and poured herself some coffee, "that it's important to have something *stable*."

"What do you think I should declare as my major, Mom?" Morgan Jo asked, all innocence and daisies.

CarlaMay looked from her daughter to Essie and back again. "Business. Then you could open up a real-estate firm." She blinked. "Or architecture. You love houses. Could build new ones if you wanted to."

In almost perfect synchronism, Essie and Morgan Jo protested at once, "*Old* houses."

CHAPTER EIGHTEEN
PRESENT DAY

Morgan Jo

Morgan finally unfastened her seat belt and got out of Julia's truck. Julia had already gone in, comfortable enough to enter the big house without Morgan or any other escort.

She took a moment to assess the property. It looked the same, just as the town looked the same. Reminding herself she hadn't been gone long, Morgan stepped up onto the expansive front porch with its lazy rocking chairs and narrow picnic table. Across the table sprawled a burlap checker set, untouched by children in years and yet still set out every spring and packed away every autumn. It was getting close to the time they winterized the place, the checker set included, Morgan figured.

Knocking was silly, and the Coyles didn't believe in doorbells. Though they did have a great big iron dinner bell swinging out at the corner of the porch, so that when someone struck it, it ran clear through the farm into the tobacco hangar and out beyond, to the fields.

Anyway, doorbell or no doorbell, the big house was practically a public space. Ever since Morgan could remember, people would wander in uninvited, unannounced, greeted with sincere welcome by Memaw or Morgan's mom or whichever aunt was flopped onto the sofa with a magazine at the time. It was the Kentucky way. Memaw always said, "Don't need to knock on my door. Just come on in and give a holler." Grandad, in life, had never tended to particularly appreciate this open-door policy. He always seemed shocked if someone actually did just swing the door open and stomp their feet on the mat. Even if it was a cousin. Even if it was Morgan Jo. Even if it was Memaw herself, he was surprised as all get-out.

Morgan turned the brass knob and opened the door. It creaked loudly, despite having only just admitted Julia.

Once inside, Morgan saw plainly that no one was loitering in the common areas of the house. She wandered into the parlor and around the wide-mouthed fireplace to the kitchen. The dining room. Through the half bath and back into the front hall. Voices registered from the east wing of the house. The first-floor master bedroom. The door sat ajar, but Morgan hesitated before it.

"Miss Essie," Morgan could hear Julia say. "It's me again, Julia Miles."

No response. Then came Morgan's mom's voice. "Mom, it's Julia. Morgan's best friend?" Shuffling. Other voices. *The aunts. A cousin? Tiffany or Amber, maybe? Rachel?*

A groan.

Morgan winced.

The groan came again followed by a slur. "Who'sit?"

It was Memaw, and what they'd all said was the truth. The old woman was in a bad way.

Morgan swallowed the urge to cry and pushed into the door. Five faces turned on her. Her mom, Julia, Aunt Barb, Aunt DanaSue, and Amber.

A sixth face remained frozen, supine on the bed, staring up.

Her cheeks gaunt and tongue working like a baby's at the brief taste of mashed bananas.

Memaw.

The black dye job in her hair had grown out, leaving behind long streaks of white. Her eyebrows, undyed or painted, were invisible over the hollows where her eyeballs ought to be. Sunken. She looked, simply, sunken. A literal shell of herself, and now Morgan understood that expression. She understood it painfully well.

Like the Red Sea itself, her aunts, mother, Julia, and Amber parted, taking to the walls of the bedroom and giving Morgan ample space at the old woman's bedside, where a chair was set facing the all-but-lifeless body.

Morgan forced herself to suck in a breath and let it out again. Without greeting anyone in the room, she crossed to the chair, lowered down into it, and collected the skeletal hand from its place atop the quilt. "Memaw?" Morgan whispered. "It's me."

And the old woman's face turned toward the soft new voice. Her eyes narrowed and her eyebrows appeared, sharp and arched and steely gray. And then, she said, clear as day, "Morgan Jo."

CHAPTER NINETEEN
PRESENT DAY

Morgan Jo

Behind Morgan, the other women twittered excitedly, rejoining the reunited pair at the bed and chattering wildly at the confirmation that *yes*, Memaw had been asking for Morgan Jo. *Yes*, she could recognize her eldest granddaughter.

Yes, there was hope for a real recovery.

CarlaMay squeezed her daughter hard. "Morgan, oh honey." Then she squeezed Memaw's hand. "Mom, it's Morgan. She's home. And you're *talking*."

The old woman's eyes rolled at this, and it was as though the stroke had never happened. At least, for that sarcastic moment.

"She did have a stroke," Morgan murmured when Julia moved into the space next to her.

Julia patted Morgan's shoulder. "This is a great start. If you can be around, it might help her find more words. The speech therapist says anything that gives a spark like this is *great*."

"Memaw," Morgan said, turning her attention back to her grandmother. "How are you doing?"

Memaw managed to scooch up on the bed somewhat seamlessly, and it reversed her poor-looking state a great deal. Then she nodded and smiled. The smile was a bit vacant, but there was no question that many thoughts fluttered lively behind Memaw's watery blue eyes. She even cleared her throat and repeated, "Morgan Jo. H—" A glance to Morgan's mom and aunts, who then prompted her.

"Hi," CarlaMay said loudly, patronizingly. "Hi!" Even louder.

"Hi, Morgan Jo." Memaw's lopsided grin grew bigger.

"Mom," Aunt Barb said, pushing through Julia and Morgan to get the bedside. Barb was every bit her name. Big and boisterous, bold and belligerent. "Let's get you up and show Morgan Jo what you can do." She threw the quilt back and shooed Morgan and Julia out of the way. "Shoo, *shoo*! Watch this woman go."

With help from Aunt Barb, Memaw inched to the edge of the bed and slid her legs over the side of it. Aunt DanaSue brought a walker, complete with tennis balls affixed to the bottom to act as gliders or maybe stoppers—Morgan wasn't sure which—close to the bed.

It was then Julia who took over, stabilizing the walker as Memaw braced her hands on it and pulled herself up. Her left side was along for the ride. It was her right side that did the work, pulling its counterpart into position and scooting across the floor in slow, deliberate steps, each one supported by Julia.

"See?" Julia gave a meaningful look at Morgan, who knew the question didn't mean, *See? She's doing great!* but instead meant, *See? She's not doing so great, Mo!*

"She's doing great," Morgan marveled as sincerely as she could muster. "Memaw, you're doing great."

The old woman waved back toward the bed, and Julia helped get her back there. "Miss Essie," Julia said a note louder than was likely necessary, "I want you to stay sitting up now.

We'll bring in a slice of pie and a glass of milk. You can eat right here with Morgan. Okay?"

Memaw nodded like a bobblehead. Julia ushered everyone out, but Morgan knew she was supposed to sit tight. Maybe see if she couldn't get the old woman to say something other than a fumbling "hi" or Morgan's name.

"Memaw, I really am glad you're okay," Morgan said, looking at a family photo that hung on the wall. It was from a time so long ago; she hardly recalled the day whatsoever. In the staged scene, Morgan sat cross-legged between Amber and Geddy. Geddy, who was born just months after Morgan, was Uncle Garold's eldest son, and brother to Earl and Jesse and a slew of others of various mothers. But it was Geddy's mother, Jeana, who'd insisted he assimilate into the family. Geddy lived a more familiar life in Bardstown with his mom while his father, Morgan's uncle, tarried about around the state with other women and children and any number of shameful acts that Memaw had never bothered to acknowledge. But it was Geddy who Morgan felt a deeper connection for. A surprising connection, seeing as their ties were so comparatively thin.

Stretching across and behind the cousins were the rest of the family, aunts, uncles. Centered and seated comfortable, Memaw and Grandad Bill. Proud. Smiling. Coy, even. Back then, Memaw's hair was raven black, and her lips ruby-red. She was a powerhouse of a woman. Not a wisp.

"Morgan Jo," Memaw said, lifting a shaky hand up to her mouth, half of which drooped like her face was melting. She waved the shaky hand over her eyes, which Morgan saw were brimming with tears.

"What is it? What?" Morgan became alarmed. *Was this another medical event? Was it real?*

But her grandmother cleared her throat and repeated Morgan's name crisp as a newly minted bill. "Morgan Jo. I. Am. So..." she hiccupped, "so—so—"

"So... sad?" Morgan tried. "In so much pain?"

"Sahh..." Memaw coughed and gave her head a shake. Then, she steadied her gaze back on Morgan Jo and tried one last time, with success. "I. Am. So-rr-y."

CHAPTER TWENTY

PRESENT DAY

Morgan Jo

Before Morgan could think clearly enough to respond, the others twittered back in, with pie and milk and sweet tea, all bubbling at this happy little reunion.

The old woman's eyes, colder now, clung to Morgan, and it was all she could do not to tear her own gaze away and run out of the big house and through the orchards and fields and fences and into that shallow little creek at the back of the property. The one that ran headlong into the lake that Morgan Jo once slid into like it was quicksand instead of water.

Her mother situated pie and a glass of milk with a straw poking out in front of Memaw, and Morgan was able to break away at last. She moved to the far corner of the room. Her forgiveness clutched so fiercely in her chest that it might never be ripped free.

"Hey, *cuzz*," Amber slurred through a prolonged slug of sweet tea. Barb's bombastic and full-figured eldest daughter ran her arm around Morgan's neck and squeezed her in, tight, tangling them up in one another almost like old times.

"Whoops." Morgan's hair got stuck in the hinge of Amber's glasses and trying to pull it out painlessly became a comedy of errors. Finally Amber took off the dated wire-rim transitional lens set and pinched the few strands, breaking them off. "Sorry, *cuzzo*. So, how ya been doin'?" She flipped her own auburn hair over her shoulder. It was a trait all of the girl cousins shared— their long reddish-brown locks. That and the famous "Nelson Nose." A prominent feature with a hook that looked better on some of them than others.

Morgan rubbed the spot of her scalp where the hairs had been tugged out and answered, "Good. Real good."

"Oh, yeah?" Amber shoveled half her pie and a great big dollop of whipped cream into her oversized mouth. She spoke before swallowing. "How's the Wild West? Hook up with any cowboys yet?" Amber cackled and whitish slobber formed at the corners of her mouth. She gave Morgan a rough elbow.

Nick wasn't exactly a cowboy. And he also wasn't a hookup. But Morgan played along for ease of conversation. She laughed and elbowed her cousin back. "What happens in the desert, stays in the desert, *cuzzo*." Then, to slather it on real thick, she added, "Man, I tell you h'what, Amber Lee, you would *love* it there."

"My hair would go pin flat if I did that. 'Sides, I got Grant." Amber, whose hair was set in big, bouncing reddish curls for this special occasion, was engaged to Grant Maycomb, who just so happened to be the security guard at Western Credit Union on Main. Amber, a hairdresser at the Cutting Edge, met him for lunch at the Dewdrop every day, where they each ordered the French dip with curly fries and extra ranch. Morgan knew this because their routine hadn't changed in about four years. And neither had their betrothal status. If Amber and Grant had one thing going for themselves, though, it was stability. And that was more than could be said for Morgan.

"Oh, nonsense." Morgan took her own bite of pie, swallowing before she went on. "But it is *really* hot there. Like, hot like you can't even imagine."

"But i'n't a dry heat? That's what Memaw says, anyway." Amber said this with an edge of condescension. As if Kentucky and its humid hot was worse than Tucson and its arid hot, and therefore Amber and Kentucky *won* and Morgan *lost*.

Morgan answered simply, "Most of the time. Yeah."

Their mothers, together with Aunt DanaSue and Julia, fussed over Memaw for a while, but before half an hour was up, every last one of them, the old woman included, had finished at least one slice of pie if not two and downed one glass of milk or tea.

It was nap time. That's how things worked in the big house. If it were the weekend or if anyone was home at three in the afternoon, they all took to their respective bedrooms and slept off lunch and a sweet afternoon snack. If they didn't have a bedroom in the big house, like Morgan's aunts didn't, then they took a sofa. There were plenty to go round, too. A red sectional that snaked through the living room, curling itself around the fireplace. It could fit no fewer than two full-size adults. Then there was the upstairs loft sleeper sofa, a corduroy number from the nineties when sleeper sofas were all the rage in Brambleberry for some reason. Down in the basement, there were two more couches, and a love seat in the bedroom down there, as well as a big heavy leather thing with reclining backs that Uncle Garold had convinced Memaw to buy when he had to move back home for some time after college.

But Amber and Morgan were young and jet lag hadn't hit yet, so they followed Julia to the kitchen, where the three washed up dishes and tidied.

Well, Morgan and Julia washed up. Amber talked. And talked. And talked. They learned about Grant's skin cancer that wasn't exactly cancer but *could* be. They learned about Tiffany having a positive pregnancy test one day and getting her period the next, and then Travis bringing around a girl all of them hated so much that one family event was enough to scare her off. She told them how Ryan had become some big-shot insurance salesman up in Bardstown, and Geddy was down on his luck, and he'd moved *out* of Bardstown and into the cabin at the back of the property.

At the mention of his name, Julia flinched.

"Down on his luck? I thought he was running a crew at the construction site in Lexington?"

For the first time since Morgan had been back, she and Amber shared a knowing smile.

"Did I say he wasn't gainfully employed?" Amber teased. "You know... I think he's home right now. I saw him this morning when I was hanging up my laundry." Morgan had a hard time believing Amber hung her laundry out to dry. So between this suspected fib and the possibility that her cousin Geddy was currently on the property, Morgan got a stirring. "Let's go say hi and find out."

Julia stammered, "Oh, n-no. Let him be. I was hoping we could go into town together. Do a little shopping?"

"Shopping? In Brambleberry?" Amber scoffed so hard spittle flew out her full, freckled lips. "You got me way too curious about Geddy. Either he's lying about being down on his luck and wanting to live off Memaw or—"

"Or Julia's got bad information?" Morgan gave her best friend a knowing look. "You've stayed in touch with Geddy, then, eh?" This would be pretty funny to Morgan, seeing as Julia and her cousins had never really gotten along quite like Morgan would have hoped.

Julia held up her hands in surrender. "I just hear what I hear. Lots of talk up at the hospital is all. And around town."

"Well, he *is* in construction, right?" Morgan asked Amber. "What'd he say to *you* and Memaw about being down on his luck?"

"I mighta exaggerated," Amber admitted. "I mighta said he was down on his luck when what I meant was he'd broken up with that girl—who was it?"

"Celeste," Julia replied, and her reply was enough to send giggles through all three of them.

And just like that, it was old times. One of them had a crush on someone in the greater Brambleberry circle, and the manhunt was on.

They went out the back door, and the memories and beauty of the rest of the property hit Morgan like a sack of red bricks.

CHAPTER TWENTY-ONE

2012

Essie

Essie and Bill sat on their back porch, in a matching pair of white wooden rocking chairs, sipping on summer's sweet tea and admiring their land together.

It was a beauty, the farm and all its pieces.

April had taken in good rain—not too much, though. They'd thrown down tobacco crops a month back. Now it was May, and the good rain had meant good sprouts. The good sprouts were becoming good crops. And good crops meant pretty wild-flowers. Not only that, but the promising weather of the first half of the year proved out that the vines and orchards had come back to life. In all, it was a scene out of a children's picture book. Essie could just imagine her own grandchildren running through the green grass, catching lightnin' bugs by twilight and blowing dandelions by daylight.

Of course, with the thought of kids blowing weeds, came the thought of Bill hollering at 'em to *Cut that out now a'fore I tan all you alls' hides. Blessed be, Ess, them kids are wild as hogs. Gon' throw my back out weeding the goddamn grass!*

Essie could see her old self, too, frowning in consternation at her husband, at his gripes, at her feelings about it all. *I'n't like we grew this grass or these dandelions, Bill. And watch your tongue. Blasphemy like, what would your'n mother say! My, Bill. My, my, my. If God saw fit to throw down grass in these here blue Kentucky hills, and if he saw fit to throw down dandelions in this here grass, then he saw fit for our grands to blow the seeds around, too. Circle of life, Bill, for heaven's sake.*

In months' time, the grass'd be brown. The dandelions naked. The crops harvested and hanging out to dry.

"Morgan comes home tomorrow," Essie said, by way of breaking their silence.

She must have stirred Bill awake, because he startled and grunted and gave out a low curse.

Essie kept her gaze on the big red barn not fifty yards off. In there, her ma and daddy used to keep the horses. They had two. Just for traveling and ploughing. Nothing fancy. They weren't no thoroughbreds. They were working horses. Out from the barn, Essie swept her eyes across the rest of the property. To the far left, a cul-de-sac of bunk houses. Three. Used to be they were for the help, back when Essie's ma used a wet nurse and her daddy kept *help* help. That's what Essie had grown to call those poor folk who were enslaved to folks who just happened to be lucky enough to be born into a bit of money. It didn't even take much at all. Land and a crop or two. A horse. Cattle, and you were set well enough to bring on *help* help.

Unease coursed through Essie every time she cast a glance out to those old outbuildings. By the time she was born, her ma had dried up so that Essie and her sister Dottie needed a proper wet nurse, but things were getting more complicated with regards to help, and so Ma Nelson had her eldest, Providence, who was seventeen at the twins' birth, feed the girls.

Across the property and northeast of the big red barn was the working part. Way, way up sat the tobacco hangar, which once was partly used as an animal keep for goats, chickens, and cattle in the winter. Off east, the orchard, a rectangular stretch of apple trees, mulberry trees, pear trees, cherry trees, and apricot trees. At the south edge of the orchard were vegetable gardens. Three of them.

Then, spread even farther east, all up and down along the property were the tobacco plants. Rows and rows of the fragrant-smelling crop, growing up nicely that year. Praise God.

"Billy." Essie stopped rocking. She wanted to talk serious to him now. "Now, listen up, Billy, honey."

Billy gave her a gruff look and leaned her way, his wiry gray eyebrows climbing like old spiders down on into his eyes. "What is it, Essie?"

"It's the kids I wanna talk to you about."

"The kids?" He leaned back into his rocking chair then gave her a sidelong look. "What kids?"

"Oh, Billy." Essie clicked her tongue. "The grandkids I mean."

"Well, what in the hell do you wanna talk about with 'em?"

"No, Billy, I want to talk to *you* about the kids." She pursed her lips and pressed on. "I'm worried." Another tongue click. A shake of the head. She rocked back and forward and sighed low and long. "I'm real worried."

"Well, why're you worried, Essie? They're fine." He waved her off and took up his drink, taking a long gulping swig. Ice clinked in the glass as he downed the rest.

After her first granddaughter, Morgan Jo, had left for college four years earlier, Essie set about putting pressure on the others. It was her daughters' children who'd stayed around town, and it was the lot of them she and Bill worried about the most.

"Tiffany'll be pregnant before she graduates high school," Essie replied.

"Pregnant?" At that, Billy let out a laugh, and this served to really piss Essie off good.

"I'm serious, Bill." And she was. She gave him a serious look to prove it. "And then there's Travis. Who knows where he is any given day." She rocked forward and back. "Amber's lazy as sin. Ryan i'n't much better."

"Well, it ain't our problem, Essie."

Billy could say this easily. In his own addled mind, their grandchildren were decidedly *not* their problem. Even their own children, the three girls and two boys, *weren't* Essie nor Bill's problem. They were irrelevant. Totally.

She wasn't exactly sure how to respond. To tell him he was wrong flat out would enrage Bill. To placate him wouldn't get her anywhere, either. She was stuck between a rock and silo. Silence couldn't help, either, but she let them be silent a minute.

Maybe there *was* another way.

"Honey, what with Amber out of the house, and Travis and Tiffany, too, well, what if we see about hiring them on here?" There. It was the thing she was heading toward, anyway. Maybe, if Essie spun it as she and Bill needed help and not that their grandchildren needed a leg up, maybe that could work.

Bill's face turned red as a chili pepper and he leaned way far forward in his rocking chair. He gave Essie a poisonous glare. "I don't need no goddamn help, Essie. I'm fit as a fiddle, and so're you. What in the hell you think? I can't run this damn farm the way I see fit? You wanna bring in *kids* to do the hard work? There's one thing you're right about, Essie, and it's those lazy kids. Barb's kids and Dana's alike. Lazy as all get-out, and you know it. Now you think they come on and get a free ride in order t'*help*. Ha!" His voice roared at the short laugh and spittle formed over his lips. *Seething* was putting it lightly. He pushed up, his back more crooked than ever, suspenders pulling his saggy-bottomed jeans way up to the top of his hard, big belly.

Essie glowered off into the distance. The sun was beginning to set out past the bunk houses. Memories of her own painful childhood washed over, hard. Self-pity surged, and as her husband left her out there on the porch alone to fester, she clung to one especially bad memory.

The worst day of Essie Nelson's life.

CHAPTER TWENTY-TWO

1948

Essie

Essie and her twin, Dottie, liked to play house, mainly. And as a precocious pair of ten-year-olds with free rein of a farm that spanned acres upon acres at the far-off edge of a little old town in Kentucky, there was a lot of house that could be played.

Essie especially liked for them to pretend the tobacco hangar was a great big old castle, like she'd heard stories of. They didn't get many stories, the Nelson kids. Only those they heard at school. Miss Tuelle, the one-room schoolteacher—who also happened to be Essie and Dottie's aunt—liked to tell stories of far-off lands, like Europe. Miss Tuelle knew about far-off lands only on account of how dang much she seemed to read. She read more than she taught, even, with a book in her hands like it was nailed there.

Miss Tuelle would tell about princesses trapped in high-up towers and the princes who'd rescue them. She'd tell about the stone walls and the dozen or more rooms with brick floors and echo chambers of highfalutin English voices. Then outside, where the vines grew like ropes—Essie loved to hear all about it.

What with its tapered shape and towering appearance, and then all those brambles that grew over the whole farm, it wasn't too hard for Essie to pretend that the hangar wasn't a cruddy old farmer's hangar but instead was a great big stone castle, where she could be a princess, and where a prince would come to rescue her.

"From what?" Dottie always asked. "What you got t'be rescued from? Our lives is just fine. We got it real good."

"We got it good enough, sure," Essie would agree. But deep down, she knew they could have it even better. "Think about it. What if we were big-city folks with lots of gold stashed in our cellar?"

"Big-city folk don't have no gold, and they don't got cellars, neither."

"Well, they don't milk cows, do they?"

"I like milkin' cows," Dottie pointed out. "I even like slopping the pigs. I like it all." She said this so proudly, that Essie knew to feel ashamed, and she did.

"Come on," Essie urged the freckle-faced mirror of herself. Both girls wore long dark braids. Their pale skin didn't prove out the fact that the duo spent every single summer day—and most fall, winter, and spring days, too—out in the sun on the farm. It was the Irish in 'em, Mamaw'd say. But that never rang quite true, because Mamaw Moira's skin had turned like leather in the summertime. At that, Mamaw'd say, "If you're Irish, you can be many a thing. You girlies is fair as fresh cream, and that's no bad way to be."

Essie flipped a braid back over her shoulder and ran into the tobacco hangar. "Come on, I said. Let's go play."

"I'm tired of playin' house, Essie," Dottie groaned, but she followed anyway, weaving through hanging dry leaves all the way to the far back of the hangar.

Essie started up the ladder to the hay loft, where they usually started off, pretending it was morning and Essie-the-mom would cook up breakfast and Dottie-the-daughter would eat it down and run off to play while Essie went to town to see about a position at the newspaper, or some other such pretendin'. Up on the loft up there, Essie kept scraps of their home life, including a rusted cast-iron pan, cloudy glasses, a decanter she'd found out in the woods near the creek, and a crumbling whiskey barrel Essie had convinced her brother to haul up to use as a table.

Also up there, she kept littler things she'd snuck out. Some of Mamaw's cheesecloths to use like dish towels, napkins, table-cloths, and even a little white apron.

They ascended the ladder one after the other, Essie's little red boots clicking on the wood until she was through the opening and hauling herself onto the splintered landing. "Careful your hands," she told her sister. "Splinters galore up here."

Dottie giggled, and Essie knew exactly what she was giggling about. Dad O'Toole had a right funny saying about splinters. They being so much of life on the farm, he'd often use splinters to insult another farmer, or one of his cousins or broth-ers. In a singsong, folksy voice he'd sing as he strummed his thumb up and down the little banjo he kept in the kitchen. "Splinters up your butt, my friend."

Essie giggled, too. "That would hurt somethin' awful."

"I can think of worse things than splinters, though," Dottie retorted smugly. That was Dottie. Always smug as a prize pony about tough-girl stuff like splinters and taking falls and getting dirty. She went to the far side of the loft where there was a crude shelf. On it, a box. She fiddled with the box.

Meanwhile, Essie wiped her hands on a grubby cheesecloth then put on her fanciful mother voice. "All right, sweetheart, your daddy will be home from his business trip today. After breakfast, let's go into town to the shops. We can buy a special pretty dress for you and a special pretty dress for me."

Dottie returned from the shelf, acting sort of funny. She pretended to eat grits out of one of the cloudy glasses with a rusty spoon. But she stopped with the spoon halfway, and then tossed it into the glass so that it clanked about hard. Then she rolled her eyes good and long. "I'm bored of this, Essie. Come on. Let's go huntin' instead."

Essie didn't budge. She was really excited to pretend she had a traveling salesman for a husband and that he was heading home to greet her with a kiss on the front porch. She'd have on a pretty checkered dress, something real expensive. And her make-believe husband would pat their daughter's head kindly, and they'd all go on about their perfect imaginary life.

But Dottie, fiery and fearless as she was, went back to the opening. "I'm going huntin'. With or without you."

Essie scowled hard at her sister. She was angry. Angry they had to make up a great life and angry that they had to pretend a tobacco hangar was a nice home in a nice neighborhood or a nice palace in a nice kingdom or *anything*. She was particularly angry they didn't have any proper play toys, too. She'd heard about kids who got to go to the Puppet Show and pick out spanking-new dollies and rocking horses and she didn't! And what was worse? Dottie didn't even care! Dottie *liked* farm life. She *liked* where they lived and what their folks did and the fact that they came in every night covered over in mud and didn't even take a bath 'til the end of the week. She liked it all.

Folding her arms over her chest, Essie dared Dottie. "Go ahead. You ain't got a gun to hunt with."

"Sure do." Dottie pulled a small pistol out of the pocket of her dress, brandishing it proudly.

Essie's mouth fell open. Her eyes got real big. Her face felt like it had stretched like rubber, wide, wide open. "Where did you get that?"

"Dad keeps it in that box. I saw him once."

"Be careful with that, Dorothy Carla." Essie's stomach knotted up. They wasn't supposed to play with guns.

But Dottie seemed unfazed. "I'm goin' on down and goin' hunting, and you can come if you want to or not. I don't *care!*"

Dottie crossed the short stretch of wood and grabbed a cheesecloth that had been tucked into Essie's front like a neat little white apron. She yanked it out spitefully. "Actually, I *fibbed*. I *do* care, and you *are* comin'!" And with that, the lithe, braver twin grabbed up Essie's fair hand and tugged her hard toward the opening in the floor. But the thing of it was, Essie may not have liked to hunt or fish or work the fields or slop the pigs or milk the cows, but she was strong. As strong as Dottie. Of course she was. They were twins.

Essie pulled her arm back hard, whipping it out of Dottie's, who sailed back across the splintered wooden landing. The next thing Essie knew, Dottie's bottom half was flying in the air like a rag doll's legs. It'd be a funny sight.

If Dottie hadn't fallen through that damn opening.

And if that damn pistol hadn't discharged straight into her little body.

CHAPTER TWENTY-THREE

PRESENT DAY

Morgan Jo

Morgan, Julia, and Amber made their way out back of the big house, cutting through overgrown grass to get to the cabins. Crossing through the grass in such a state made Morgan feel sad. It made her think of Grandad Bill, who mowed that grass so religiously, she wondered if he'd been a barber in another life. His work ethic was just one of the many qualities Morgan admired in her grandfather. Another was his commitment to family. Though her grandmother and aunts and especially Morgan's mom were equally dedicated to putting one another first, Morgan couldn't help but feel Grandad particularly espoused family values. Maybe not in his day-to-day behavior, which could cast him as a cranky old man, but rather in his big actions. His move to the farm to uphold the Moonshine Creek Farm traditions. His support of all their children, financially and in other ways, too. There wasn't nothing Grandad would not do for family.

Morgan hoped she was the same, but she feared she wasn't.

"Who's doing the groundskeeping?" she asked Amber out of curiosity, not judgment.

But Morgan should have known better. Now that she was back at the farm, everything came under shadows of judgment. Every single thing.

Amber snorted. "Well, it's hard. This place is huge. I mean, we're responsible for the fields, the barn, the hangar, the big house, the bunkhouses... not to mention the orchard and the vegetable garden. And that doesn't even include mowing the *grass*," she whined.

Julia glanced at Morgan, who should have known better than to even ask. A year before, when she was back here, living full-time, all of that had fallen to Morgan. No, she hadn't been alone. Her mom had helped. And back then, Amber, Travis, and Tiffany all helped. All of them pitched in. They hadn't hired anyone, and they hadn't yet needed to. The tobacco field only needed tending so far as cutting back the plants—since they were no longer harvesting. The trees in the orchard were handled by a group effort to bring in friends and extended family. Everyone was invited down to clear the trees. Thereafter, aunts and cousins and friends of the family would be set with fruits to can or turn to pies. They'd pull vegetables for stew, too, as the garden often overproduced. Other than that, what, with no animals to tend, the keeping of the barn and hangar was no big fuss whatsoever. So long as no one was planning a big event like Memaw used to do, they just kept the buildings padlocked. Simple as that.

"Amber," Morgan argued, "nothing's changed since I left. It's just mowing. You've got the ride-on in the barn."

Julia gave her a look, and Morgan knew what that look meant. It meant *knock it off right now. It's not worth it.* And she was right. It wasn't. But that didn't mean Amber should just get off the hook.

Amber's face twisted defensively. "We're planning the

wedding. That's what's changed."

Morgan slowed. "So, you've got a date, then?"

A great big smile grew across Amber's mouth, but it flickered out as some other emotion took over. *Confusion?* "Your mama didn't tell you?" she asked this so quizzically that Morgan knew she'd get her mom into trouble if she was honest.

Instead of telling the truth, Morgan shook her head dumbly. "Oh, my word. Of course she did, Amber. I've just been—work is crazy!" She laughed lightly, stealing a look at Julia as they approached the first cabin out back.

Amber startling prattling on. September of the next year. September ninth, which was a great date because they could write it *nine-slash-nine.* "Isn't that a great wedding date? Grant hasn't totally agreed yet, but he thinks next fall is perfect."

"Plus," Julia replied, "that Grant could use any help he could get with the anniversary reminders. So, yes, Amber. It is great."

Amber beamed goofily at Julia's encouragement, and there they were, deposited through the grass at a gravel drive just outside of Geddy's supposed cabin.

"Go on, Julia." Amber prodded her playfully. "Knock."

"I'm not here to see him," Julia shot back, stepping back into the grass that lined the gravel. "I don't even know why we're out here."

"I wanted to see him," Morgan said. "I haven't seen Geddy since Grandad's funeral."

The other two fell silent. No one much talked about Grandad's funeral. It was a hard time in all their lives.

Especially Memaw's.

And especially Morgan's. Because Grandad's funeral wasn't long after the time she got hurt. In fact, it'd just as easily have been Morgan's funeral at which she was last with her cousins.

Not Grandad's.

CHAPTER TWENTY-FOUR

PRESENT DAY

Morgan Jo

It was Amber who ended up knocking on Geddy's door. He answered lazily and shirtlessly, and Morgan could feel Julia ripple with excitement behind her.

"Geddy Coyle." Morgan smirked and clicked her tongue. "Get dressed, you slob."

Geddy's face lit up at the sight of her, but when he noticed Julia, Morgan could see his expression twist into something else. Morgan looked at Julia, who acted so suspiciously innocent that the whole of their recent history was immediately clear.

Morgan's cousin and her best friend had hooked up.

Disgusting.

Morgan shook her head at Julia, who shrugged, but she couldn't wipe the smile off her face with a washrag if she tried.

As for Geddy, he turned his mouth up in a broad smile and dipped his chin. "Julia." Then smiled even bigger. "Morgan Jo. What in the world are you doing here?"

"I think you know what she's doing here," Amber answered, pushing past Morgan and into the cabin. Morgan and Julia followed as Geddy pulled a white T-shirt over his head. Geddy was the opposite of a slob, actually. Fit as a fiddle and tidy to boot, he made even grass-mowing-obsessed Grandad seem sloppy.

"Aw, yeah. Ol' Essie Coyle." Geddy, being a hair removed from the family on account of his father's philandering, had never taken to calling their grandparents by their proper grand-parent names. Nope. It was Essie and Bill to Geddy. "I haven't been up today. How's she doing?"

"Didn't you hear?" Amber asked sourly. "She asked for Morgan. That's why Morgan's here."

"Oh, right." Geddy tugged his shirt down and gestured toward the leather sofa that cut the room in two. "Have a seat, ladies. I'm off work today. Can I get anyone a coffee?"

"It'll keep me up," Morgan declined.

Julia and Amber, however, each accepted a fresh mug and they hunkered down for a spell. After small talk and catching up, Morgan learned that Amber was half-right, and Julia was half-right. Geddy was working construction, as a lead, on several projects. Since he was moving around the state so much, he sublet his townhouse up in Bardstown and moved into the cabins, becoming Amber's often-absent neighbor.

"So," Morgan interrupted, "when did you move in here?"

Amber answered for him. "A week ago, right, Ged?"

"Five days, to be exact. I'll stay through the season. Once winter hits, I'll return home. Anyway, Amber, Tiff, and Trav could use my help around here." He gestured with his own coffee mug out the window toward the property.

"That's good." Morgan tried to be even-keeled on the subject. "They could use the help, I know."

"After you left, sure." Geddy was maybe the only family member of Morgan's who wasn't afraid to talk about the serious thing. The big thing. The *bad* thing. He pointed to Morgan's midsection. "How is it?"

"My hip?" She feigned ignorance.

Geddy scoffed then spoke to Julia. "Are you working with her?"

"It's fine. *I'm* fine," Morgan insisted.

"She's fine," Julia agreed, "but she limps."

"I saw." Geddy stood up and held his hands out to Morgan. "Get up. I want to see you walk."

"Geddy, shut up." Morgan slapped him away, but he persisted.

"Get up, Morgan Jo. I haven't seen you since it happened. All I've heard is lies from Amber and company."

"Lies? What lies?" Amber protested, grumpy and edgy and probably regretting that she even brought Morgan and Julia out here. Geddy was a pistol. They all knew it. Amber just chose to ignore the bad in life. Like the rest of the family seemed to. It was a Nelson-Coyle family epidemic, ignoring the bad in life.

"Listen, I don't want to get into all the things wrong in this family. I just expect a little more honesty." He pushed his hand through his hair and gave up on trying to get Morgan to parade her wounded gait around the room. "I got a lunch date."

Julia was quick to jump in on that one. "A lunch date?"

But Geddy gave her a wry look. "Yes. A *lunch* date. You know, Jules, the kind where two people aren't scared to be seen in public together? Eating a meal together? That kind of lunch date."

Julia's face turned to ice, but Morgan spoke up on her best friend's behalf. "Who is it? Who're you taking to lunch?"

"Actually," Geddy said teasingly, "someone you all know." He folded his arms over his chest, smug with a morsel of gossip for the trio of girls.

"Oh, just give it up, Ged," Amber said. She was sick to death of being there under such awkward pretenses. "Who is it?"

Geddy turned a sharp gaze on Morgan. "Emmett Dawson."

Emmett Dawson. It was a wonder what a name could do to your insides. If Morgan believed in things like *the one who got away*, Emmett would be that person to her. Handsome but boyish, kind but smart, Emmett was everything and nothing to Morgan. That was the thing of it. Emmett was the sort of boy, way back when, who Morgan suspected was perfect. But for everything he ever was, he was too perfect.

Emmett was nice, but was he a pushover? Would he have given in to Morgan like Nick did? Telling her if her hip hurt, she ought to nap, not stretch.

Emmett was cute, but too cute. Those blue eyes and his dimples—there was no telling how they'd play out as features on a middle-aged man.

Emmett was smart, but too smart. He became a lawyer. Morgan could have skipped college all together and it'd make no difference on her life, but Emmett was a reader. She knew this about him. Remembered it. She recalled him swallowing up news and spitting it back like he must have had a photographic memory for the serious stuff in life. Though he never treated anything too serious. See, now, that was another problem with Emmett.

Her mind skipped through time and space to the last time she'd seen or talked to him. Emmett had gone to law school somewhere out east. But he'd come back after. Not to take a job, but for a visit. And for a party. Morgan's college graduation party. The last party that Memaw would host on the farm. The last party she could remember, period.

CHAPTER TWENTY-FIVE

2012

Essie

Over the course of that summer, Essie had set aside the conversation about bringing on some grandkids to help out on the farm. Bill was convinced he could handle ever' last system from mowing that damn grass all the way down to harvesting a small section of the tobacco, which they didn't sell on a grand scale anymore. But it was what Bill liked to do. It made him feel potent and capable, Essie figured. So between that, the animals they kept on, and her vegetables and the fruit trees, the couple maintained a self-sufficient lifestyle even into their seventies.

But there was more to the farm than all those things. Ever since that first child's birthday party—Morgan Jo's—a few years ago, Essie had gotten real good at throwing hootenannies. She'd cleaned the place up so spotless you could lick the floor. Her daughters mostly helped, except for Barb, who was more often than not off chasing a man. Bill worked the grass. DanaSue's husband—whichever one she had at the time—would corral the teen boys into setting up fold-out tables and chairs. Essie and DanaSue and CarlaMay would head out with baskets of paper-

THE HOUSE BY THE CREEK

ware, and they'd smooth across checkered tablecloths. Essie set out sweet tea and mixed in sugar and baked up pies and cut up fruit, and everything would be beautiful and so perfect you could cry.

They hadn't had a hootenanny in over a year. As the grandkids got older, birthday parties weren't exactly birthday parties. All the grandkids who lived in Brambleberry had graduated from high school. But now, one of them was back.

Morgan Jo.

And there was a great big cause to celebrate. She'd been the first in the whole wide family to graduate college traditionally. No night school or internet degree. She'd gone to the University of Kentucky and had followed her mother's advice. A degree in business with a minor in architectural studies. It was all the family could have wanted for Morgan Jo, and it was all Morgan Jo could have wanted for herself. She was ready to tackle the world, one home project at a time.

The only thing of it was, Essie had her hesitations. She wanted Morgan Jo to be the tough nut Essie knew she could be. Anyway, she reminded Essie of Dottie in so many ways. Scrappy. Unafraid of anything. Hardscrabble. Essie might have been those things, too, but Dottie was always *more* of them. More tough and more gutsy and more tomboyish, just like Morgan. And though Essie had outgrown her girlish freckles, Morgan Jo had not. They carried right on past teenagehood and into the girl's twenties. Sometimes Essie really wondered if Morgan Jo was Dottie reincarnated. That's how alike they were.

And that was why Essie didn't want the girl screwing around in old, tumbledown houses.

Essie figured the graduation party was the perfect opportunity to warn Morgan Jo about this very matter. But she couldn't do it alone. She'd need Billy.

"Billy." She found him tinkering on the Gator out back of

the barn. "What in the hell are you doing? Party's starting in half an hour."

"I gotta fix this, Essie! Engine's screamin', and it needs fixin'."

"You can do that later, Billy," Essie told him, hands on hips, a dishcloth in one hand. "I need to talk to you about something important."

Bill pinched his voice tight and made a mockery of his wife. *"You can do that later, Essie."* He propped his hands on his hips then laughed at his own cruel, childish joke.

She took a deep breath and closed her eyes. Now wasn't a good time to make a fuss out of Bill or what he was or wasn't working on. Now was the time to come together as one and talk serious to their granddaughter. It was important. It really was. And if Bill was in on the conversation, Essie knew Morgan Jo would listen better. That's just how these things worked.

"Billy, I'm sorry. You're right. If you need to work on that, go right on ahead. Can I talk to you while you work?"

He gave her a suspicious scowl and dropped back into the engine bed of the vehicle, tinkerin' and toilin' and sweatin' and stinkin'. "Go on. You got me here. I ain't got nothin' better t'listen to."

Billy wasn't a sports fan or a television watcher or even much for the radio. He liked his records, which he kept inside, neatly in a stereo cabinet he'd built himself. It was the most high-tech thing the man had ever done in his life. No one except Bill was allowed to touch the stereo cabinet or the records. It was his special thing. But out here, Essie knew he preferred the sound of the wind through the trees, the cows groaning out in the pasture, and the songs of birds in the sky to anything else. Maybe especially her own voice.

She had no choice, though. They had to stick together on this one. "What do you think Morgan's going to do with her degree now that she's all done with college?"

"Oh, Essie," he grunted. "I don't have a damn clue what she's gon' do. I don't care, either!" He didn't have to pull his head out of the hood of the Gator for her to know his face was mottled red. His lips wet in spittle. The silliest things sent him hard into a tizzy. She knew she'd better walk on eggshells.

"Well, honey, I just think she's dead set on fixin' up old houses."

He snorted. "If she's gonna do that, then she can start on the hangar. Needs sanding and needs to be stained. Switch out some rotted old boards, too."

Essie couldn't help it. She smiled a real coy smile and seethed back at him. "I thought you didn't *need* any help."

It was too far. She'd gone too far.

Bill straightened up and wiped his hands on a rag so greasy he may as well not have wiped them at all. His voice was calm like the still-water lake up north of the fence. "I don't give a damn what that girl will or won't do. Fo' all we know, she'll run off just like her mama. Get pregnant. Then h'what, Essie? Then you'll bring her here just like you're won't to do with the other'ns. You save everyone, Essie." Then, his tone broke and his face did, too. He dropped the rag to the grass and closed the hood of the Gator. Billy gave her a soft but earnest look. The same kind he'd given her that day so many years ago when he proposed. Or when he sort of proposed. Whatever it was. "Essie, you don't got to save no one. Not me. Not them. No one."

Her throat dried up. Not because he was right, which he was. Not because he was hot and cold and up and down and kind and cruel, which he was.

But because no matter if Bill Coyle was right or wrong or mean or nice, no matter Bill himself, Essie did have to save someone.

She had to save Dottie.

If only it weren't too late.

* * *

The guests trickled in during a half-hour wave between two and half past the hour. Essie was dog-tired by then, but the warmth of company helped to fill her up with a second wind.

She was sitting with the special guest, Morgan Jo, talking about life and what was next. Essie had a piece of advice for Morgan Jo she was itchin' to get across.

"I know you didn't ask, Morgan Jo," she started, her voice taking on a sharp tone, but she had to so that the girl knew she was serious. "But I want to tell you something about life and being a woman."

Morgan Jo, bless her heart, returned Essie's stare with one as earnest as the day was long. "All right, Memaw. I'm listening."

"You're going to want to have babies and settle down—" Morgan Jo started to cut her off, but Essie wouldn't let her. She sliced the air with her hand. "Now, hush, Morgan Jo. I'm serious talkin'. You don't have all the time in the world like people say. I mean when it comes to startin' a family of your'n. You make sure whoever you pick, honey, that he likes to skinny-dip—"

"*Memaw*," Morgan Jo hissed at her and looked around, mortified probably.

Essie didn't care. "Morgan Jo, this is important. I want to tell you somethin'. When I was young, just eighteen years old, I met a man named Robert. He was a hard man in some ways, Morgan Jo. He'd had a rough childhood. He worked on his folks' ginseng farm up north when we met."

Boy did she have Morgan Jo's attention now. Essie went on. "He was a stern man, but he was *fun*. He was a hard worker, Morgan Jo. He was a black-and-white person, you see. He wanted to do life with me."

"I thought Grandad Bill didn't want you foolin' around anymore. When were you with Robert?"

Essie considered this. "No man wants you to be foolin' around, I 'spose. Anyway, Morgan Jo. I met Billy after Robert had ended things with me. Later on, I mean. Anyway, this Robert fella, he was first a good man. Never lied. Never a hurt a woman. He'd have laid down his life for me."

"He sounded perfect," Morgan Jo whispered.

Essie pressed her lips into a line. "Well, I didn't knowd that, Morgan Jo. What I knew then was that Robert wanted to take me dancing and skinny-dipping, and I couldn't go."

"Why not? Your parents?"

"No, because of my morals."

"Oh." Morgan Jo nodded.

Essie swallowed down the last of her lemonade. She just had one more thing to say, and she'd better say it quick because someone was coming over and Essie knew who he was and probably what he wanted, and she wasn't want to stand in the way of Morgan Jo and her future. "I thought that doing things right meant to do things better. Always, *better*. I thought I needed a man whose parents were married true and who was a good Christian. I thought, Morgan Jo, that I needed a man who knew how to farm and didn't need me to teach him. I figured I'd need someone to teach *me*. I never thought that it'd be okay if we learned about life together. That's why I ended up with Billy. He was capable and had know-how. Robert was hard-working, but he didn't have the know-how, and he was a little wild, and that scared me."

"Okay, Memaw."

The visitor was upon them now, so Essie made sure she'd better wrap things up. "I want you to find a man who'll learn life with you. Whatever it is you want to learn, too. Maybe that's about houses or maybe it's about raising kids, but the man isn't going to know everything. He's not going to hold your hand because you need help, but because he needs your heart. Does that make any sense?" She laughed a little and looked up, and there was Emmett Dawson.

"Am I interrupting you two ladies?" Emmett asked.

Essie watched as Morgan Jo turned to see him. Essie knew right then, at that very moment, that her granddaughter would one day go skinny-dipping with Emmett Dawson.

She nodded as Emmett asked if he could steal Morgan Jo away. And as she watched them walk off together, heads bent in, Morgan Jo's arm looped through Emmett's, Essie smiled.

CHAPTER TWENTY-SIX

2012

Morgan Jo

Despite the heat of the sun, Morgan's skin tingled with goosebumps. Sudden self-awareness flushed her neck, and the contrasting feelings gave her anxiety. She hadn't seen Emmett since they ended things, unceremoniously, the summer before college.

Maybe her fresh nerves spilled out because things had never come to a head. They'd never addressed the fact that they were officially *over*. The whole thing had been like the appearance of a tick. One minute you were out in the woods, happy and carefree, and the next minute you walked into the house and looked down at your arm and there it was. A bloodsucking little bug you never knew had latched onto your skin. You pinched it off, but something about the encounter dragged you into a world of dread. How could you not realize it? How could you just pluck the thing off and flush it down the toilet like it never happened? Would there be repercussions? Would you get a disease later on and wake up one day and say to yourself, *it was that dang tick.*

That's what breaking up with Emmett had been. A mild trauma that lived just below the surface of Morgan's skin, undetectable until provoked.

They walked quietly and slowly in the same direction they used to. Along the bramble vine-laced fence. Morgan could smell him, but it wasn't Emmett she smelled. It was someone else entirely. Someone who wore cologne and took two showers a day and didn't get his hands dirty. He wasn't the same.

"Why'd you come?" Morgan stopped at the opening of the fence. Next, they would pass through it and wander around the orchard, looking for any ripe fruit to nibble. At least, that's what they used to do.

"To congratulate you, of course." He didn't look at her. Instead, Emmett stared across the farm, back at the party as if he wasn't sure they should leave the safety of others.

Morgan didn't believe him. "You could have called."

His tongue ran over his lips and his hands disappeared into his pockets. She saw he wore slacks and a button-down. Not the jeans and T-shirts he liked. "I'm going to law school next semester."

"What does that have to do with anything?" She turned from him and looped her arm around the fence pole. A blackberry caught her eye, wild and deep purple. She wanted to grab it and spin back to Emmett and pop it into his mouth.

She didn't.

"I don't know. I figured you didn't know what I was doing with my life."

Should she care? "Okay. Well. That's great. I'm really proud of you, Emmett."

His hand landed on her shoulder and a soft tug tore her away from the view of the orchards and vines and back to him. Emmett looked... sad. "Actually, I just wanted to know what you were doing. Where you're going next." She watched him close his mouth, swallow. She felt his hand slip away from her shoulder. "I wanted to see you again?" It was a question, somehow.

"Okay." She blinked and fought the urge to fall into him and tell him she still loved him and was stupid to let things fall apart. On the other hand, though, Morgan carried anger toward Emmett. As much as she'd turned indifferent toward him, he'd done the same toward her. "It's good to see you." She looked him in the eye and kept her face as expressionless as was possible.

His mouth whipped into a tight rope. "Yeah. It's good to see you, too, MoJo."

Was this a dare? Was he testing her? To see if she'd break first? Memaw's advice swirled in her brain like a mobile hanging over a crib, distracting her from the reality that she was tired or hungry or suffering from some other basic biological complaint. It got all jumbled up inside of her mind. Feeling scared or trusting or infatuated or in love. Morgan didn't know *what* she'd ever felt for Emmett. Not scared, even though he could be a little wild. Not that he didn't have know-how. All she could pinpoint about Emmett was that she couldn't pinpoint anything at all. Four years ago, Morgan had loved Emmett. She didn't question it. And now, she felt the same. And maybe that was the problem. Maybe Memaw's advice was that if you weren't questioning it, then it was too safe.

Morgan narrowed her gaze on Emmett and offered a tense smile of her own. "I'd better get back to the party."

CHAPTER TWENTY-SEVEN

PRESENT DAY

Morgan Jo

Morgan spent her first evening at home settling in. Napping hour was finished by the time she and Julia left Amber to get supper ready for Grant.

Julia had to get home. She worked the next day—which would include a lunchtime pit stop at the farm to check on Memaw's progress with the other therapist.

Morgan's aunts bid their farewells, promising to drop in the following weekend, or sooner if anything new developed. And then it was just CarlaMay, Morgan, and Memaw again. Almost like old times.

Almost.

"Does she come out of the room at all?" Morgan asked her mom, who set about fixing ham sandwiches for supper. So much for any hope of a big roast dinner. Things were different now.

CarlaMay glanced in the general direction of the first-floor master bedroom, Memaw's room. Then answered absently,

"No, but she wasn't coming out for supper even before the stroke."

"What do you mean?" Morgan tucked into the sandwich, surprised at how satisfying a quick meal could be, so long as it was homemade by her mom.

CarlaMay joined her at the table and took a bite, too. After a while, she answered, "Things have gone downhill. I've told you this, Morgan." Her voice was stern.

"But I thought you meant in terms of her... *emotional* state. Not her ability to join you for dinner."

Morgan's mom just nodded, blinked, took another bite. After some moments, she answered, but her tone remained tense. "It's just been real bad is all." She blinked again and dropped her sandwich to her plate, letting out a mirthless laugh. "I guess maybe I'm not so used to having a real supper anymore myself."

As though an eclipse had struck the house, shrouding the two of them in an unnatural and eerie darkness, Morgan's stomach roiled. "Mama," she said with great worry in her chest.

Her mom didn't answer. Tears had sprung up in her eyes, and she was blinking and looking off into the distance, wiping away the salty wetness.

"Mom?" Morgan rested her hand on her mother's. "It's okay. She'll be okay."

A sob let itself out of the older woman's mouth, but CarlaMay caught it in her hand before breaking down and crying into her shirt.

"Mom, it's okay." Morgan stood and rubbed her back in circles, tickling the hair that fell in sweet tendrils down her neck. It wasn't chestnut anymore. It was streaked in gray, and the thought occurred to Morgan that the three of them—Memaw, CarlaMay, and herself—were like that photo of evolution you see on T-shirts, what with the monkeys turning into humans.

The final result not being a biped who could walk and talk and think, but instead being a wacky old lady with a penchant for outbursts who the family suspected had a light case of Munchausen's syndrome. If there were another figure that came after that final form, it wouldn't be an even *more* advanced human being, either. It'd be a fragile, white-haired woman who'd succumbed to her neuroses. Bedridden and speechless and with nothing to mull over except all the bad she'd done in her life.

Morgan swallowed that all down bitterly. Memaw couldn't be that bad. She *wouldn't* be. Maybe it was Morgan who could flip things around a bit. Improve her mother's outlook and her grandmother's forecast.

"I'll talk with her tomorrow. A *real* talk. Maybe we can take her out for lunch?"

CarlaMay looked up, hope filling the spots where tears were drying off. "You will?" But just as soon as that hope swelled to life, her eyes fell to Morgan's hip. CarlaMay's hand flew there, too, lifting up her daughter's shirt.

The scar wasn't as bad as you'd think. Nothing much more than a thick purple stripe across her hip bone. At least, that's all you saw from the front. The stripe wound around her backside, deforming her right butt cheek in a downright weird way. She couldn't wear cute tight leggings anymore. She couldn't wear slinky skirts—not that she ever had, but... you start to want to wear certain things when you *can't* wear them, apparently. At least, that's how Morgan had felt lately. Angry. Angry that her butt didn't dimple from fat and cellulite, but from a mutilation, of sorts.

It embarrassed Morgan.

But it mortified her mother, who had now fully changed the subject to Morgan's injury. "How's it feeling lately? Are you in pain?" She looked up with pleading eyes.

Morgan shook her head. "Naw. I mean, sometimes I do get a little shooting pain, yeah. But it's really fleeting. No big deal."

"And your therapy? Are you keeping up with it?"

Morgan sucked in a sharp breath. "I haven't been. Work is crazy."

"But you can work. That's good, right?"

Morgan shrugged. "I'm living a normal life, Mom. Just happen to limp a little."

"Julia says that'll get better with time and more therapy. If you're really serious about your recovery, you can go back to normal."

Ah yes. Normal meant Nick and selling houses and living in a handicap-accessible townhouse in the arid desert where humidity wouldn't come to bother her hip half the year. She'd spoken with Nick earlier in the day, and their conversation was brief. Not cold, but a little short. He had paperwork and signatures to send out for. She'd promised she missed him.

"What's normal, anyway?" Morgan said this with a wide smile now, and at once, both women looked to the sign that hung above the kitchen sink. A conspicuous comedic sign that Barb had bought Memaw back in the good days. When the kids were still kids and before Memaw started having TIAs and strokes and palpitations and falls.

Morgan could hear her mother chanting the phrase like some sort of mantra. CarlaMay took it a little too seriously, but that was part of the fun in it, maybe. *Remember, as far as anyone knows, we're a nice, normal family...*

"*Who's* normal, anyway, you mean." CarlaMay sighed all her breath out and grabbed Morgan's hand, kissing it. "Talk to her tomorrow," she said, taking them back to Morgan's promise. "Then we'll do lunch. Maybe pick something up for a proper dinner. Have the cousins over? Your aunts, too?"

Morgan sucked her lips into her mouth. "Yeah. Like old times." *Old times.* Like back when they still could pretend that they were a nice, normal family.

· · ·

The next morning, Morgan woke up with a headache. A bad one. Her mother cast it as jet lag, but Morgan knew better. After graduating college and before she left for Arizona, she'd gone through cycles and cycles of headaches. They'd come in waves, days on end of head-splitting pain that wouldn't let up unless Morgan followed the perfect routine, a system she'd figured out after trial and error and practice and practice. By the time she left for Arizona and stopped having headaches and looked back on those days, she might have considered her perfect routine to be less a routine or medical treatment plan and more like a witch's spell.

So, after chugging down two ibuprofen and three mugs of coffee, she filled the upstairs tub, a beautiful porcelain clawfoot that was quite possibly Morgan's favorite thing in the whole house. She dipped her feet in first, then wrapped her neck in the first towel, a wet one. Then she applied a Ziploc bag of ice to the base of her neck and wrapped a second towel—also wet— around the bag, securing it in place. She sat at the edge of the tub like that for five minutes, until the water was no longer scalding. Her feet were fire-red and burned so hot they felt colder than the ice on her neck, but that was the routine. Emmett Dawson had taught her it over the phone once. Said he'd picked it up in undergrad when the history readings made his eyes blur. A smile danced over her mouth at memories of back when she was still in touch with Emmett.

Morgan let them drown away, though, as she submerged herself under the water. After ten minutes, she got out and went back to bed. On the edge of her nightstand, her mother had left a tall glass of ice water. The second-to-last step in the routine. CarlaMay knew because Morgan had taken Emmett's headache wisdom and spread it far and wide, like wildflower seed. Morgan downed the water as fast as she could, then lay down and pulled a pillow tight over her face.

Sleep must have come quickly, because when Morgan

stirred awake sometime later, she didn't remember lying there, fitfully, willing it to come to her. And when she woke up, her headache was gone.

Memaw was sitting on the edge of the bed.

Morgan screamed when she saw her. Then Memaw cried, then CarlaMay came in to see about the fuss and to explain that Memaw was ready to get up and about and wanted to check on Morgan to find out how she was coming along.

"So..." the old woman tried. "I'm. So—"

"She's sorry, Morgan," her mother begged.

"It's okay." Morgan forced herself to breathe normally and returned the old woman's intense gaze. The two of them locked eyes and behind her grandmother's watery-blue irises existed something more than the dull stare of a stroke patient. There was more there than the search for the right word. The pain and anguish of trying to string together an entire sentence.

Behind her eyes, Memaw was deeply... sad.

Morgan glanced at Memaw's hands and grabbed them both. Then, she looked back up. "Memaw, it's *okay*."

The old woman blinked. The last of her tears spilled down her cheeks, but her blue eyes were drier now. She mopped her face with a dish towel. The sight of her using it as a handkerchief made Morgan feel worse; it made the fragile, aged lady seem pathetic. Discomfort roiled deep in Morgan's chest.

"I'm starving," she managed.

The fraught moment passed.

CarlaMay got Memaw to her feet on the walker. "Should we go eat?"

"And..." Memaw stammered. "And. Sho..." Her eyebrows pinched together and she shook her head, cocking it and looking at CarlaMay who surely could read the woman's mind.

"Shopping," CarlaMay said firmly. "Say it, Mom. Shopping."

"Shopp-ing." Memaw smiled, and gone was the consternation.

"Great," Morgan replied. "Let me get ready. Meet you at the truck in five?"

Lunch could take place at only one spot if they planned to hit the market after. That spot was the Dewdrop, at the corner of Main and Eighth Street. With her mom there, Morgan felt more comfortable to broach the past and discuss things with Memaw, but it occurred to her also that maybe now wasn't a good time. The woman could hardly speak. *What would she say? What would she want to say? What if she couldn't say it?*

Every few minutes, between sips of tea or bites of the burger Morgan split with her mom, the woman would give her meaningful glances. As if to say: *Do it. Say it. Come on. Now.*

Morgan wasn't ready, though. And Memaw seemed content. She worked on a vanilla milkshake, which was supposed to be exciting because it'd help her reclaim some of the muscle memory in her mouth. Also because not one of them could ever remember Memaw having had a milkshake, least of all Memaw, of course.

They finished lunch having discussed little more than the weather. Next up came the market on the opposite corner. They'd have to either get in the truck and re-park or walk a distance that'd put Memaw to the test.

"I say we drive," Morgan asserted. "Anyway, my hip..." But she stopped short. Now wasn't the time. Nor place. Not to talk about her own personal issues. It wasn't right.

Her mother clued in immediately. "We'll drive." And so they shuffled into the truck and back out again just half a mile north of where they first parked.

Main Street between Eighth and Tenth Streets was the heart of Brambleberry. Pretty brick storefronts sat back behind a tree-lined curb with grass in-between the street and sidewalk. Flower boxes hung off just about every shop window, and you could be certain they were all gifted to the business owners by Fullton's Florals. CarlaMay drove slow, and Morgan looked at the windows and at the signs. Just like the farm, everything was much the same. Antiques Attic bled into Clancy's Women's Wear which bled into The Cutting Edge. They stopped at a stop sign at Ninth, and pedestrians crossed casually, not a care in the world. Morgan longed for a time in her life when she'd be a pleasant walker, taking in the sights and sounds of a quaint downtown district such as this. It felt like a far-away dream.

CarlaMay accelerated carefully through the intersection and they drove past Western Drugs, the bank, and other critical businesses of a flourishing town, small or big.

At the southwestern corner of Main and Tenth sat a storefront that gushed memories like a spigot. Olde Towne Video. The Blockbuster of Brambleberry, Morgan hadn't been immune to the Friday night fever felt across town every week of her life from the age of about eight until Netflix became a thing when she was in high school. Even then, she and Emmett had spent their share of weekend evenings combing the shelves looking for the perfect date-night flick to canoodle to.

Morgan shook her head. It was getting impossible to avoid the memories.

Another block up, and CarlaMay turned into a long, shallow parking lot that trimmed the front of Market on Main, where they could get nearly all their shopping done. Back when her mom was a kid, the market was simply named Brambleberry Grocery, but since then, it had been sold off and updated by a young upstart. Morgan was silently grateful for a change of scenery. Something different so she could pretend like she was just a visitor. A tourist, even.

Memaw used her walker again in the market, and they trudged up and down aisles, picking out all the things that would help pull together a nice big family dinner. Like old times. When they were a *nice, normal family*. Or rather, when they could pretend as much.

A marbleized roast, collard greens, potatoes, carrots, yeast rolls, noodles and cheese for Aunt DanaSue's *macaroni a la queso*, and tea bags and sugar filled the cart. "Barb'll bring a pie," CarlaMay announced as they loaded up the conveyor belt at the checkout. "Morgan Jo, why don't you take Memaw to the truck ahead of me? You two take your time. I won't be too long." CarlaMay gave Morgan a look.

"Fine," Morgan muttered, petulant as all get-out. "Come on, Memaw." She guided the old woman gently with a hand on the small of her back, and they wove down an empty checkout aisle and to the front doors, which whooshed open with such gusto, Morgan worried Memaw would get the wind knocked out of her. But she was stronger than she looked and forged ahead, almost faster than Morgan could keep up.

After some wrangling, Memaw was secured into the front seat. Her walker leaned against Morgan's knees in the back seat. Morgan gripped the handles and held it against her legs, feeling the cool metal and wondering if she, too, would one day use a walker. And if it'd be sooner than later. She'd already had experience in the aftermath of the accident. She'd been in a wheelchair first. Then on a walker as she fought through the pain and deadness that shot through her right leg like lightning bolts.

"Morgan Jo," her grandmother said, crisp like a freshly sliced apple. The next sentence came out a mixture of slurred jumble and staccato sounds. "I wanna talk t'ya."

"Okay, Memaw." Morgan didn't bother congratulating the woman on stringing a sentence together. It was no great feat, apparently. She'd had good moments and bad. "I'm listening."

The old woman twisted in her seat, gripping the headrest with her blue-veined hand. She needed a manicure. "The tryst."

"The *tryst*?" Morgan made a face. *Tryst* was a fancy word

for a stroke patient to use, but that wasn't why. "What in the world?"

Memaw shook her head. It looked as if pain was shooting through her brain in fits and spurts. At last, she gave a second shake then narrowed her eyes on Morgan. "No." She garbled a sound or two then repeated herself more clearly. "The *trust*."

CHAPTER TWENTY-EIGHT

2013

Essie

Bill was worsening. His quick-to-anger temperament turned into anger all the time. The slightest thing would set him off, reddening his already-ruddy cheeks and sending spittle to his lips. Essie stepped on eggshells every day of her life. But even though she'd been stepping on eggshells, there were good days, too. And love? Well, she and Bill had that aplenty. It was possible to love someone and be irritated with them. It was even more possible to love someone and irritate them right back.

That's how it'd been between them, sure. But woven throughout the rocky spells were great spells. Like when Bill wanted to make Essie's Daddy proud and took up winemaking in earnest. Essie remembered the day clear as if she were looking through a just-cleaned window. It wasn't all that long ago, in fact. The kids were all grown.

Before that, Bill had dabbled here and there, trying his hand at the whiskey still down at the crick, but then, years on, when the barn wasn't used as much as it had once been, he set up a little winemaking area. It had all begun with some woodwork.

Bill needed a cask, of sorts. Several, in fact. He hewed the wood and wrapped the barrels with metal braces. Then there had to be a workstation, and Bill already had one for tools. He needed one for wine, too. So he made that with felled oak timber from the property.

By the time Bill was situated with everything that could be done with what he had had on the farm, he asked Essie if they couldn't take a trip up to Louisville to get the wine supplies. There was a store there called Restaurant and Beverage Supply, and he was betting on them for everything he'd need from clean funnels to a fermenter to bottles and corks. Essie told him he'd have to scrap the bottles and corks, because they couldn't just sink a fortune into a hobby. It didn't work like that on a farm. And anyway, where had he gotten all this know-how? Cousins, he'd said. It was sweet, Bill's excitement back then.

The shopping trip went well. They'd even gone to lunch after, and Bill told some dirty jokes that Essie didn't know he'd had in him. They'd gone home and before he stole away to start fiddling with a cousin's recipe, he'd kissed her and they rolled in the bedsheets like young lovers. It was probably one of the best days of their marriage, and Essie clung to that memory with every fiber of her being.

* * *

One clear, warm June day, Essie decided she was going to take a trip up north. A day trip to visit Morgan Jo, who worked on the Bourbon Trail, slinging amber fluid in shot glasses to a string of tourists at one of the many distilleries. "Did Bill want to come along?" she had asked.

"Not particularly."

But he hadn't no other choice. Essie was his wife, and she needed his help. That was Bill's opinion on the matter, and

Bill's opinion was fact. Didn't matter he didn't want to go. He had to go.

"I could take CarlaMay," Essie pointed out.

"CarlaMay's got a job to go to, Essie. I'll come with you. I'm driving. And you'll just shet up and come along."

"I wanted to spend the night."

"With Morgan Jo?" He was incredulous. "I'm not doing that, Essie."

"I can drive up alone just fine."

"Does she even want you to come?"

"She doesn't know I'm comin'." Essie figured Morgan Jo would be excited to see a familiar face. From all accounts, she wasn't very happy, in general, and least of all with her job at the distillery. Therefore, a little surprise was in order. Essie hadn't even mentioned the idea to CarlaMay, who'd no doubt try 'n' talk her out of going at all. CarlaMay liked to play mediator, which just about maddened Essie.

Bill threw his hands in the air and just about threw a fit. "She doesn't know you're comin' and you wanna drive up there! What if she's workin'? Or what if she doesn't want to see you, Essie? Ever thought of that?"

"Of course she does. We're close as two peas in a pod, Morgan Jo 'n' me."

By some miracle of God, Bill gave in and got the truck keys. They gassed up off of Rolling Fork and took to the backroads up the way toward the general area of Morgan Jo's new home. She'd gotten an apartment somewhere near the distillery. According to CarlaMay, she took the job seriously and hoped to move up in the company. Only problem was that bourbon wasn't exactly Morgan Jo's passion. Of course to Essie, passion didn't matter. Having a good secure position that brung in money and was safe—that's what mattered.

They arrived at the distillery just before closing, and Essie convinced Bill to walk her in. When it came to public places,

Bill was only a degree better behaved, but Essie took what she could get.

She approached the person who stood behind the ticketing desk. "Hello. My name is Esther Coyle, and I'm Morgan Jo Coyle's memaw. Is she here today?" Sweet as honey butter, Essie knew her charm would prevail.

But the young man behind the ticket desk didn't look all too charmed. Mainly annoyed. "She's workin' right now, leading a tour." He pushed a fat ol' thumb back down a dark hall. "If you want to book a tour, the next one leaves in ten minutes."

"Will Morgan Jo be the guide?"

The chubby boy made a face, pushing pudge around his cheeks like he didn't understand the question.

Memaw lifted a dark eyebrow and repeated her question, capping off each word with sickly sweet clarity. "Sir, can you assign Morgan Jo as our tour guide?" Then she looked to her husband. "Billy, wouldn't that be fun?"

He grunted "No," then turned a curious face to the wall of information behind them. Blown-up pictures of whiskey barrels and men in overalls enchanted Essie's husband, tearing him away from the desk.

The chubby boy had moved on from Essie, apparently, fiddling with his phone. Essie pointed her red-painted nail. "Young man, you put that down. It's *rude*."

At this, the boy's cheeks turned pink. He shoved his cell phone into his pocket, though he couldn't get it too far in. It was like his jeans were pushing that phone right back out and crying, *There ain't no room in here!*

"Now, I'm talking to you, boy," Essie said, sharp. "You don't pull your phone out when someone's talking to you. I want to see my granddaughter, and even better, I want to get put on her tour. If you want to keep your job here, you'll help me do just that. Else I've a mind to call the boss of this here distillery 'n' have him string you up by your toes and whip ya with a wet noodle." Fire blazed in her eyes. Nothing worse to Essie than a lazy, unhelpful person.

The boy tried with all his might to fold his arms over his chest. Then, a little smile danced on his puffy face as he looked beyond Essie.

Essie followed his gaze to see an even fatter man descend from a staircase that apparently wrapped around behind the wall Bill was studying. "What's all this?" the man bellowed. He wore a collared shirt and his baggy jeans looked special made for extra-big people. Memaw hated him, and she hated Bill for being useless, and she was startin' to hate Morgan Jo for taking a job at such a disgusting place as this.

It didn't occur to her who this man might be other than he was clearly a boss or a manager, and he clearly got wind of the altercation forming at the front desk of his boozy ol' establishment.

Essie put on a sweet smile but washed it off with as serious a face as she could muster. "Hello, sir. My name is Esther Coyle. This here," she held out a hand toward Bill, who'd now begun to shuffle back to her, "is my husband, Bill Coyle Sr. We've come to see our granddaughter Morgan Jo Coyle. She works here, taking people on tours."

"And?" the man barked.

"And?" Essie barked back. "Your front-desk clerk is being rude, to put it plain. Won't let us see our granddaughter or so much as confirm how we can go about it."

The man ran his hands inside the waist of his jeans and tugged them up higher on his gut. "I'll handle this." Then, he waddled off down the hall that led into the magical part of the factory where bourbon was made.

Essie glared at the chubby boy, still unaware that he and the man shared their girth out of more than coincidence. "Son," she said, "I do believe you could lose your job today."

The boy glowered at first, but then a smile curled up his lips and he took out his phone, once again pounding pudgy fingers on the screen like it held the secret to the world.

In minutes' time, the older, heavier man re-emerged from the hall.

Behind him, Essie could see a panic-stricken Morgan Jo.

"There's my girl," Essie cooed, on the brink of thanking the big old man and spitting in the face of the younger one.

It wasn't to be, though. Something was wrong. Very wrong.

"Here she is," the big man declared. "All yours." Then he waved a hand toward Morgan Jo who stepped up like a prize pig aware she was headed for slaughter. Tears welled in the girl's eyes. Fear stretched her mouth into an odd oblong shape.

"What's wrong?" Essie asked, confused and worried. She glanced from the boy behind the desk to Morgan Jo to the big man.

The big man grinned broadly. "We don't tolerate abuse to our employees," the man boomed. "And you yourself needed to see Morgan Jo so bad. She's *all. Yours.*"

Billy spoke up then. "We ain't takin' her."

Essie pressed her mouth into a tight little knot and stared daggers at her husband.

Morgan Jo started to cry.

The big man bellowed again, "She's fired."

The drive back to Brambleberry was riddled with argument. Bill was mad at Essie, blaming her for the world's problems. Essie was mad at herself, but most she was mad at the two heavyset men from the distillery. "Morgan Jo shouldn't work there anyway, if that's how awful they are!" she argued.

Morgan Jo had left for her apartment, and a cell phone call to CarlaMay revealed that while she wasn't altogether crushed, she was at a loss at what to do next.

. . .

A week later, Morgan Jo had returned to the farm, and Essie figured that was as good a chance as any to reveal her big plan for the farm and for her daughter and granddaughter.

They sat around the table one night, Morgan Jo picking at her food, still sore over the whole mess. Bill was complaining there was too much salt on the potatoes. And CarlaMay stretched precariously between them like a safety net for the whole thing.

"I have an idea," Essie declared once she'd started in on her pork chop. "Morgan Jo, you're going to work here. On the farm. You and me, we're going to open our own distillery."

Bill just about choked on his potatoes. "What in the hell, Essie?"

"It's possible!" Essie declared. "That's what my daddy did down the crick there. He don' bootlegged. Made a devil's amount of money. We can do that, too."

"Memaw, I don't even like whiskey," Morgan Jo complained.

"Mom," CarlaMay said low, "Morgan Jo wants to do something with houses. Remember?"

"Of course I remember," Essie shot back. "This isn't dementia talking, this is a smart idea." Essie was the producer of smart ideas. She'd turned the family farm into what it was today. She'd made something out of nothing from Bill, a surly, spoilt child with parents who'd coddled him into oblivion. She'd created the empire that was the Moonshine Creek Farm, and if she had a great idea, then whoever got in her way was just plain stupid. "And 'sides. You want to work a house. We've got plenty here, Morgan Jo." But as she said that, Essie knew to tread lightly. She didn't want Morgan in the hangar or the barn. The bunkhouses were fine. The big house, sure. But the safest place would be if they erected a new building. "I think we should build something new here. Don't you all? It's about time we

THE HOUSE BY THE CREEK

added on to this here farm. So with Morgan Jo's help, I think we can make a distillery. From the ground up. Brand new."

No one had anything much to say. Morgan Jo played with her food. Bill issued yet another gripe about the salt and the potatoes. CarlaMay clinked her fork on her plate uselessly, and the whole thing was a great big letdown to Essie. So much so that she felt outright angry.

"Memaw," Morgan Jo muttered weakly. "I'm really sorry. I just—I don't want to stay here. I want to see other places, remember?"

Essie remembered all right. They'd had this conversation before. Essie had even encouraged her. But things had changed. Morgan Jo was having trouble finding and keeping a job—no thanks to Essie, sure, but... An idea struck. Something that was sure to lure Morgan Jo back into the fold. "Did you know what I heard?"

"What, Memaw?" Morgan Jo's tone was patient, but she was pushing her food around like her appetite had jumped up and left.

"Emmett Dawson's coming back to the area. He finished law school."

Morgan Jo looked up fast, real fast. "He is?"

CarlaMay, dimwitted as she could be, said, "Oh, no. Uh-huh. He's doing a spell up in Louisville first."

"Oh," Morgan Jo's face and voice fell, and her fork clattered to the plate. "Well, anyway, Memaw, I really do want to go away, I think. Remember?" She looked with hope at Essie, and Essie knew better than to press an idea that would cut her granddaughter's legs out from under her. Far be it from Essie to handicap the girl's hopes and dreams.

"I remember, all right. I'm just saying think of your goals."

"I don't—" Morgan Jo started, but CarlaMay cut in again.

"Mom, Morgan wants to date. There's no dating scene here.

She wants to start a career, not a family business." This was all very bold of CarlaMay, and it pissed Essie right off.

Essie leveled her chin. Bill glanced up at her. She could read in his eyes what he thought about all this. He was happy. Happy as a damn clam, that man. Happy to keep Essie all to himself and to keep the farm all to himself. Happy to keep things just as they were. That's what Bill wanted.

"Well, then," Essie said, staring at Morgan Jo with all the mercy of Mother Teresa of Calcutta. "Go on ahead. Leave. I'll be sure to make that change in the *trust*."

CHAPTER TWENTY-NINE

PRESENT DAY

Morgan Jo

Dinner was planned for five o'clock. Morgan was responsible for the roast, which she'd started just as soon as they got home. CarlaMay handled sides. Barb was arriving early to fix the *macaroni a la queso,* and DanaSue promised to bring "something good." No one knew what.

As for Amber and Grant, Tiffany, Travis, and now Geddy, they were just supposed to show up. Nothing more.

Nothing less.

By five minutes to five, everything was set, including Memaw, propped at the head of the table acting miserable.

Since their conversation in the truck outside of the market, tensions were tight between Morgan and Memaw. Memaw didn't have the words to explain what she meant, but Morgan felt pretty sure she knew. Memaw wanted to change the terms of the family trust. A trust that was written years earlier, when things were different. When Grandad Bill wasn't at his worst, and when Memaw wasn't at her worst, either. When Morgan Jo was still young enough to admire her grandparents like a little girl fawning over a special, fragile doll.

CarlaMay had arrived at the truck before Morgan could make sense of the old woman's mutterings, and the matter was put to rest naturally, by virtue of a third party's presence.

Now, though, with Morgan sitting at Memaw's left, it was apparent both could feel the titterings of things left unsaid.

Geddy came almost late, knocking on the front door like an outsider. "It's Geddy!" Travis hollered inappropriately loudly. "Ol' fool." Travis let him in and Geddy waved awkwardly to everyone. Apparently, living on the farm hadn't yet granted him comfort among the family. It was an odd thing, Geddy's relationship to the group.

When Geddy sat down at the other end of the table, next to Amber and Grant, Amber asked him so that everyone could hear, "How was your lunch date?"

"Date?" Aunt Barb asked. "Geddy, you got a girlfriend?"

Geddy waved her off easily. "Can you pass the rolls, Aunt DanaSue? And no, no girlfriend. Not unless Julia Miles has changed her mind." He smirked and winked at Morgan before biting into his roll.

"No!" Memaw screeched, pointing a finger at him. When they'd returned home, CarlaMay had painted her mother's fingernails red, to bring back a little life to the woman. All and all, Memaw was on the upswing, and it was best everyone acted like it. At least, this was the general consensus.

"What?" Geddy looked left and right, but his gaze returned to Memaw. He wasn't afraid of her. He didn't know to be afraid of her.

CarlaMay used a soft voice to say, "Grace. Honey, we say grace before a meal."

"Oh. Grace." Geddy put the roll down and clapped the crumbs from his hands before holding them up, as though he were the new Grandad, what with sitting in the old man's spot and leading them easily in a simple rendition of the usual meal blessing. Morgan held her mother's hand on her left and Memaw's on her right, and Memaw's grip was as strong as ever. Surprisingly so.

"Bless us, O Lord, for these thy gifts, which we are about to receive from thy bountiful hands through Christ, our Lord."

"Amen," everyone said in unison. Memaw managed the amen seamlessly, but Morgan noticed her mumbling through the prayer itself. A pang of guilt and pity washed up through Morgan, but she didn't say anything. She didn't say she was sad Memaw couldn't say a simple thing like a memorized blessing. She was sad for a lot of reasons.

But on the whole, Morgan still had hard feelings toward her grandmother.

Even after all this time.

Even after the stroke.

And even after the infamous summoning: *Morgan Jo.*

"Geddy went out to eat with an old buddy," Amber said once they all started in on supper. Amber would reignite the conversation that would serve only to put the spotlight directly on Morgan. Morgan threw her a glance, but the girl didn't notice and finished her sentence. "Emmett Dawson. Remember him, Mom?" She looked at Barb.

Aunt Barb looked at Morgan. "Emmett Dawson. That ol' hound dog?"

Morgan rolled her eyes. If anyone was a hound dog, it wasn't Emmett. Now Nick—he fit that bill, what with his flirtatious sales persona and metrosexual attention to his presentation, as if his main goal in life was to look good enough for the opposite sex. "Emmett's not a hound dog. He's—"

"A lawyer," Tiffany said, sucking on the rind of a pork chop. A lascivious smile spread across her face as she said it. "In *Bardstown*, by the by."

"Bardstown?" Morgan swallowed. She didn't know Emmett

was back in Bardstown. She'd figured he was visiting family and set something up with Geddy before he left to go home—wherever home was for him. Maybe Louisville, still. Maybe with a wife. Someone pretty who'd look good skinny-dipping. Morgan shook off the self-pity.

"With a cousin on his daddy's side. Dawson and Dawson Esquire."

"That's not the name of the firm," Geddy said, wiping his mouth with a paper towel. "It's Dawson and Dawson, Attorneys at Law."

"Same difference." Tiffany picked at a stubborn strip of meat with her long nails.

"Have you talked to him, Morgan?" Aunt DanaSue asked.

Morgan shook her head no.

Silence spilled over them, as if everyone's appetite and chatter had been suspended in the air above the table.

After several awkward counts of that, Amber asked, "Does he know what happened?" She was as dense as pumpkin pie. Morgan glared at Amber hard, trying to bring to her cousin's attention that *now* was *not* the *time*.

But Tiffany was just as dense as Amber and doubled down on the topic of conversation. "Do you mean does Emmett Dawson know what happened to Morgan?" Wide-eyed with the wonder of a promising sprout of gossip—*oh, Tiffany*.

Morgan tried in vain to thwart the whole thing. "This isn't the time."

Memaw, however, spoke up. She cleared her throat and held the edges of the table, as if gripping would help her gain some stability of language. It worked. "Time. For. What?" she croaked.

"Nothing, Memaw," CarlaMay replied. She was the last person who wanted to dredge up the whole miserable memory.

Geddy ignored Morgan and Memaw in favor of answering

Amber. "Yep. Emmett Dawson knows what happened to Morgan."

"What exactly does he know?" Morgan asked, her stomach churning uneasily at the thought of Emmett Dawson picturing her with a limp. Picturing her as an invalid. A maimed woman. "You told him? What did you tell him?" Anxiety wormed around inside of her like a pack of nightcrawlers escaped from their styrofoam cup.

Geddy shrugged and gave Morgan a soft, pitying stare. "I told him the truth."

But this wasn't good enough, because in their family, there were shades of truth. "What *exactly* did you tell him, Ged?"

He shrugged again. "I told him you were in a shoot-out."

Gasps sucked the air from around the table, and Morgan braced herself for an implosion from the center of it. Like a shotgun had been discharged right then, Morgan flinched, and pain coursed up her leg, pooling in her hip. It throbbed. A wonder, what the human body could do if enough emotional trauma was inflicted on one's heart. And doubly so when the emotional trauma came from an actual physical wound.

Barb snapped, "What in the *hell*, Geddy?"

CarlaMay hissed, "You didn't. Geddy, tell me you didn't tell Emmett Dawson that Morgan was in a shoot-out, for goodness' sake."

Geddy laughed. "Don't worry, I'm not that crazy. I didn't tell him nothin'. All I said was that Morgan is back."

CHAPTER THIRTY

PRESENT DAY

Morgan Jo

After dinner, Geddy cornered Morgan in the living room. "I don't want to get caught up in you all's business, but here." He offered a scrap of paper.

On it, ten digits. "What's this?" she asked.

"Emmett's number. He says to call if you want to. No pressure."

Morgan had gotten a new phone not long ago, and with it, she'd let old numbers die off. Maybe Emmett knew as much. Maybe he'd tried to reach out unsuccessfully. After all, their last communication, which had been at her graduation party, only carried forth the sense of unfinished business between them. It'd make sense that he'd come around at some point and shot off a text or put through a call, only to find out that she was uncontactable. Maybe he'd even looked her up online to see if he couldn't find a phone number for her on one of those useless pay-for websites that promised a background check and everything. Then again, if he had been trying, he could easily have asked any of her family for her new number. Maybe he hadn't tried to contact her at all.

Maybe Morgan had even regretted getting a new phone and new number. A new life...

As if by magical coincidence, her pocket buzzed. She pulled out her device. Nick. She hadn't talked to him aside of short texts and that one phone call since she'd been in Brambleberry for the past week. "I gotta take this."

"Sure," Geddy answered and left. Geddy was a funny one. When he said he didn't want to get caught up, he meant it. He did things on his own terms, like a rogue or a renegade. It was part of what made him interesting to Julia, maybe. But to the family, Geddy was little more than a boxcar kid, jumping from place to place, never happy. Never quite normal.

Morgan pocketed Emmett's number and accepted Nick's call. "Hey," she said, heading upstairs into her room for privacy.

"Babe, I *miss* you. Just hearing your voice. Wow."

Morgan couldn't quite pin down the emotion that descended like a shroud on her at the sound of his voice. *Was it repulsion? No, couldn't be.* "I miss you, too," she managed. "How's, um, how's Arizona?"

"How's *home*?" he corrected, chuckling. "Well, things are heating up, babe."

"What do you mean?"

"The market. October, November. We're rolling into the eye of the storm. As soon as you can, you really should get back."

"Yeah. I think... I think that'll be soon. My grandmother is doing pretty well."

"Then why'd you even go?" He laughed again, a snorting laugh.

Morgan tensed. "Um—"

"I know. I *know*. I just *miss* you. And the market, Morgan. I mean, we're expecting some prime properties to come our way.

I'd hate to let them go to other agents. You could be killing it right now."

"It's barely October. I have time. Like I said, Nick. I'll be back soon. Memaw's on the mend, I think. Just a matter of finishing up."

"What are you finishing?" Nick pressed.

She put him on speakerphone. Then, Morgan tugged off her jeans and sweater and pulled on a white lace-trim nightgown from when she was a teenager. Miracle of miracles, it still fit. Comfy as ever. She slipped under the crisp sheets and pushed her feet way down deep beneath a quilt and heavy lace bedspread. She was tired, inexplicably so. Tomorrow the plans were to head out to the property with Geddy and come up with a game plan for sustainable groundskeeping and care of the property. They would also talk seriously about living arrangements. This all came from CarlaMay and Memaw—although with the latter who knew how much had actually been said so much as garbled.

"You know." Morgan yawned. "Just... spending a little time with her. Visiting family. Might as well make the most of things."

"Okay, well. Sure. And I *get* that, babe. Just—maybe book your flight home?" Another little laugh. "Have a plan, is all I'm saying. An exit strategy, right?"

"Yeah. Right. I'll, um, book tomorrow. Maybe I'll shoot for Wednesday?"

"Wednesday's great. You'll be home before the weekend. Before a big crush of looky-loos hit us up for showings."

"Okay. Well, good night, Nick."

"Oh, yeah. Right. Okay, babe. I, um, hey, I *love* you, Morgan."

Morgan squeezed her eyes shut. This was a first. Well, a first for Morgan and Nick. Morgan bit her lower lip, holding in her breath.

"Babe?"

"Mhm. Yeah. I'll talk to you soon," she answered distractedly, ending the call and thinking back to that day's outfit, tossed carelessly to the ground. Inside the front pocket, Emmett Dawson's number.

Morgan climbed back out of bed, dug her hand into the pocket, pulled out the scrap of paper, and inserted it into the book on her nightstand. For now, she didn't need that number. Wouldn't touch it. Wouldn't dare. Not while her emotions ran so high.

But she sure could use a bookmark.

CHAPTER THIRTY-ONE

2015

Essie

The trust. Essie and Bill had accumulated enough wealth to establish a significant trust, which safeguarded the profits of decades of hard work on the farm. Profits from relationships with cigarette and cud companies and national distributors of tobacco-based products. That was in addition to some of the dregs of a savings account Daddy Nelson had left behind from his bootlegging days. Bill tried to pick that up, but with wine, and he hadn't had as much success.

All told, the sum of cash wasn't as much as might earn itself being called a trust. However, together with the farm, well, the Coyle family trust wasn't nothin' to sneeze at.

Logically and fairly, everything would be split even-steven across the kids. To make this happen, Essie and Bill had a couple of options. They could sell off the farm and everything on it, move into an old-age home, and leave cash in the trust. They could figure the worth of the farm and everything on it, then designate each asset fairly, split six ways. Or they could do some combination of the two. It was a hassle any way you sliced it, Essie realized.

The last thing she wanted was to move off the farm and live in an old-age home.

Billy was just as well ready to move back into *his* family's tumbledown house up north. It hadn't been bulldozed yet, but it ought to have been. Shingled and rotten from the inside out ever since his parents passed some thirty years back, there was no chance in hell either one of them could bring that little shanty back to life. If he wanted to keep his own family history alive, he'd have to enlist the help of his cousins, because Essie had enough on her hands with the property they already lived on. It would have seen them at an impasse, what with Essie preferring to stay on and Billy preferring to move off, but Essie flat out put her foot down. Not only was the farm their livelihood, their hobby, their *world*, but it was Essie's history. Her legacy to her children. The farm could not be sold.

She and Bill found as cheap an estate attorney as possible—a feller who worked just south of Main Street, not far from the courthouse. CarlaMay and Barb had wanted to be involved, to help, but Billy had said no. It was a matter best handled in private. Essie didn't agree, but because she was about to get her way with keeping the farm and letting the Coyles' homestead sink into oblivion, she went along with him.

"Mr. Bill and Esther Coyle to see Mr. Loggerman."

The secretary didn't look up, and that outright pissed Essie off. "I'll take you in to see him shortly."

Shortly turned out to be a good ten minutes, by Essie's watch. Then, the heavyset woman waddled out from behind her desk and summoned them back through a narrow door. And in they were, seated in no time as an oily-haired lawyer swiveled around like in one of them movies with gangsters. "Mr. and Mrs. Coyle." He opened hands, not bothering to stand. "Glad to be of service today. What've we got?" He clapped those soft hands together and rubbed them like a crook. Essie didn't like him. Billy, however, was enchanted.

He blushed like a schoolgirl and hemmed and hawed, ever impressed by educated folk, though he wouldn't admit that to anyone. Not even to the oily-haired crook with soft hands. Least of all to him.

"I reckon it's time we lay out our last will and testament," Bill said, formal as he could muster.

"Right-o! What're we looking at? Maybe a little home in the countryside? A car? Do you have a savings account at Western Credit Union? If not, we really ought to consider—"

Essie cut him off. "I'm Essie Nelson." She didn't mean to undermine her husband's God-given authority as man of the house, but this clown of a lawyer needed a wake-up call. "Essie Nelson of the Moonshine Creek Farm."

The lawyer used the tip of his pinky finger and scratched an itch beneath the oil slick of his hair. "Right-o—"

"We need to settle plans for the farm and its assets, including equipment, our money—which *is* in Western across three accounts—as well as some acreage we own north and east of Brambleberry." She pulled a battered envelope from her lap. "Our finances are organized in this packet. My daughter helped me."

The lawyer accepted the paperwork and shuffled through it with more interest than he probably wanted to let on. After reviewing each page, he looked up. His face lost the smug scowl, and a prong of his oily hair broke loose from the top of his head and fell across one eye. He pressed back where it belonged. Essie guessed this feller was no older than thirty-five. "You mean you own the *farm*. The one up in the northeast corner of town. The tobacco farm."

Essie and Bill nodded as one.

"All right. What do you have in mind for this will? I know you have children." His tone was more serious, and Essie felt easier now that he wasn't the goof he'd at first seemed to be. Sometimes all a person needed to take you serious was a little kick in the shorts. Essie's kick to this Loggerman's shorts was her family fortune, as it were.

Essie glanced nervously at Bill then back at him. "We'll create a specific list of who gets what."

Bill sputtered a coughing, choking sound. "Essie," he wheezed.

She ignored him. "It's the best thing. We'll be fair as the driven snow. Each of our children will get a sliver of the pie. And our grandchildren, too."

"What about..." Bill started, but Essie held up a hand, silencing the old man next to her.

"We'll start with CarlaMay and go on down the line. And that's that."

"Garold, too?" Bill's face reddened in anger. "He's off the God-blessed map! We don't even know where the hell Garold's done gone to!" He referred to Geddy's dad, who was their eldest son. And everything Bill said was true. Garold could be dead of an OD in a ditch somewhere, and they wouldn't know. More likely, he was up north, living off the land like he always said he would. That's what Essie prayed for anyway. Sometimes, a mother's mind made up what her heart needed to feel. It was no use searching for Garold. He'd get in touch with Geddy in fits and spurts then fly off the map again. Essie had nothing to do but to respect his need to run. That's what she'd come to, anyhow.

"If I may," the lawyer interrupted, smoothing his tie and all but licking his lips over what a slam dunk the Coyles would turn out to be.

Bill's fuming tapered off, but he kept his lips tight and his eyes bulging. "Go on, now. Go on ahead. I'm just here to listen, I guess!" His hands flew up from his lap, and Essie tried to calm him with a simple pat on the knee. He shook her hand away and gave her a sharp look.

"You'll want to include everyone who might *think* he or she may have a claim to your estate. You'll want to pass down *something* to ever' last one. Even if it's something small. Garold is your son, then?"

"Our eldest. Haven't seen him in years, I hate to even say." Essie didn't explain why, and the lawyer was good enough not to ask.

"All right, well, especially any children. Grandchildren are less likely to come for something, but you have how many *children?*"

"Six. Three boys and three girls," Essie replied.

"Then we start with them."

"Okay," Essie answered. "Do we leave the properties in their names? Divide the land?" What with all of Essie's older siblings dead and gone, the farm belonged solely to her. And Bill, naturally.

"Well, one option is to elect one or two of your closest relatives, perhaps children, as trustees. These are different than beneficiaries, as they'll help manage your assets. But you seem healthy." He gave them each a harder look. "Could be a long, long while b'fore any of this comes to pass, so to speak. Years and years. And over time, well, a lot can change."

"What'll change?"

The lawyer rocked from side to side and narrowed his gaze on some invisible feature off in the distance of his bland office. He then returned his stare to Essie, pinning her with it and saying, "Your assets may change. Your money. But the biggest change that can affect a trust, especially one of this size, isn't the money or the assets."

"Well, then what in the hell is it?" Bill roared.

"It's your relationships."

CHAPTER THIRTY-TWO

PRESENT DAY

Morgan Jo

CarlaMay woke Morgan up the next morning by sitting in wait on her bed. Naturally, this scared the bejeezus out of Morgan, who gasped awake. "Can you be normal and just... wait for me in the kitchen, or something?"

"I have an idea," her mother said, ignoring the request.

"What?"

"Now that you're home, we're going to put on a family reunion. Mom's doing well enough to enjoy yourself. It'll mean a lot to her."

Morgan needed coffee before she could tackle *this* level of confrontation.

They both made their way to the kitchen, CarlaMay dressed and ready for work and Morgan sheathed in a flannel robe that hung behind her bedroom door. Probably one of Grandad Bill's leftovers. Though odd for it to have been in her room and not Memaw's.

"Mom," Morgan said through swigs of black coffee with

sugar. "A reunion sounds great, but I have to get home. Especially now that..." Did she really need to finish the sentence?

"Now that Memaw's better." CarlaMay poured herself a cup, too, and joined Morgan at the table. "Well, we'll pull it together fast. I mean—it's not like you have to report to an office. Not like me."

"But I do. Nick called last night. He says things are heating up. He can't just cover for me forever."

CarlaMay seemed to think this over. "Okay, we make it happen lickety-split. Fast. How's Friday?"

"It's almost a week away. I told Nick I'd look at flights for Wednesday."

"What's an extra day, Morgan?" Her mother set about wringing her hands and bristling like a girl scorned.

"That would be an extra two days. Three, depending on what time this little shindig is at. I don't want to catch another red-eye if I can help it. The first one was bad enough."

"Okay, Thursday might be good. I know the girls don't work on Thursday. Tiffany and Amber. That way they can help set up."

"Mom, it sounds like a *lot*. A lot of work." Morgan, who generally enjoyed putting together events and hosting—she couldn't wait to host her first open house—was suddenly exhausted. The emotional toll of returning, coupled with the weirdness she felt about Emmett Dawson being little farther than a stone's throw away... well... Morgan had to get out of there.

A painfully beautiful memory surfaced in her mind. Emmett and Morgan after they'd just started dating. He'd come over to the farm—he always came to her. They went for a long walk along the fence, cutting through the orchards until they found a blossoming peach tree. They were holding hands, their fingers laced together, and he pulled her down to the ground at the base of the trunk, the low part where it was thick and not spindly and pink above. He pulled her face to his and kissed her, hard. She remembered thinking that Emmett's lips were perfect. The feel of his mouth on hers, delicious. She remembered wishing then that they could run away, deeper into the woods beyond the farm and live happily ever after, her picking fruit for pies and him hunting geese for a holiday supper. It was idyllic, and she knew that, but it also somehow felt within the realm of possibility.

After he'd kissed her, Morgan remembered she picked up a twig from the bed of grass and traced it down the trunk.

"Here." Emmett had withdrawn a small multitool from his back pocket—no country boy left the house without some version of a pocketknife.

"What are you doing?" She'd gasped.

"Same thing you are. But more permanent."

He pressed the razor-blade edge of his knife to the brown bark, making thin, shallow cuts.

"Wait." She stopped him, her hands on his shoulders, pulling him from the tree. "You'll kill it."

"It won't kill the tree. She'll heal."

"How do you know?"

"You've never seen buck rub in the woods?"

It sounded familiar, but she'd shaken her head.

"When bucks scrape their antlers off on tree bark."

"It can't be a good thing."

"Not everything in nature is mutually beneficial." His big words had contrasted his woodsy knowledge. Morgan had liked this.

Morgan hadn't thought that their initials in the bark of a peach tree was beneficial to anyone. But who was she to thwart true romance? She'd smiled wide and nodded him on, her insides melting like butter.

When he was finished, the tattoo was small and simple. *M+E*. No heart. Just them. An incomplete equation.

"Will it go away?" she'd wondered aloud.

"Never."

"So it just stays like that forever?" she'd looked at him doe-eyed.

"It'll change. The tree will heal over it."

"Like a scab?"

Emmett had kissed her. "Like a scar."

Morgan shook the memory.

Yes, she had to leave.

Before she did something she regretted.

Like turn that bookmark into a phone call.

"The girls and I will do everything. If we make it for a little later, Dana and Barb'll help, too. And, of course, Geddy, now that he's back. You can stay in here and watch Memaw."

"She needs *watching* now?" Morgan groaned inwardly, but she knew the woman could use company, if nothing else.

"No. I can't. I can't stay. Nick needs me back."

"For Nick? Or for your job?"

Morgan held her mother's gaze. "Both. And for *me*."

* * *

Despite Morgan's declination of joining in the reunion, CarlaMay decided it was still a good idea. She pushed it out to Saturday, though, in order to accommodate all the family she could. Meanwhile, Morgan had booked her flight for Wednesday afternoon.

Tuesday, she and Julia planned for a girls' night out together. Dinner and drinks up in Bardstown. Brambleberry hadn't attracted much in the way of ride-shares yet, so although Morgan was hoping it could just be her best friend and her, they needed a driver if they were going to enjoy even just a glass of bourbon. Travis agreed to tag along. He had a friend he liked to visit in town. *Friend. Right*, Morgan teased him. But once Tiffany and Amber caught wind of Travis taking Morgan and Julia uptown, the jig was up. It became a party.

Since Morgan wouldn't be around for the reunion, she accepted that this was just as easy a way to keep things pleasant between her and the family, so she even invited Geddy, too. He declined, though, on account of an early morning the next day.

The group stopped first at The Colonel's Cousin, a KFC-origin-story knockoff that sat exactly halfway between Bramble-berry and Bardstown. Just like old times, Morgan and Julia ordered a Colonel Chicken Basket, which amounted to a menagerie of chicken parts, deep-fried into oblivion. They added on top of that a bowl of coleslaw to split and Colonel Biscuits, flakey and buttery and oh so good. Sweet teas rounded out their main course, and for dessert, the table shared a lemon-meringue pie. After the pie, coffee.

Then, once Travis got them into town, they swung into the Blind Pig Speakeasy, a bourbon bar that stayed open until ten on weeknights. One shot in and tensions had cooled—if there were any. Morgan wasn't sure.

Julia was whining to Amber about how Geddy shoulda, coulda, woulda come. Amber was whining back that Grant shoulda, coulda, woulda come, too. They basked in one another's misery. Tiffany eyed a cute stranger down the bar. This left Morgan to try to fit herself into Julia and Amber's conversation.

At first, it was easy enough. "So, the wedding, Amber. What are the details? Have you got a locale?"

"I asked Memaw if I could have it on the farm," she said through slurred speech and bleary eyes. Morgan wondered how many bourbons she was into the night. Probably more than two. Grease for the words, Grandad Bill always said.

Morgan raised her voice above a roar over some game on TV in the opposite corner. "That's a good idea."

"I thought so, too," Amber hollered back. "But apparently, it's not." She sliced a chubby hand across her throat.

Julia spun on her barstool, suddenly interested anew in their conversation. "Miss Essie said no?"

The roar from behind them tapered off. Morgan could talk normally again. "Is that true, Amber? Memaw said you couldn't host the wedding on the farm?"

"Right." Amber pursed her lips. "She says it's a working farm now. Not a play farm."

Julia snorted a laugh, but Morgan didn't. "It's not a working farm. It's defunct. All it's good for is playing. What did she mean?"

Amber shrugged.

Morgan looked at Julia. "Do you know what she could have meant?"

"Psh. How would I know? She's getting older. More persnickety and all that. Probably just doesn't want a wedding at her property."

"That doesn't make sense. Memaw *loved* doing events."

"But Grandad didn't," Amber pointed out. Then her eyes grew big. "Maybe she doesn't realize he's dead!"

Morgan and Julia scoffed in unison. "She's had a stroke, but she doesn't have dementia."

"She could have dementia," Amber argued. "She's gotten mean."

"Mean? She's always been a little mean." Morgan swigged from her glass then rolled the amber fluid around, studying it as if it had the answers to the world. Maybe it did. "Remember how Memaw told us those stories about her daddy cooking up whiskey on the creek that runs along the property?"

Amber smiled, the memory fond in both their minds, since with that story came the girls' first sip of the hard stuff. Each at the ripe, ol' age of sixteen. "How could I forget?"

"Maybe that's what Memaw thinks about sometimes. How

the land is so rich. I mean, just think about all they've grown on that farm. Tobacco, sure. Vegetables and fruit, too. Grandad himself made wine out of the grapes from the vines. Some of the berries, too."

"I forgot about the wine." Amber looked sad over the memory. "Grant keeps our bottle on top of the fridge."

"You still have yours?" Morgan asked, panic gurgling up inside of her. She thought back to that dinner with Nick and how even he'd warned her not to drink the last of it. She was drinking away a part of her history. Her grandfather himself, like Jesus's blood in the wine at Communion.

"Yeah, of course. We like beer better. But anyway, it's Grandad's wine. You know? Tiffany and Travis drank theirs, if you can believe it. What a pair of jerks." Amber had never been one to judge, especially where her own siblings were concerned. She was fiercely loyal to them. But here she was now, ragging on them for sipping away their sole inheritance.

That reminded Morgan of something, and now was as good a time as any to change topics. "Grandad left us each a bottle of wine." She paused thoughtfully. "I wonder what—"

"You're talking about the trust, ain't ya." Amber got her drawl going, and Morgan knew a fight was coming on.

Morgan shook her head. "No, I don't mean... it's just there's one thing..." It was useless. No sense in dredging up topics like this in mixed company.

"You want to know what'll happen with the farm, don't you?" Julia asked.

Morgan didn't care about the farm for many, many reasons. But there was *one* reason that did get to her. Her mom. Her mother had never known another home. Her mother didn't even *want* to know another home. CarlaMay Coyle was comfortable, but something told Morgan her mother wasn't going to get to keep her comfort, or her home. It was something that worried her.

Julia understood Morgan, even better than her own kin, Amber, ever could.

Amber bristled. "I would think the farm'd go to us."

"What do you mean 'us'?" Morgan asked.

"Tiff, Travis, Grant, 'n' me. We live there."

"So does Miss CarlaMay," Julia pointed out.

But Amber was already shaking her head and working her mouth into a half-cocked answer. "Four on one. We'll let CarlaMay take one of the cabins. She's just one person. Rest of us is four. And what with Grant 'n' me getting married, I reckon I'll get pregnant right away. We want to have a lot of kids. Like maybe four or five."

"So what?" Morgan was devolving into defensiveness, and she could hear in her voice that she was about to argue uselessly, but still she pushed on. "Who cares if you have kids? Just having kids doesn't mean you get the big house if that's what you're getting at. *I* grew up in that house."

"And just 'cause you grew up in it doesn't mean you and your mom get to take it. I never did think it was fair that you got to live there all your childhood. And my mom says it's not fair that CarlaMay lives there still, just living off of Memaw like that."

This was just *rich*, Morgan thought. Just positively *rich*. "Coming from you, who also just lives off of Memaw, that's pretty funny." She simmered now. "And you know what's not fair? Not fair is not having a daddy. At least you all had one of those."

"Not our fault your mom tramped around and got pregnant." Amber's eyes were glassy and cold and cruel, and Morgan felt like she could scream.

Instead, she pushed her glass away and grabbed Julia's arm. "We're leaving."

"What?" Julia juggled her own glass until she downed the last of it.

Morgan pulled her away, not bothering to tell Amber that they'd find another ride. Not bothering to so much as say good-bye. Morgan would leave Brambleberry and the rest of Kentucky behind the next day.

And maybe she'd never, ever come back.

CHAPTER THIRTY-THREE

2016

Morgan Jo

A year after Morgan left for Louisville, off on another attempt to get a job good enough to pay well *and* make her happy, things started shifting around in Brambleberry. Not necessarily in and around the big house, per se. There, things were pretty much the same as ever. Bill ran the lawn mower once a week. CarlaMay lived in her girlhood bedroom, working during the day and sharing her wages to cover groceries and some other essentials. The others, save for Garold, would visit once in a blue moon.

But there was a shift on the farm itself. The vines were over-grown and, true to the town name, had turned from fruit-bearing beauties into thorny brambles. Once the last of the chickens died off, Essie decided no more animals. The bunkhouses were falling into disrepair, as was the barn, as was the hangar.

Essie only knew that the hangar was in disrepair because Bill had said so. Last time she'd set foot out there was years and years back. She hated the hangar. Not what it stood for, but what had happened there.

That's when she made a shift herself. It was the Friday following Thanksgiving. A Thanksgiving for which only a handful of their children and grandchildren had attended. Seeing as Essie's brothers and sisters were all dead and Billy didn't have any siblings, the gathering was small, and it felt incomplete. But the most important ones had come: CarlaMay, always, Barb and DanaSue. Their kids.

But the absence of so many others together with the absence of Morgan, who'd gone up north to her new home after Thanksgiving, well... it all had Essie feeling down the next day.

That Friday morning, Essie washed dishes by hand at the sink while she gazed out across their land. "I want it torn down," she told Billy one day, referring quite plainly to the old hangar that was in such bad shape it could practically tear its own self down.

The weather happened to be bad that day. A storm was rolling in and the air was thick with the promise of a heavy rain. Bill loved a good storm. It was something that lived deep down inside a man, he said. A love of rain. Rain meant life on a farm. As long as the rain came and went as it was supposed to.

Rains that stayed, now that was a different matter. Rains that stayed meant flooded crops. Root rot. Miserable livestock. Now, the Coyles didn't have to worry one iota about crops *or* livestock, and yet Bill's feelings about rain remained unchanged. Exciting to start. Worrisome in the middle. Dreadful down the line when it looked like the sky wouldn't let up none.

"Torn down!" Bill cried, tearing himself away from the picture window at the front of the house, his post during times of storm. "Are you getting on about that hangar again?"

Essie worked a dish towel into a glass mixing bowl. She'd stowed leftovers in Tupperware in the fridge the night before but felt too tired to do the dishes. Usually, the girls'd do the dishes, but CarlaMay worked bright and early that morning, so Essie had shooed her to bed. The others managed to escape without so much as an offer.

"Of course. It's dangerous. What if somebody's children wander in there?" She shuddered at the thought. "I want it gone. I'm sick of the sight of it, Bill. I can't take it no more."

Bill scratched his head, and if he'd had much of a brain in there, he'd think to ask, *Why now? Why all of a sudden are you ready?*

But he didn't have much of a brain in there, and he didn't ask, so Essie said it, anyway. "Last night at supper, you know who was sniffing around out there at the hangar? DanaSue, that's who. She came in here and asked me if she could have her wedding out there. Said it was too pretty a place to go to waste like it was." A bitter taste rolled over Essie's tongue. *Pretty place.*

The worst part of it all was that DanaSue knew well and good what'd happened in there years back. She knew her Aunt Dottie had died in that there hangar. She knew it, and she didn't stop and think what she was saying. So it had to go.

Bill had a soft spot in his heart when it came to dead people apparently, and especially dead children, because his face broke a little. "All right, well, once this storm lets, we'll go take a look. That suit you, Ess?"

"I don't know what there is to see. It's a damned ol' building, and it needs to go."

"I want to take a look. See how we could pull it down. If we'd need a 'dozer or h'what."

And it was settled. Billy would think about taking down that ol' damned hangar. Essie could finally move on. Maybe she'd put something out there in the place of it. Maybe the grandkids would come together and build a greenhouse or another cabin or something useful. Something with happy memories, where people came together.

Not a place where Essie's life stopped. Because if you had a twin, and she died, you couldn't just go on living. You were broken in two, if she died. You were split down the middle like a fire log headed to the hearth. When you had a twin, you weren't just one whole person. You were half a whole.

So, if your twin died on ya, then you weren't whole. And there weren't nothin' that could fix ya.

The storm died out before a single bolt of lightning even cracked across the sky. Essie did the wash, which was mainly made up of dish towels and washrags and the table linens. When it came to the kitchen linens and cleaning linens, she preferred to do it by hand, soaking them in the washbasin in the mudroom. She'd scrub the fabric together and work borax mixed together with baking soda. The white suds and hot water were a therapy to her, though not the skin of her hands, which had gotten paper-thin in the past decade or so.

Once the wash water ran clear as a fresh spring, Essie rang the linens out good and pinned them up to a line she'd hung across the windows in the mudroom. Nothing better than fresh wash soaking up the sun *inside* the house, where it could make everything smell good and clean.

She dried her hands off on her apron to find another dish towel she'd missed, tucked into the apron, wedged along her belly. It was her favorite one. The one with the funny embroidery. *If Mama Ain't Happy, Ain't Nobody Happy.* Essie smiled at the dish towel, she always did. Then she folded it up to return to the kitchen—she'd wash it a different day. But just as Essie moved toward the kitchen, the back door flung itself open.

Billy stomped on the mat, his feet cocked outward. He was in a state. "Well?" he grunted.

"Well *what*?" she spat back.

"We gon' go look over the hangar or ain't we?"

Essie folded the dish towel once again in her hand and followed him back out. They shuffled through wet grass and across a strip of gravel past the barn. Then onto the now-muddy spread of dirt that washed across from the grass line onto the hangar. It used to be a drive for tractors and equipment. Now it was just a sandlot. It could do with grass seed. Keep the dust down back in the house and whatnot.

They stopped short in front of the big doors of the broad-faced building. Rust had crawled up and over the sides and roof like a virus, eating away at the metal and proving Essie would be right about this. The structure had to go. If it wasn't dangerous before, it sure as heck was now.

Bill stepped up to the sliding door and rested a hand on the rust-red handle. Essie had a mind to warn him off of it. "You'll get tetanus, Bill."

He waved her away, and so Essie joined him. Bill heaved his weight into the sheet of metal, rolling it wide open and letting loose the smell of must and mold. Essie pressed the back of her hand against her nose for a moment. "When was the last time we was in here, Billy?"

"Hell if I know. Been years. Last event, maybe?"

Essie found that she considered the hangar to live like a nightmare in her head. The most terrible nightmare a person could ever have. It hung around up in the rafters of her brain, reminding her of the worst thing that could happen in life. So, even though she hadn't stepped foot here in years, the hangar was inside of her all the time.

"I'll be damned." Bill let out a long, low whistle once the sun poured into the gaping space. Long gone were sheaves of tobacco. The clips to hang 'em with remained, like rotten teeth dangling along the top half of a man's jaw. Scraps of hay covered the dirt, but it had formed little piles here and there.

Something rustled in the far corner.

"Back up, Essie," Bill commanded, pressing her behind him

with one hand and reaching into the waist of his jeans with th'other. He drew out a pistol, some old relic of a weapon that he'd once used as a manner of defense back in the days he was a huntin' man.

He pointed the thing in the corner where they both had heard the rustlin'.

"Probably just a mouse, Bill, for heaven's sake, put that thing down b'fore you shoot yourself or me."

Bill lowered the gun and tucked it back into his waistline. Whatever was inside couldn't be no bigger'n a racoon at best. More likely it was a squirrel. He left Essie near the door and treaded deeper in, specifically back toward the corner loft. It was as though he wanted to prove something out, Essie figured.

"What?" she asked, waiting for him to explain why he was studying the wooden rungs.

"I'm gonna go on up there," he answered as he tested out the first rung. The same one Essie climbed down another lifetime ago. The one she'd almost never been able to climb down. But climbing over her unconscious sister's body and down the ladder was the only way to get help. The only way to bring in an adult who could press his ear real close up against Dottie's face to listen for a breath. Of course, by the time Essie had worked up the courage to move her sister's legs aside and descend down that ladder and run like a fox into the big house to summon someone, anyone... and by the time she found her daddy and dragged him back to the hangar, afraid for her life that if Dottie wasn't already dead, he'd sure as heck kill 'em both for playing in the *damn* hangar... by the time she'd gotten him there and up that narrow stairway, it was too late.

"The hell you are!" Essie hollered at Billy, who was wobbling on the second rung.

He didn't look back at her. Couldn't look back. But he hollered in reply, "I want to see what all the commotion is about this place!"

All the commotion. All the commotion? Essie seethed so hard she thought a vessel in her head might burst.

She wanted to scream, but the memories were rushing in hard, like a pack of goblins trying to get at her. Essie fell back a step, but something caught her heel, and she went sailing through the air. All she felt, at first, was losing grip of the dish towel. It must have gone sailing, too, flying through the air like a little ghost all its own.

Landing with a thud, Essie expected to call out or wail. But instead, it was a low and long groan that escaped from the very bottom of her belly. She stayed on the ground for a moment, wondering what was going to hurt first. It scared her, the thought of getting up. She had little choice except to call for Billy to come help.

"Bill!" she hollered, but it came out weird, like a growl. She cleared her throat and called up louder. "Billy, help!"

She watched his feet re-emerge on the rungs of the ladder, but they didn't move fast. She wasn't sure if that was because he could not move fast or because he *would* not move fast.

By the time Billy made it over to her, she'd sat up and begun to assess her injuries. Essie couldn't be sure, but it felt as though she'd broken her damn back. It felt crooked and sore and all kinds of painful, from stabbing and stingy to throbbing and pulsing.

Bill lowered to her. "What happened?"

"Billy, I fell," she managed, rubbing her hands over her knees and keeping herself as upright as she could.

"How?" He glared at her and stood back up, shoving his hands under his armpits and giving her a cold, rough look. But it wasn't an angry one, oddly. It was a suspicious one. His lips weren't pressed into a tight line, spittle clinging to the corners. His face hadn't gone red and ruddy in raw madness. It was a calm, strange face that Billy showed her now, staring down at her. Like he thought she'd done it all on purpose, falling and getting hurt.

Maybe she had. Maybe somewhere deep down Essie fell as a way to tear her husband off of that haunting corner of the hangar.

But even if she did it on purpose, so what?

Essie, more determined now, reached her hand out, but Bill didn't take it. He kept his arms crossed, hands tucked in his armpits like an ol' farmer.

"Well, I didn't *see* you fall. I was up there!" Now the rage came, as did the spittle and red cheeks and bulging eyes. He threw a crooked finger up to the loft.

"I told you not to go there. Why'd you have to go up there? This is just crazy talk! Crazy stuff, Bill. Why'd you have to go up there! You know what happened. What, you think she's still there? You think my Dottie is still up there or something? Or you just want to drive a stake in my heart about it all? You just want to scare me off of tearing this place down so you can pretend you still run a tobacco farm. You are livin' in the past, Bill Coyle." Essie's mouth quivered, but she wasn't going to cry. Essie didn't cry. Not even about Dottie. Not anymore. She'd cried so much way back when that there were no more tears left in her body or soul. She'd never shed another tear again. No, siree.

After she finished her piece, Bill simply turned to go. On his way to leave her, he stopped, bent over, one hand pressed on his back like the old man he was. "You hang on to your sister like she *is* still up there, Essie. You never moved on. You never let me make this farm into something great."

Essie remained seated, just listening. Watching her prideful husband who seemed to have something to prove. "She was my other half. You don't understand." Her voice was cold as ice.

Bill swung his free hand down and collected the dish towel —her favorite one, he must have known—and then pulled his gun out from his waistband. Though she couldn't see his face, she knew her husband was wincing at the pain of the forward bend.

"It ain't that I gotta see where she died, Essie." He said this without facing her. "It's that I wanted to see *why* in the *hell* you can't seem to live." His voice broke in half. "She's not your other half no more. She's dead. I'm supposed to be your other half. So what could be up there?" He pointed a crooked finger to the loft. "You want to tear this thing down, but you don't want me to touch that loft. You wanted me to grow your parents' 'baccy but you wouldn't let me see where Dottie died."

"What's there to see?" Essie cried out. She knew. Of course, she did. What was kept up on that loft was Essie's last memory with her sister. It was her heart, hanging up there. If they kept the hangar, then she'd have to face it. Share it. With Bill and everyone. If they kept it closed or, even better, tore the whole thing down, then that secret final memory could live on inside of Essie. And somewhere deep down, Essie knew that it about killed Bill that she had a private memory that he couldn't. And it didn't make her feel sad for him one bit. No sir. What was more, *he* knew that she wanted it secret, and he couldn't stand that.

A heavy scowl turned his face ugly. "Nothing, I guess. Nothing you ever wanted me to see anyway."

Bill spat on the ground then made a show of holding the gun out as if he needed a good hard look at it. Then he turned to her, with a sneer for a mouth, and shook out the dish towel. Bits of dust got caught swirling in the sunlight that streamed in from any number of cracks and crevices that ran along the lengths of the hangar. When the towel was good and shook, he wrapped the gun inside of it. Then he said, teasing, "I needed a gun rag."

CHAPTER THIRTY-FOUR

PRESENT DAY

Morgan Jo

The argument with Amber at the bar hadn't only pushed Morgan to leave, it pushed her to call Nick.

As soon as she and Julia made it back to town in an over-priced ride-share that dropped Julia off at her house first, Morgan took a hot shower. She thought long and hard about her life, her family, and, mostly, her future.

By the time her skin was scrubbed raw and her finger pads were pruned up like raisins, she pulled on her white nightgown and slipped under the heavy quilt, fumbling with her phone to find Nick's contact—the only other number she'd called in quite some time. Being home did that to a girl, Morgan figured. It meant there were no more phone calls. Not when your best friend was a text and a car ride away. Not when your mama lived in the room next door. It was just the boyfriend who needed phoning.

"Nick?" she whispered, keeping her voice as low as possible once he answered. "You're awake?" She squinted at the cuckoo clock that hung on her wall, but it was too dark to make out.

"It's only nine here, remember, babe?" His voice calmed her. It transported her home to Arizona, which officially *was* going to be her home. It was going to be her home just as soon as she delivered the news to Nick that he wanted to hear. The news that she wanted to give him.

"Right. So, how's everything?"

Nick replied, "Good, except for your absence. It's *felt*, really it is, babe."

"Right." Morgan shifted in the bed, wiggling down deeper and finding the sweet spot where her body belonged in that old mattress, in that old house, on that old farm. "The market? Any new leads lately?"

"Well, every day a new lead crops up. That's why you need to get back here."

"*That's* why?" Morgan was flirting, but somehow it didn't convey.

Nick's sigh was audible through the line. "You know what I mean, babe."

"Right. Listen, about your... proposal." At the word, she choked out a small cough. "You know what I mean."

"Moving in? Renting out your place? Yeah." His pitch rose.

Morgan sucked in a breath. "My answer," she began, chewing over her lip then letting out her breath little by little, "is *yes*."

* * *

Morgan went to bed and promptly found herself in a nightmare.

She typically didn't sleep well. Pain from her hip made sure of that. But this was an especially fitful, painful night.

In her dream, Morgan was back in Arizona, but this time with Julia instead of Nick. They were at a bar, drinking bourbon, and Amber showed up. She had a gun, a rusty old pistol, and she was aiming it directly at Morgan's heart. Morgan froze at the sight of the gun, unable to defend herself or disarm her crazy cousin.

Julia threw her body in front of Morgan's just as Amber pulled the trigger, but instead of hitting Julia *or* Morgan, the dreamscape suddenly changed, and it was Morgan pointing the pistol at Memaw. Just when she pulled the trigger, she woke up.

The now-familiar and ever-present throbbing in her left side was gone. That was the first thing she realized. But just as soon as Morgan realized her hip felt okay, the nightmare and all its scariness heaved back into her mind, removing the surprising new relief entirely.

Her whole body was damp from sweat, and her nightgown clung to her clammy skin. It was early, painfully so. Before dawn, even. There was no going back to sleep after that one, and Morgan felt the hot fear of the nightmare. Her heart pounded. The memory of the make-believe world of her dreams still fresh and real in her mind. She wanted her mom.

She wanted Memaw.

Slipping out of bed, still in her sweat-soaked nightgown, Morgan crept out of her bedroom and down the hall, stopping first at her mother's bedroom. She listened in, starting to open the door. But a better idea came to mind. Something that would make her feel much better, probably.

She closed the door carefully, one hand pressed against wood so old it belonged in a museum.

Then, Morgan moved to the stairs. They creaked badly, but Morgan knew if she stayed at the inside edge of each step, she'd descend silently.

The big house smelled different at night. Gone were the scents of home-cooked meals, grease, sugar. Gone was the fleeting whiff of one of Morgan's aunts' perfume, or her mother's. Gone was Memaw's smell—the smell of a long life, a hard life, a good life, and so many other things it was hard to pin down exactly *what* the old woman smelled like. She smelled like a grandmother, probably. But then again Morgan hadn't smelled Memaw moving through the house in a long while.

She made it to the first level and swung quietly around the banister, taking care to tread across the runner that would carry her from the staircase to the bedroom.

The door was wide open, and it made Morgan feel weird about standing in there in front of it. Like she was watching something she shouldn't. She stood in the doorway to Memaw's bedroom and just watched for a few moments. The dream remained fresh, and Morgan's heart pounded more heavily now than when she'd first awoken.

Memaw's form lay in the dead center of the bed in repose beneath a heavy quilt. Under that were layers of blankets, Morgan knew. She was cold all the time, Memaw was. Her hands were tucked beneath the blankets, but Morgan could see them, a pile of skin and bones poking up on her chest. Memaw's face was slack, and a very low, very soft snore came and went.

Next to Memaw on the bedside table was her alarm clock—unlikely to be set. Also, a baby monitor—CarlaMay's idea. The coordinating device would be upstairs in Morgan's mom's room. Morgan wondered if there was a shift over the sound waves of the monitor. Did CarlaMay hear that Morgan was standing in the room? Would she hear anything if Morgan stepped *into* the room?

On the far side of Memaw's bed, some medical equipment. The oxygen tank that the doctors cleared Memaw of using. Another taller and more complicated-looking monitor, the function of which Morgan couldn't remember, also sat unused. A little heart monitor was attached by glue or something to Memaw's chest, but otherwise, she was generally quite healthy.

Morgan moved into the room all the way, on the balls of her feet, like a child on Christmas morning, waiting for Santa to pop out of the fireplace. Or, worse, waiting to see that it was her father there, hiding presents beneath the tree. And that it was her father all along.

But Morgan didn't have a father.

She had a mother.

And she had Memaw.

The nightmare crept up Morgan's spine and flicked her in the brain. It was that kind of nightmare, the kind that felt so damn real that you never shook it. Not for a day or more.

Morgan found herself at the foot of Memaw's bed. The woman's snores remained consistent. Comforting, even.

"Memaw," Morgan whispered in spite of the baby monitor, in spite of herself... in spite of a *lot*. "I'm sorry."

Of course, Morgan knew that's not what her grandmother wanted to hear. Morgan eased onto the bed, sitting there on the edge like her mother had done that very morning. It felt all wrong. Her nightgown was still damp, but Morgan had stopped caring about that. She pulled back from the bed and lifted the corner of the covers, then slipped her body carefully in, nestling far enough from her grandmother so as not to disturb her or wake her, but close enough that she could reach over and rest her hand just near the quiet, slumbering body. "Memaw," she whispered again, forgetting entirely about the baby monitor and the heart monitor and the oxygen tank and everything else in the world. "Memaw, I forgive you."

CHAPTER THIRTY-FIVE
2017

Essie

Morgan's tenure with the firm up in Louisville was short-lived. She was flounderin' around, and her mama wanted her back home to figure things out.

Essie was glad of this. She thought maybe Morgan could apply some of her learning and skills to projects on the farm.

Namely, Essie wanted to convince Morgan to find a way to get the hangar torn down. Bill was against the idea, of course. He still carried dreams of making the farm into a great tobacco growing operation, even greater than when Essie's parents had it going. It was the man in Bill. The provider. It was the desire in him to do something so big and glorious that people would love him the world over.

It was also Bill's driving hunger to have more of Essie, to have her past, somehow.

But he was never going to have Essie's past. It was locked away in the wooden casket with Dottie's body.

Essie's next move was to just tear down the hangar anyway, but this was probably a bad idea. Still, the farm and all the property was Essie's family home, and the hangar was *her* misery.

Convincing Morgan to take on odd jobs at the farm would be the hardest part. And Morgan, like Bill, was a sentimental gal. She longed for the history of her life and the history of others. That was what she said was her professional mission: "to resurrect history." Sounded like blasphemy to Essie, and dangerous, to boot. But Morgan was a go-getter, and she was *good* at what she did. Essie just knew it.

Essie didn't bother to approach Bill with the news of Morgan's return, much less news that just as soon as Morgan arrived, they'd head out back to the hangar and brainstorm a good way to handle the macabre business of it all.

"Memaw," Morgan said once they were out there. It was a cold day, bitter cold for Brambleberry. Essie knew that if rain happened to make its way to Kentucky, they'd get snowfall, and that was a relatively rare occurrence for the southern town. Morgan pulled her down jacket over her front and zipped it up to her chin before tucking her hands deep in the pockets. She looked at her grandmother, and Essie looked back. Morgan, apparently satisfied to have her full attention, continued. "You could easily get this thing torn down if you just hire it out to a construction crew. Isn't Geddy doing that sort of work?"

"Well, the thing of it is, I wanted your perspective, Morgan. Because what I think is that we put something in its place."

Morgan kept her voice soft and gentle. "You mean, like a memorial? For Aunt Dottie?"

Essie had taught her children and grandchildren to properly refer to the aunt they'd never met. It was only right, after all.

"No." Essie shook her head. "Her memory is here." Essie tapped her heart. "I want this to be something for *you*, Morgan Jo."

"For me? Memaw, that's... generous. But it isn't fair. What about—"

"What about who? Your cousins? They hardly come a'calling. You're looking for a career to settle into, and I think you'd do well as a businesswoman, Morgan Jo."

"I never saw myself as a businesswoman. Or a business owner. I want to work on houses."

"You can do both, you know."

"How?" Morgan Jo wrinkled up her nose, and if she were any other grandchild, Essie would consider it the face of a lazy person who thought they was about to get into a spell of hard work. But this was Morgan Jo, and the wrinkled-up nose wasn't a sign of laziness. It was a sign of *thinking*. Probably, Morgan Jo was thinking right clear through to what she could bring onto the farm and whose help she'd need.

Essie said, "I can help you. Your mama can, too. Hell, you're right about Geddy. He can do the teardown and build."

"Build? But Memaw, that's not exactly—"

"I know—you want an *old* place. Well, what if we reused the materials from the hangar? Turned 'em into something new but still historic?"

Morgan Jo's face cleared a little. "It's not a *bad* idea. But... what would the business be? What I wanted to do was buy and resell houses. Fix them up. Restore them, you know? This is on family land. It's not like you're going to parcel off the land and sell it."

Morgan Jo had a good point about that. Essie had no intention of selling off anything, and Bill wouldn't stand for that even more than he wasn't standing for a teardown of the hangar. "Well, you could do any business you've a mind to do!" Essie pronounced with all the confidence of a desperate, desperate woman.

"But, Memaw, I don't have a, like, *business* in mind at all. I just want to work with houses."

Essie could feel herself losing her grip.

"Well, I have an idea, then." A shiver coursed through Essie. She was cold as all get-out standing out there staring up at the old metal thing that once was a playhouse. Now, little more than a dangerous shed. "Let's go inside. I'll make sweet tea and get a fresh loaf of bread going. And we'll talk."

Morgan Jo was fairly easy to convince. She loved sweets and bread, and Essie was going to use this to convince her to roll out something in place of that ol' hangar.

They set about heading to the big house, Morgan Jo walking slowly while Essie clung to her elbow. They talked about Morgan Jo's love life, some—there wasn't much to say in that regard. They talked about family and how Amber, Tiffany, and Travis hadn't done much with their lives, yet. Neither had Geddy or anyone else. It had been only Morgan who'd tried to make her way and then looped back for visits. One might think a grandparent would love for her grandkids to stick around close and visit often, but actually it was the opposite. A memaw wanted her grandkids to head off in the world and only ever come back to say that they'd made it. Or, the other option was for them to come back and say, "Let's make it together, Memaw." Dreamers could dream, Essie figured.

"What about you build a place and let it out?" Essie suggested, delivering a glass of tea for Morgan Jo and setting one down for herself. She returned to the bread maker, dumping in ingredient after ingredient and finishing it all off with a heaping spoonful of sugar, for good, southern measure.

"I'm not sure I want to deal in property management. Seems like a lot of work. And I don't really think strangers should be living on here. Do you want strangers living on here, Memaw? It might not be safe."

"Well, that's true. Now if it were family we could let to, well, then that'd be a conversation." Essie gave it another think. She snapped her gnarled fingers together, but the sound was rubbed out by her dry skin. Even so, she had an idea. "You know what could be *real* lucrative, Morgan Jo?"

"What?"

"You know." She smiled mischievously. "That whiskey business. Or bourbon or whatever. We're on the bourbon trail, or not far from it, 'least. You could have a tastin' room! You know my daddy bootlegged whiskey."

Morgan slugged back her tea then offered nothing short of a look of exasperation. The whiskey business was an idea they'd already discussed and set aside. Morgan knew where it came from, too. "Memaw, I know about Great-Grandad and his whiskey creek."

"Then you know how much money he made. He built this place up on the profits of slinging that ol' drink." She punched the air for emphasis.

"Memaw, I don't know a thing about liquor."

"I've seen you drink a bottle of wine over the course of a few days, Morgan Jo, so don't you start in on that nonsense. You know a thing about wine."

Bill came in, cranky as all get-out. "What about wine?"

"We ain't talkin' about your pastime, Billy," Essie replied, sharing a knowing look with Morgan Jo.

But Morgan Jo had no interest in the business of her grandparents' brittle marriage. "I'm gonna take a bath and a nap. I'll let you two duke it out."

She left, and Bill scowled something awful. "What are you schemin' on, Essie Coyle?"

Essie pressed her thin lips in a line, closed her eyes, and shook her head. There wasn't no use in prolonging the inevitable. And it *was* inevitable, tearing down that eyesore. That death trap. "We're taking it down. The hangar. And Morgan Jo is going to open a new business. Probably a bourbon shop."

Bill laughed, a searing kind of laugh. "No you ain't." He sneered and ran his tongue about his mouth. "You ain't taking it down. I still use it."

"What in the—no you don't, Bill. You don't use it, and you haven't since we stopped growing. I've had it up to here with this conversation. It's my property. We're taking it down."

Bill seethed. Blood crawled under his wrinkled neck skin and shot up his cheeks. His glasses fogged up. Spittle formed at the corners of his mouth. "I wish to God I never met you. You were always interested in *you, you, you* and your dead sister. Well, I reckon you killed her the way you carry that guilt that hangs off you like a big ol' bag a'lard."

"What in the world made you so hateful, Bill Coyle? Was you always like this? I really want to know, was you always this way? This mean?"

He moved cud around in his mouth, and it was the first time she realized he was chewing again. He was supposed to have quit years back, when they got word that the stuff would eat away the insides of his mouth and could cause cancer, too.

"Are you chewin' 'baccy again?"

He leaned right, toward an ol' brass spittoon that was just for looks and had been for years. Then, he spit into it before running his hand against his mouth to clear the left-behinds. His face wasn't red no more. His mouth was clean. His mind seemed clear, even. It was the worst-case scenario. If it were dementia Bill had, Essie could understand it. Her own mama had the disease.

They'd been to doctors going on three years now, though, and every last scan, questionnaire, and check-up revealed that Billy Coyle wasn't brain-damaged. He was an asshole. Probably, he'd always been one.

The thing of it was, Essie kept that side of him as hidden and tied up as she could. She talked him up to everyone from her own parents down to her grandchildren. And they were all convinced. Every last one of them believed their grandad was second only to Saint Nick. Even now, Essie imagined Morgan Jo was rolling her eyes on her grandad's behalf. *Poor Grandad, about to be bossed 'til kingdom come!* Essie hadn't been the bad guy for all their marriage. She'd taken the faults. She'd been the perpetrator. To everyone else.

Not to Billy, though.

"If you touch that hangar," Bill went on, his voice pitching up and down like he was gon' lose control again, "then you'll be sorry, woman!"

"What?"

His threat was empty, of course. But it wasn't the first. And after years upon years of even the emptiest of threats, well, they wore a person down. Even empty threats got to ya. Bill had laid so many empty threats on Essie, that it all rolled into one big and very real threat, in fact. And while Bill wasn't an abusive person, she was starting to see what people talked about when they said emotional abuse. This was a concept so foreign to Essie and her generation, that it might as well be something made up. In fact, Essie had been fairly certain that something like emotional abuse *was* made up. You couldn't be victim to emotional abuse unless you were a weakling, and since Essie wasn't a weakling, she couldn't rightly be a victim of emotional abuse.

But there it was. She was fed up. She was aggravated, and just fed right on up.

Bill left the room without another word, off to go tinker on something. Off to gripe and moan and groan soon again, no doubt.

Essie realized in that moment that she hadn't ever really got Bill's *attention*. Maybe the problem wasn't on Bill's bad behavior but rather Essie's tolerance for it. She'd let him beat her down with his words and his red face and trembling wet lips. She'd let him. So now, she'd better go on and *stop* letting him.

She'd better get his attention.

CHAPTER THIRTY-SIX

2017

Essie

Essie first went to the shed just outside of the big house. Red like a miniature barn, it was the best kept-up structure on the farm, because that's where Bill usually tinkered away. But he wasn't in there now. He was in the parlor, fiddling with the record player.

She looked around for a long while but didn't find what she was looking for. Ten minutes in, she worried he'd come out lookin' for her, so she moved on to the real barn. There wasn't nothing much in there 'side from heavy machinery, so she moved on fast from the big barn. The hangar, Essie didn't dare to enter. She made her way back to the big house, moving room to room, methodical-like, but avoided the parlor. The kitchen didn't have it. Neither did the bathroom or the front room or the living room. Their bedroom didn't have it, neither. It wasn't shoved in his bedside table drawer or wedged betwixt the mattress and box spring like men usually did. There was only one logical spot left to look, so Essie made her way out there. To the big ol' truck that was Bill's pride and joy.

She opened up the driver's-side door and first peered beneath the seat. Her back ached from all the hunting, so she pushed her hand in and kept on. The thing wasn't beneath the seat or behind it. It wasn't in the console, neither.

Lastly, she popped open the glovebox. Sure as a dairy cow lets milk, it was there. 'A course, Essie wouldn't have even known what she was looking at if it weren't for the incident in the hangar, when he stole her favorite dish towel. It got her all fired up again, seeing grease on that towel. She took the towel and the thing inside of it, slid it down into her front apron pocket, and ambled back into the big house.

Worn out, she stopped in the front room, which was just adjacent to the parlor and just around the corner of the staircase. So far as Essie could tell, Morgan was fast asleep upstairs. It left only Essie and Bill down there to get this good and over with.

To get his *attention*.

She lowered into a rocking chair that once belonged to her grandmother, which was an incredible feat of woodwork, Essie figured. Then she took the thing from her pocket and pulled her dish towel off. Far as she knew, it was loaded. But Essie wasn't an idiot, and she could handle a gun well enough. She set it on her lap, pointing outward, then draped the dish towel back over the top.

"Billy!" she sang out, sweet as honey. "Come're a second, sweetheart."

She sat, waiting patiently. Her back burned from walking all over the place, bending this way and that. Her hand remained perfectly still beneath the dishcloth, fingers like lace around that dang nab pistol.

"What ya need now?" he grunted, emerging with a record in his hand.

Creaking pulled Essie's gaze past him and toward the front hall, but she didn't see nobody.

"I want to talk to you about how you treat me, Bill." Her saccharine smile fell away, and in its place, Essie put on a very serious, very earnest expression.

He frowned at her hand, or rather, the dish towel.

Essie went on. "Now, you see here, Bill Coyle. You've got me real aggravated. I'm tired of your griping. It's wore me out." She pulled the dish towel off without any flourish. It fell to the ground. Bill's eyes seized upon the weapon in Essie's hands.

His look turned scornful, though. "You don't even know how to work that thing." A laugh erupted up his throat and fell out his mouth.

Essie cocked the gun.

"Essie, *dammit*!" he roared, and that funny ol' laugh was yesterday's piss in a pot. Essie was in charge now. She was the one who held the cards. "You're gon' kill somebody!" His voice was loud and terrible, but Essie was frozen in this moment. She had his attention. Her work was done.

She went to *un*cock the gun, but just as she turned the thing in her hand, a blur emerged out of nowhere. Before Essie knew what happened, she was toppled out of the rocking chair. The pistol loosed out of her hand. A shot had gone off, ringing so loud in Essie's ears that she was deaf to any noise that came after.

But she wasn't blind. Clear as day, she saw Bill crouched, fussing over something on the floor. He hauled it up, and that's when Essie seen what she'd done. In his arms, Bill held a stunned and bloody Morgan Jo.

CHAPTER THIRTY-SEVEN

2017

Morgan Jo

Memaw went to jail, naturally. Grandad had called the police and the ambulance, and they arrived with a stretcher for Morgan and handcuffs for the grandmother who'd shot her. Morgan, probably numb from shock, sometimes could manage to forget the pain of that night. But she never forgot Memaw's wails. The worst, most awful sobs a human ear could register.

The aftermath was as brutal as one might expect. Morgan went into surgery then stayed at the hospital for weeks—months —as she worked on regaining the ability to walk.

In that time, the family was split worse than a brittle strand of over-processed hair. Sure, every last one of them worried over Morgan. They felt sorry for her, visited her—even the cousins did. They sent cards and flowers and poured sympathy over her like warm maple syrup. That part, Morgan had to admit, felt good. It felt good to have doctors and nurses caring for her in the hospital and her family caring for her from afar and in the way of daily or weekly visits. But the visits tapered off. By the end of Morgan's hospital stay, it was only Julia and her mom who'd still come by on a regular basis—on a daily basis. To his great credit, though, Grandad came every other day. He didn't say much, if anything. But he pretended to check her vitals on the monitor and fuss with some part of the hospital bed that wasn't electronic but mechanical.

No one had mentioned a word to Morgan about what had become of Memaw. And Morgan hadn't had the guts to ask. But the day she was released, the day she was set to return home, it was inevitable.

They had to talk about it.

Because Memaw would be there. At the big house. Waiting like a wretched ol' woman, weak from a lifetime of guilt. She'd been released on bail the day after her arrest. Grandad had posted the bill, scraped together from a savings account that was supposed to carry the two through their funeral. This part, Morgan had heard.

The family had pooled some of their funds, too, and seen to it that Memaw didn't have to stay in jail. The rationale being that Memaw wouldn't survive in a cold prison. She wouldn't sleep, wouldn't eat, wouldn't talk. Wouldn't live, in a very literal sense. And her death, well, no one had been quite ready for that.

What bugged Morgan, though, was that nobody stopped to wonder if Morgan was going to survive. Maybe that was what youth got you. A guarantee on surviving a gunshot wound that hadn't penetrated the head or the heart or a main artery.

Then again, the gunshot wound might have hit her hip, but it *shattered* Morgan's heart. Some days she lay in her hospital bed with a book, scanning words on pages while she wondered if maybe the doctors could perform a heart transplant while she was there. Because she sure as hell couldn't imagine how she'd ever care about someone deeply again. Not after that.

The drive home was agony. Morgan ought to have accepted the offer of an ambulance ride instead, but she didn't want anymore bills piling up. The nurses got her as comfortable as she could be lying down on the back seat. Her mom and Julia sat in the front.

"So, she's going to be there? At home?" Morgan asked her mom. She was referring to Memaw, of course, but Morgan wasn't quite sure what to call the old woman. In her head, she was a criminal, a person who had drawn a gun on another person and managed to pull the trigger. Morgan knew she was the victim of that crime, but she wondered sometimes about Grandad. Was he a victim, too? Or was there more to the story? Why had Memaw been pointing the gun in the first place? What in the world had happened between those two? What was the *truth*? It was lost, that's what. Lost to the trauma of the blast. Nothing was excusable or explainable. There was no acceptable reason, in Morgan's hurt mind, that that woman should have been holding and pointing a loaded gun at anyone. Least of all her husband.

CarlaMay shifted audibly in her seat. Julia looked back at Morgan and rested her hand on Morgan's arm. "We already figured it out. We moved Miss Essie to one of the bunkhouses. She's not even in the big house. You don't have to see her if you don't want to."

Before Morgan had a chance to reply, her mom asked, "Do you want to?"

"Want to what?" Morgan replied.

"Want to see Memaw?"

An eye roll would go unnoticed. Silence was useless. Sarcasm was Morgan's last remaining weapon. "What do you think, Mom?"

"Okay. Well, maybe in time." All three were quiet for a moment, but then CarlaMay spoke again. "Morgan, she is so sorry. She is a wreck. Miserable. I know we haven't talked about it yet, but she's in a bad way, hon."

"I would be, too, if I'd shot my granddaughter." Morgan said this without mirth. Her throat turned dry. She felt like crying, but it wasn't worth the effort or energy.

"What about Grandad?" Morgan wanted to know. In the crisis, he'd been her savior. He'd acted fast, pressing a dish towel to her wound to stop up the blood and holding her close as he fumbled with the nearby landline and dialed 9-1-1. It was a miracle, really, how much Grandad managed to juggle all at once. He wasn't known for multitasking. And then his regular visits to the hospital, well, it meant something to Morgan. Really, it did. The accident had made them closer.

"Grandad?" Morgan could see CarlaMay turn to Julia, who shrugged in reply.

"Is he staying in the big house or in the bunkhouse with Me... with *her*?" Morgan felt this was an important question. She needed to know where he stood. She needed to know where *everyone* stood, actually.

"He's in the big house, but he checks on her. We all take turns checking on her. She can't go anywhere off the property, really, not with her probation order in place. And she can't even leave the bunkhouse once you come home. She knows that. We told her so."

Morgan considered this. *Probation.* For discharging a weapon and severely maiming one's own kin. *Nice.* She scoffed. "She's not going back to jail, then? Or prison, I guess?"

"She'll have a trial," her mom acknowledged. "But the attorney thinks she'll get by on probation based on her clean record..." CarlaMay broke off at that point and cried.

Julia tried to calm her, but Morgan couldn't muster up anything worthwhile to say. Morgan just needed the information. "Based on what else? I mean, what she did was serious. Does anyone even know what happened?"

Julia answered, "Well, probation and maybe no more time in jail based on the fact that she's nearly eighty years old and harmless. She *is* harmless, Morgan. I know... I know. It's crazy to say, but we've been checking on her. She's the same old Memaw, the same old Miss Essie. It was just one crazy moment. Crazy moments happen, Mo."

Morgan disagreed. "And, anyway, why does she even need checking on? She wasn't hurt."

No response came.

Morgan let out a sigh and squeezed her eyes shut. *What a mess.* And to think there was such hope before all this. She was going to think up some grand business scheme and stay on the farm while starting her career in earnest. She was going to do something great. Something her whole family would be proud of, and something Morgan herself would be proud of. Now she was a cripple. An invalid. All those dirty words you weren't supposed to say about someone who couldn't walk or function normally. Not only that, Morgan's whole future was called into question. Yes, she'd been making good progress with taking steps and could get around on a walker. But no, the doctors weren't sure if she'd have other residual issues. Like, for example, fertility problems. Morgan hadn't yet known if she ever wanted to have children, but now she was already mourning the loss of children she might have had.

From the front seat, CarlaMay cleared her throat. "Morgan, you know that Memaw, um, she wrote you a letter."

Julia twisted in her seat. "You don't have to read it until you're ready." She passed Morgan a cream-colored envelope, thick with folded pages inside. Or maybe something other than paper, even. Who knew?

More to the point, who *cared*? She let the envelope drop into the paper bag that housed the clothes she wore into the hospital along with few personal effects she'd accumulated during her stay.

"She's really not going to prison?" Morgan asked again.

Julia looked at her. "Do you want her to go to prison?"

Morgan shrugged. "I don't know. No. I mean... I don't know."

"Memaw still could go to prison," CarlaMay said. "Her age and clean record alone aren't all that will keep her out."

Morgan knew her mother well. There was more to be said. "What are you getting at?" Morgan was so interested in this, in fact, that she pulled herself upright. The pain meds they'd sent her home with were still in effect, but it was an awkward position. Once up, Morgan saw her mother's hands twist on the steering wheel. "Mom?"

"Once it goes to trial, you know," CarlaMay replied.

"No," Morgan answered. "I don't."

"Well, it depends on who testifies, Morgan Jo." Her mother's tone sharpened.

"You mean, who would testify *against* her?"

Julia turned. "It's on the prosecution to prove she's guilty."

"Guilty of what, though?"

Julia looked at Morgan with a gentleness. "Assault with intent to murder."

Morgan felt her heart skip. "Intent to murder? I don't think she *intended* to *murder*..." Morgan's voice fell away, though.

"Exactly," Julia said, but her voice remained sympathetic and clear of judgment or *told ya so*-ness. Julia was good like that. She saw the whole picture. She saw it from every vantage point and every perspective. But, ultimately, she had Morgan's back. Morgan knew this. And Morgan knew what both Julia and her mom were getting at.

They turned onto the Coyle family property, the tires crunching over gravel and the view of the broad-faced white farmhouse stretching out as they neared it. Once parked, CarlaMay and Julia hopped out and came around to the back to help Morgan get out and on her feet for the trek inside.

Once inside, they settled Morgan on the pull-out sofa in the parlor. It'd be her recovery room, so to speak. They'd furnished it with a dresser just to the side of the bed, where she could take meals if need be, and keep things. Her mom and Julia left her momentarily to go get the sweet tea. In that time, Morgan pulled the letter out of the brown paper bag. She studied the envelope. Her name was scrawled in Memaw's penmanship, a little shaky: *Morgan Jo.*

Even just *thinking* about reading the thing gave Morgan fits. She opened the top drawer of the dresser, saw a stack of Memaw's old doilies, and shoved the letter deep under all of them.

Her mom and Julia returned with a sweaty glass of sweet iced tea. Julia flipped the television on.

Morgan figured now was as good a time as any to answer her mom and her best friend. It wasn't a snap decision, or, at least, it didn't feel like one. It was a decision from deep down inside of Morgan. Her mom was about to head to the kitchen to start on supper. Julia mentioned she had to get back to work. Before either left though, Morgan stopped them. "About the trial, whenever it happens," Morgan said. Even though she was hard-hearted—or maybe even broken-hearted now—she wasn't cruel. She wasn't totally heart*less.* "You don't have to worry. You can tell *her* not to worry."

"What do you mean, Mo?" Julia asked.

Morgan stared at the TV, unwatching and unhearing and having decided she wouldn't ever read that damned letter. It could rot under the pile of chintzy crochet rags. "You can tell Memaw that I won't testify against her."

CHAPTER THIRTY-EIGHT

2018

Morgan Jo

A year after "Memaw's Incident," as it became known to the family at large, Grandad died. He'd been diagnosed with throat cancer sometime in between that day and just before his death. He'd passed on chemo, citing his age and general contentedness with how his stay on earth had gone. According to Morgan's mom, Grandad said he was done with this life and "ready to get on with it."

Morgan couldn't help but wonder if he'd have accepted chemotherapy or any other measure of prolonging his life if the argument with his wife hadn't happened. And if his granddaughter hadn't been accidentally shot. It was sad, Grandad's passing, and it was also a reminder that sometimes you needed a big change to get over a hard thing.

Morgan moved away, chasing another dead-end job that was only loosely related to her passion. She was staging houses for a high-end rental agency. Home design wasn't Morgan's thing, and the funeral was an added reason to go back home, see if she could maybe stand to live in Brambleberry for good, even if not on the farm proper.

But the funeral proved that simply couldn't be. It was a challenge to come face-to-face with Memaw. Everything about that awful day was too close to Morgan. It was too hard to remember. To dwell on.

And yet, there were the cousins, champing at the bit to finally have a chance to bombard her with questions.

Morgan saw them approach at the tail end of the service, so she veered off to the coffin. She'd wanted to go up with her mother, but her mother had already been there, kissing Grandad's cheek and sobbing into a handkerchief. Now, though, CarlaMay was laughing at some memory with her sisters, and Morgan was left to either face Amber, Tiffany, and Rachel or woman-up and take the moment to talk to the man who saved her life.

She focused her gaze on the polished dark wood, and in her periphery, the vultures scattered.

Coming up on the tufted satin, Morgan felt tears threaten to burst through. So far, she hadn't cried. Not when she got the news he'd died, and not all through the wake and service. But now, being so near the shell of the man who'd raised her as his own, more or less, it was hard to push away the sadness. Even a man like the cranky Bill Coyle had shared sweet moments. Especially with Morgan.

She squeezed her eyes shut and thought back to a million times he'd smiled. A hundred hugs he'd given, even though they were often awkward and stiff. She recalled how he'd shown up to every important even in her life, from her first communion to her college graduation. He'd been there for her.

And now here she was, for him, even if it didn't feel like the figure lying prone in the coffin was *really* Grandad.

It was, though. It was Grandad there in the coffin, all formaldehyde and makeup and hairspray, all sewn up and buttoned up and stapled up, it wasn't *him*. He was like a wax figure of himself.

Morbid curiosity got the better of her, and Morgan reached in, pressing the back of her hand to his cheek. The cold of his skin froze her hand for a moment, but she jerked it away. A single sob crept out of her throat, and she quelled the sound with the back of her hand—the other hand, not the one that she'd just rested against death. A pair of tears trickled from her eyes, one on each side. Once she was sure she'd muffled the cry well enough, she pushed the wetness away and bent down lower. "I love you," Morgan whispered to him.

Then she spun around and took a deep, long breath.

"Morgan." Amber stood there, fanning herself with the In Memoriam paper that everyone received upon entering.

"Hi, Amber." They hadn't yet done more than a fleeting greeting when Amber and Grant had shuffled into Morgan's pew, late to the service.

Amber's eyes got watery, and that made Morgan's eyes water, too. Though they weren't very close anymore, they shared a past so tight-knit that a death could rupture any lingering tensions. It enmeshed them, Grandad's passing. Morgan pulled Amber in, and they hugged for a long while.

At last, upon releasing one another, Tiffany and Rachel appeared. Morgan hugged each of them, too. And they wiped their tears and laughed at length. "Can't believe he's gone. I never thought he'd actually *die*," Tiffany remarked.

"Yeah. He was a strong person," Amber said weepily.

The four of them left the coffin, each one's eyes lingering on the man lying prone at rest. Outside, the sky above St. Mark's was white-blue and Morgan wondered if that was half the reason folks wore sunglasses to funerals. On the one hand, you could hide your tears. On the other, you could shield yourself from the light when you finally emerged from the darkness.

They huddled near a memorial bench situated between two

great big ceramic flowerpots with fresh, colorful flowers. Did flowers really make people feel any better? Or were they like another set of sunglasses, meant to hide away something too ugly to see?

Rachel struck up a new angle of the conversation. "Honey," she said then dropped her voice low, "*Morgan Jo*, how *are* you? What really happened?" Her face glowed with the excitement of gossip. Tiffany and Amber leaned in, too, their faces suddenly dry, their mouths shut, their eyes big.

Morgan swallowed. There was no real use in putting them off. And, anyway, whatever they *did* hear about the incident was already spreading around town like wildfire. Morgan could set them straight or confirm what they'd already divulged. What did it matter anymore?

"I came downstairs from a bath. I wanted to get a drink. I heard Grandad hollering in the parlor, so I walked in. And..." Morgan felt herself freeze up and stare off, one hand in the air as she was describing the scene first in her mind's eye. She blinked. Looked up. "And... and Memaw was holding a gun at him. I just... I just reacted. I went to grab the gun from her, and she pulled the trigger."

"She pulled the trigger?" Amber gasped, her hand to her mouth. "I heard it just went off. The pistol, I mean. That it was an *accident*." Her eyes were wide, and her mouth remained a perfect oversize O.

Morgan ran her tongue over her lower lip then chewed it. She swallowed and shook her head. "It *was* an accident. I meant that the gun went off. She didn't—I don't think she was trying to shoot me. Probably not even trying to shoot him." Morgan jutted her chin toward Grandad in the coffin. "But it was just—bad." Her eyebrows knit together. She looked at each cousin in turn. "It was just real bad, you know? Just... *bad*."

"Poor thing." Tiffany rubbed Morgan's lower back.

Rachel's gaze flew beyond the others. "Here she comes."

"Who?" Amber turned, oblivious to Rachel's subtlety.

But before an answer came, Morgan felt a tug on her elbow. She turned.

Memaw stood, crookedly, behind Morgan. "Morgan Jo," she crooned. "You came." Memaw was a woman who had herself fixed up for events, especially funerals. Morgan could distinctly remember all throughout her life how her grandmother would make a hair appointment far in advance of a birthday party. She'd call upon her daughters to help her with her face. It may have been the result of having grown up a scrappy farm girl or in spite of that, but Morgan knew that Essie Coyle was one to have her hair washed and set and her makeup done. Her outfit, if not newly purchased, would be a special favorite, pulled from the depths of her closet and sent to the dry cleaners. Extra ironing for any cotton or linen. Perfume. Jewelry.

Now, the woman was almost unrecognizable. At least twenty pounds lighter—and twenty pounds she didn't have to lose—and half a foot shorter because of her poor posture. Her hair was recently dyed, it appeared, but not fixed. Black and wispy, it lay flat and stiff around her head. Her mouth was pale, and Morgan couldn't distinguish the shape of the woman's lips from the rest of her sallow, sunken face.

She wore transitional glasses which were sitting in the odd shade between indoor and outdoor, a yellowish brown.

Memaw did not smile.

Morgan looked for help from one of her cousins, but each was slowly moving backward.

"Why wouldn't I have come?" Morgan asked, laughing nervously and looking from side to side.

Memaw pressed her mouth in a harder line and clasped her hands in front of her, full of repentance and guilt—her own and a heaping dose for Morgan, no doubt. "Well. *Thank you.*" And just like that, Memaw moved away. No apology. No nothing. This is the first time the two had seen one another since the *incident*, and all that woman had to say was "Thank you." A pitiful, manipulative thank you.

But that wasn't the reason Morgan decided the funeral was it. After that, she'd find a job somewhere else. Somewhere on the West Coast, maybe. Far away. A new beginning. A fresh start. All those things that pretty young girls in movies talked about when they broke free of the nest and chased after their dreams along to a chipper musical number.

No, that wasn't the reason.

The reason Morgan wouldn't stay was because of what she observed the remainder of the funeral, and the service, and the day after.

Not once did that woman cry. She didn't cry at her own husband's death. She didn't cry at the loneliness that would succeed it. She didn't cry out of the remorse for what she'd done, or what she'd *almost* done.

Morgan was already dealing with a broken heart, after all. She didn't need to harden what she had left of it.

CHAPTER THIRTY-NINE

PRESENT DAY

Morgan Jo

Morgan woke up the morning after climbing into Memaw's bed, and she felt like she'd been drugged. She was disoriented, first. Tired, mostly. But after that, she felt a little like maybe she'd been reborn. Like maybe her time on the farm hadn't been all for naught. Morgan felt like she'd go back to Arizona and maybe book another visit to Brambleberry. For Christmas. Or even Thanksgiving.

She stretched beneath the layers of sheets and blankets and quilts, pointing her toes as long as they'd go, rolling her wrists. Morgan felt her hip, working it from behind like she did most mornings. It, too, like the rest of her, felt *good*. She twisted in bed, ready to repeat what she'd said to Memaw. Ready to start her new beginning now, with a hug and a proper, loving goodbye.

Something was weird, though. The air in the room, too still. The sunlight streaming in across specks of dust that fell gently down, entirely undisturbed.

No sound came from the kitchen or the parlor or front

room, or anywhere else in the house. No creaking floorboards or fridge gasket whooshing as the door swung open and closed. No percolating coffee. Morgan eased out of the bed, careful not to wake Memaw, who remained motionless on her side of the broad bed.

Morgan figured she might whip up pancakes and bacon before she left for the airport, and so she padded to the door, opening it slowly, slowly, and squeezing through a narrow crack before closing it again behind her.

In the kitchen, her mother sat with a mug of coffee, the newspaper laid out on the table in front of her.

"You're up," Morgan greeted, smiling. "I didn't hear you." She glanced at the clock. It was early. Much earlier than Morgan had been waking since being home—or, rather, since being in Brambleberry.

Her mother smiled back. "You're—different. What's different about you?" Then she looked past Morgan. "Where did you just come from?"

"I had a terrible nightmare, Mom." Morgan poured her own mug of coffee then lowered into the chair nearest her mother. "It was terrible. It was—" She stopped short, shaking her head. "Just real, real bad."

"Aw, i'n't that the worst?" CarlaMay clicked her tongue and flipped a page over before taking a long sip. "You gonna get ready soon?" She then glanced at the clock. "We need to leave in a couple of hours. I figure you're not packed quite yet."

Morgan gestured behind her to the kitchen. "Actually, mind if I make some breakfast for you all?"

"Who all?" her mom replied, rearing back.

"You, Memaw. Heck, let's bring Amber and all of 'em on over." She didn't exactly want to see Amber, but something about that dream and last night's deep sleep in Memaw's bed had changed Morgan. Like a softness had grown inside of her.

Her mother stayed unconvinced, though. "What's all this

about?" She pushed the paper aside, and her coffee cup.

Morgan felt suddenly emotional. "It's just—you know—I've had it hard these last years, and... I just feel like I don't want to leave here again with a bad taste in my mouth." She hesitated. "I want us to be a proper family again. You know, *nice and normal?*" She laughed a little, but her mom gave her a suspicious look.

"What happened last night? At the bar?" CarlaMay glanced toward the living room. "Did Julia stay over? Is she okay?"

"Nothing happened." Morgan took a beat. "Amber just, well, I just hate to think about what's going to happen when Memaw dies. Amber thinks she and Grant and Tiff and Trav are going to get the farm, all of it. It worried me to pieces about you. If they kicked you out. And if they did, it'd probably be because you're just one, and they're four. I want to be in the loop and available. I want to have a stake in this place, Mom. And that means getting along. I know it does. Putting the past in the past and getting on with everyone."

Her mother rested her head thoughtfully on the heel of her hand and drummed her fingers along her cheek. "That's sweet, Morgan Jo, but you don't have to worry about *me*. I'll be fine no matter what happens."

"You've lived here all your life, Mom."

"And I'll stay here until it's time for me to go. Whether that be when Memaw dies or sooner or even later. Who knows? But as for getting along, well, that's just plain noble." She stood, reached over, and mussed Morgan's hair, then moved to the pantry. "Pancakes and bacon. Why don't you text your cousins, then you can wake Memaw up. Get her in here, would you?"

Morgan ran upstairs first, to retrieve her phone. She sent a group text to the bunkhouse crew and got changed into her traveling outfit, a light sweater, yoga pants, and canvas shoes that'd be easy to slip in and out of. She threw her hair into a pony, forwent any makeup, stuffed her things into her duffel and all but jogged back downstairs just in time to see Amber barging through the front door with Grant, Tiffany, and Travis sleepily in tow.

"Hey, you all." Morgan dropped her bag at the foot of the stairs and rushed towards Amber, hugging her hard. "Sorry about last night's conversation. I was being uppity."

Amber relaxed in Morgan's grip. "Oh, cuzzo, it's no big deal. Who cares about the trust, right? Let's just be friends, okay?"

"Yes, please," Morgan answered. "Mom!" Morgan raised her voice as they left the front hall and headed back toward the kitchen. "Do you want me to strip the bed, or..." They arrived in the kitchen, and a single pancake was burning on the griddle. Blackened at the edges and smoking, it was about to catch fire. Morgan grabbed an oven mitt and flung the charred disc into the sink before killing the griddle and whipping around to the others. "She was just here. I was gone upstairs packing, for like, a few minutes. Ten at most." Morgan looked out the window then went for the back door, but it was locked. She spun around and raised her voice again, but not as high this time, as she was nearer to Memaw's bedroom and more likely to wake her if she was still asleep or startle her if she wasn't. "Mom!" She directed her holler to the far side of the house, toward the living room and away from Memaw's.

No response.

"What in the..." Morgan whipped around to again face her cousins, who looked at her uselessly. Tiffany shrugged. "She was *just* here. Ugh." Morgan groaned and strode in leaps toward the front of the house, and the parlor. No one. No one in there or in the living room. "Did you see her out front?" she called to Amber, who'd followed dutifully.

But Amber just shook her head lamely. "Nuh-uh."

If CarlaMay had come upstairs, Morgan would've seen and

heard her. Hers was the first room at the top, and she hadn't closed her door. Not even when she'd changed out of her nightgown.

"Hang on." She brushed past Amber and back the way they'd come, from the heart of the house, beyond the fireplace and toward the kitchen. But she turned right, down a short hall and into Memaw's room.

The door sat partway ajar. Inside of the room, the overhead light was glaring bright. Morgan's gaze flew across to the bed. Her mother lay on her stomach, at an odd angle, almost sprawled across the bed, her head up toward Memaw, her legs down by the footboard.

"Mom?" Morgan asked. She could feel Amber's presence behind her and the others crowding in the doorway. It was in that moment that Morgan was able to pin down what she'd sensed when she'd woken up.

The drifting dust.

The still air.

"Mom? Is she...?" Morgan rushed the bed just as her mother pulled her body up, monstrously. Her face was red and she was crying so hard that no sound came out.

Morgan's hands flew to her mouth as she digested the shocking, horrid news. Tears sprung up to her eyes. She turned weak and slid to the floor as her cousins rushed to the bed.

A new wail pierced the confusion in the room, and Morgan realized with a fresh horror that it was her own wail. "Mom!" she sobbed, forcing herself up off the floor and over to the bed where her mother still sat, head in hands, as the cousins started in on their own bawling. "Mom," Morgan said again, her voice growing hoarser with each repetition. "I thought she was sleeping. I thought—"

Her mother shook her head miserably. "She's not sleeping, Morgan." They grabbed each other, a hard, fierce embrace. "She's *gone*."

CHAPTER FORTY

PRESENT DAY

Morgan Jo

The days following the sad discovery of a wakeless, lifeless Memaw were nothing short of a blur. Fortunately, the woman had left firm plans in place. Morgan's mom and aunts coordinated the funeral like a Broadway musical. Morgan's uncles, Garold included, pulled off all manual labor at the farm, where the reception was held.

After the wake and service at the church, the procession wove back through town, depositing everyone at the Moonshine Creek Farm. There, they had an event to make the old woman proud. Everyone came. Cousins from here to Tennessee and the Gulf Coast. Friends from church. Locals. The mayor herself made a touching appearance and even had a word or two to share before they dug into all of Memaw's favorite dishes.

Just out back of the pond, about fifty yards north of the farm lay a small family cemetery, as was common for the area. It was back there that Memaw was laid to rest next to her sister, Dottie. The reunion of the twins felt particularly emotional as the priest made his commentary on how important family was—

be it siblings or cousins. Morgan, Rachel, Amber, and Tiffany had gripped each other through sobs. Once it was over, and each family member had the chance to drop a handful of earth on the polished wood coffin, Morgan had a moment to think about just how much an impact Dottie's death had probably had on Memaw. More than she had ever realized. Thinking about the death of one of Morgan's cousins or of her best friend Julia struck her as an impossibility, and therein lay the shock.

After the burial, however, the funeral's tone lifted, and entirely absent was the tension of the previous several years. Like a heavy weight lifted off of Morgan's shoulders, and even her mothers' and aunts' and cousins', the affair was free from the feeling that something was hanging over their heads. Morgan could easily ascribe the old kismet as her rocky relationship with Memaw and the fact that Grandad could be so dang grouchy. Even before the *incident*, Memaw was unpredictable, at best. Moody, at worst. She was up and down, and sticking on her good side was a challenge unmet by anyone, save for Morgan.

Why Morgan had become the prize pony of the bunch it could only be guessed at.

CarlaMay always said it best. "Morgan Jo," she said, when they found a moment alone together at the wake. Morgan had come upon her mother in the living room, with a box of doilies Barb had unearthed the evening before. Without discussing it, CarlaMay and Morgan sat down together and began to sort through the box. "Do you know why Memaw loved you so much?"

Morgan pulled a doily from the stack that sat on the sofa between them. Many of the little hand-crocheted table spreads and trivets were made by Memaw's mother and hers before her. Some by Memaw's sisters, who'd died long since. And while they couldn't very well keep every last small heirloom, Morgan and CarlaMay were dead set on keeping most.

"No," Morgan said, studying the pattern. She didn't know much about crafts, but the little rivets that came and went looked a lot like seashells. "Was it because she burned other bridges? Like, she could be a little mean. Amber and Tiffany got the brunt of it, but I always felt that Memaw didn't... didn't respect them, maybe?" Morgan took a beat, then added, "Although, I don't know how she could have respected me. I was the opposite of Memaw. Moving all around. Can't keep a job."

"You can keep a job. You just haven't found one you like." CarlaMay folded a doily and smoothed it down on the pile they'd made for keepers. "Although, seems like you like Tucson. And Nick?"

Morgan should have felt a tickle in her gut, a flutter in her chest. But instead, she felt a groan. Memaw passed the morning Morgan was to return home. She missed her flight and didn't call Nick until later in the day. When she had, he was less sympathetic than he was irritated.

"So, you're not coming home?" he'd asked before backpedaling. "I mean, I get it. But, babe."

What came next was what she expected. The Nick version of a guilt trip. Reminders that Memaw had "shot her point-blank." Reminders that Morgan, "didn't owe that woman anything."

Ultimately, the greatest reminder was that Nick didn't know the full story. How could he? Morgan had only given him brief, tragic glimpses into her relationship with Esther Coyle.

Even so, Morgan *had* expected Nick to book the next flight out. This was his chance to meet her family. Their chance to reunite in what was shaping up to be a rough patch in Morgan's life—the death of a grandparent was never a *good* thing.

"He's not here, is he?" Morgan asked her mom. She couldn't quell the bitterness that burned on her tongue.

"Funerals are hard for *family* to attend. I wouldn't discount him just because he wasn't comfortable having his first foray into the Coyle clan at its matriarch's final memorial. Cut him a little slack. Plus, didn't you say it's busy season out there? Snowbirds moving in, and all that? Your new home is like a beacon of hope for northerners."

Morgan set a doily on her lap and spread it across with her fingers. Arizona had become a place she loved. A couple of years in, and she felt that in many ways. She felt it in finally having the money to buy her townhouse and do something with it. She even felt it in the real-estate business, to a degree. But it wasn't home.

She tuned into the moment at hand, feeling every lump and bump of the ivory yarn that wove in and out of the doily. She felt her hip, and the fact that the pain really had ebbed, even days after the nightmare that seemed to almost reverse everything that had happened before.

"I'm not so sure that Arizona—or Nick—is home, after all." Morgan let out a breath she didn't know she'd been holding. Maybe she'd been holding it for days. Weeks. Maybe a lot longer than that. She peeked at her mom. "It felt really good to say that."

CarlaMay moved the box of doilies to the floor and scooted over, reached an arm around Morgan, and pulled her in. "Oh, honey. It's not working out?"

Morgan felt herself start to cry, and the very idea of crying anymore reminded her of Grandad's funeral and how Memaw didn't cry. It reminded her of the last time that she ever saw Memaw cry. The *incident*. The thing that had changed everything. That had pushed Morgan even farther away from Brambleberry despite the fact that, at that time, Morgan was almost positive that Brambleberry was where she *was* supposed to be after all. And within Brambleberry, *here*. On the *farm*.

But there was still one problem.

She wiped at the tears and sniffed. "Mom..." Her voice

cracked, but Morgan pushed through. "I just, I really just want to be *here*."

CarlaMay devolved into a blubbering mess, too, and they held each other and cried. Into Morgan's neck, her mom whispered, "You stay, then, Morgan Jo. You just stay right here. Don't you worry about Tucson or Nick or your job there. We'll make it work *here*. We will."

"But how?" Morgan pushed her mom gently away and ran a hand over her eyes, smearing tears across her face. "Amber says she's getting the farm. She and Grant, and Tiffany and Travis. Since they live here. I just, I was actually worried about *you*, even. So how could *I* stay? It would cause a ton of drama, and—"

CarlaMay held up a hand. "We're not going to worry about that. The will spells everything out, Morgan."

Morgan perked up. "You've read it?"

"Read it? I'm a trustee. Barb and DanaSue and me, we all are. You can stay as long as you'd like."

It was a start, Morgan figured. Maybe not a long-term plan, but it was a start. She could stay, for a while. She could think of her next steps. She could sublet the townhouse in Tucson and finally decide where home really was. One thing still bothered her, though. And maybe it always would bother her.

"Mom?"

CarlaMay was clearing the last of her own tears and preparing to get up from the sofa. "Hmm?"

"How come Memaw didn't go to jail after what happened? And... why did she do it to begin with? Why did she have a gun? Why was she pointing it at Grandad? Why did she pull the trigger?" Morgan asked these questions in rapid succession, without any hint of emotion. They were questions she carried like a wallet, for reference. For currency, even. They were questions that, once answered, might put a lot of hurt to rest.

They were questions that Morgan didn't need answered in

order to forgive her grandmother. But they needed answering if she was going to move on.

CarlaMay frowned. "I thought you knew."

"How would I know? We never talked about it."

Her mom gave her a funny look. "Morgan, the letter."

"What letter?"

"The letter she wrote you. When you came home from the hospital, Julia and I—we passed along the letter. I just assumed Mom explained everything in there. Or, at least, some things. And since you never brought it up again—I didn't want to stoke the fire. I figured you'd gotten enough closure. Especially after you told me that you'd gone in and told Memaw that you forgave her. The night she passed, when you slept in her bed, I..."

But Morgan had stopped listening. She was up and moving, through the front hall, to the parlor where she'd spent her recovery. She couldn't well climb stairs back then, so they'd set her up on the pull-out. The only thing was—did they move that dresser out? The stout one with the...

Morgan froze. She turned on her heel.

Her mother remained at the sofa in the living room. In her hand, she held up the envelope.

Morgan walked slowly back toward her, eyes on the thick cream-colored rectangle. It had worn only slightly, maybe not even at all, having been preserved so neatly and for only a few years now.

"You found it," she said.

Her mom shook her head. "Barb did. When we went through the dresser drawers last night to look for some paperwork." Her mother held it out toward Morgan. "We didn't open it."

"Then how do you know what it says?"

CarlaMay shrugged. "I don't. But I know my mother. And I know she wouldn't have left you to wonder."

"But I did," Morgan murmured, mostly to herself. She'd been left to wonder ever since. By her own volition, her own pain. She'd been left to wonder why such a tragedy befell an otherwise happy, successful family.

And now she very well could have her answer.

She looked up as her mother rose from the sofa. "I'd better go back out there." CarlaMay indicated the reception out the window. "If you need anything—"

"I'm here." Julia appeared at the door. It was all so *coordinated*. Like they'd planned it.

Maybe they had.

Morgan and Julia sat on the sofa, Morgan's hand as shaky as her grandmother's stilted lettering. She pushed the tip of her finger beneath the flap and slid. The glue came up easily. It was long dried out. Brittle.

She peered inside. Together with the letter, a cloth of some kind. Morgan frowned at it then glanced at Julia, who gripped her leg. "Go on," Julia said. "See what it is."

Morgan pulled the cloth out first, unfolding it into her lap like she'd done with the doilies.

It was stained. Yellowish blobs that had clearly been scrubbed out. Morgan didn't know what from. Maybe bacon grease, she hoped.

Across, in threaded script, was Memaw's favorite saying: *If Mama Ain't Happy, Ain't Nobody Happy*.

A small laugh escaped Morgan's mouth. "This was her favorite dish towel. She always said so. It was, like, a *thing*."

Julia kept quiet but smiled encouragingly. Morgan left the towel on her lap and pulled a thin, single page.

She unfolded it, her hands quaking now at the sight of her grandmother's handwriting in full form. A page worth of slanted, careful words.

A page worth of their relationship. Grandmother and granddaughter.

Morgan read it to herself.

Dear Morgan Jo,

Words have no meaning anymore. Life barely does, neither. What happened, or what I done, it was wrong. Flat out wrong and I'm sorry to the bottom of my heart, Morgan Jo. I want you to know the truth about it all from start to finish, but it's so much to write or to say. I don't know if I can do it. Here is what I want you to know.

I want you to know that I lost someone before. I guess you know this, but I lost my sister, Dottie, and she was like my other half. That's what they say about twins, and it was true as the day is long, Morgan Jo. It don't excuse what happened between your grandaddy and me or what I done, but there it is. When Dottie died, something in me was changed for the rest of my life, I think. I wish it weren't that way, but there it is.

There's something else I want you to know.

I love you and your cousins and your mama and your aunts and uncles to the moon and back. I love you all just as much as I love your grandaddy, which is a whole great lot. The thing is though that your grandaddy is a hard man, Morgan Jo. I love him for it but he is a hard man. He can be a rough person on other people, but especially on me. I'm not writing this as an excuse as to what I did but just to tell you that you had nothin to do with what happened other than you tried to save him. If I was really going to shoot him then I would hope you would save him. But I wasn't. I was aggravated with him and I needed him to know that he was making me feel bad for something. Well, it was for Dottie's death. There you have it.

I write all of this down for you, Morgan Jo, because I didn't serve my time that I should have. Not in a jail cell, anyway. I served it in my heart and mind and I'll serve it until I die. I don't ask you for your forgiveness for what I done.

But I do want to ask you one thing. I want to ask you that you marry someone who treats you right. If you don't, then the hardness starts to rub off on you, like it has on me. A hard life will rub off on you and then you pass it on down and that's just wrong. So if you find a man and you decide you're going to love him, don't say yes unless you know for a fact that he will treat you nice. Always. Even when the going gets rough, which it will.

Morgan Jo, I don't know if I'll be around to see you get married or if I'll even be invited if I am. But aside from your wedding, if you'll let me be part of your life, I promise you, I won't ever do anything so wrong again. You can always open your business here, whatever it is you want to do. This is your home, Morgan Jo. Not only Moonshine Creek Farm, but Brambleberry, too. I hope you know that you can always come home to Brambleberry.

I love you with all my heart and all my soul, just as much as your Grandad did.

Memaw

CHAPTER FORTY-ONE
PRESENT DAY

Morgan Jo

After Morgan and Julia had both spent all their tears and hugged and laughed over memories of Memaw—good ones, bad ones, and everything in between—they rejoined the rest of the funeral. Amber and Grant were taking the mayor on a tour of the grounds. Julia exchanged a knowing eye roll with Morgan, but they pressed on, walking without true aim, but generally in the direction of the back field, where the hangar was.

"You gonna get that torn down?" Julia asked as they stood in front of it. "Now that you're back for good?"

"Yes. I'll ask Geddy to help."

"What'll you plan to do with the space?"

Morgan didn't know. And it wasn't only up to her. "Maybe something Memaw and Grandad would have liked."

"And your lil' Aunt Dottie?"

"I don't know what she liked."

"Maybe it's time to find out." Julia squeezed Morgan's shoulder. "I'm going to go get some food. You coming?"

Morgan shook her head. "I think I'll go in, explore a little."

Julia left her, aware that Morgan meant she didn't need anymore company. She was ready to face the past, alone or not.

But as Morgan picked her way across decades-old hay and rusted farming doodads inside the hangar, a voice echoed in from behind her. "Mo?"

There was only one other person who ever called Morgan *Mo*, besides Julia.

And he lived in Bardstown. Morgan turned slowly, bracing herself.

"Emmett Dawson."

Dressed in a black suit that fit so perfectly Morgan wanted to bite down on her knuckle, Emmett struck a remarkable figure in the wide-open doorway of the hangar. Beyond him, Morgan could make out the lines of the fence with its vines creeping like a web over wood so old it was a wonder to remain standing. And beyond that fence, the orchards.

Morgan looked again at Emmett. Her heart caught in her chest. His eyes fell sorrowfully above the mouth she used to be so familiar with. Once upon a time, Morgan had tasted that mouth, those lips. She'd curled her body into Emmett's and felt his heat and hers mix and match and make her insides go all gooey. Even though it was all so long ago, they'd had something. He'd *meant* something.

"Morgan Jo Coyle." Emmett matched the cadence of his own name on her tongue. He swallowed and cleared his throat. His Adam's apple bobbed up and down beneath a strong jaw. Practicing law hadn't affected that boy's athletic build. She imagined he probably spent his early mornings out in the woods, on a run. Thoughts of them as kids racing across the farm, her giggling and him kicking his knees up high and pretending he couldn't catch her when in truth, he always could have.

She pushed all those thoughts away and took a step toward him, but he met her more than halfway. His oncoming figure making her weak in the knees and sad all over again. It was hard, talking to people who knew Memaw way back when but maybe not so recently. Their memories of the old woman were only good ones. "What are you doing here?" she asked him, her voice catching.

"At Miss Essie's funeral? Geddy told me about it. Although, it made the papers up in B-Town, you know."

"But—"

"Why'd I come? Well, mainly to pay my respects."

"Were you at the service?"

"I stayed in the back." His hands were tucked deep in his pockets. He was taller than she remembered. More handsome, too. His blond hair had turned darker. His blue eyes were set deeper. His tan persisted, highlighting teeth so white he could star in a toothpaste commercial. "I hoped I'd get a chance to say hi to you."

"Well," Morgan replied, her own arms wrapped around herself protectively. "Hi."

"How's Arizona?"

She silently accepted that Geddy had probably filled him in. Maybe he even knew about the incident. But that was okay. It wasn't a family secret anymore. Not since Morgan had told the one adult man she thought she'd marry: Nick. But that was foolish. Just as soon as Memaw had died and Morgan called to tell Nick she was staying for the funeral—*would he come?* He'd laughed and said she wasn't the girl he thought she was. Nick only ever made Morgan feel ashamed of her family. It was like he couldn't understand how families work. That they could be broken but still intact. They'd split up over the phone. It was a later phone call after the one about the funeral. The conversation had been far easier than Morgan could have imagined. Apparently, when you weren't meant to be with someone, the break-up wasn't so traumatic. Nick must have had the same thought because he'd taken it all in stride, responding that he agreed they were "on different paths." Indeed, they were. While Nick was trying to shoot up to the sky, Morgan was hoping to ground herself here, on earth, in Brambleberry.

After that, Morgan had felt a new light about everything. The incident, though objectively bad, wasn't necessarily something to feel shameful about anymore. It was just part of who Morgan was. A fact of her life. A fact of Memaw's life, too. A fact, indeed, of their bond. "Arizona is in the rearview." She hadn't expected she'd get to share this news with Emmett. She held her breath for his reaction.

Surprise lit up his face. "Oh? Where to next?"

"Here."

"The farm?" He stepped closer.

"The farm. Brambleberry. Kentucky. Yeah." She let go of her arms and let her hands slide to her sides, opening her palms in vulnerability.

A broad smile grew over his face.

Morgan took a step closer. They were just about a foot apart. She could smell him. He smelled just like she remembered. Whiskey and wood and a little bluegrass. He smelled like Kentucky. Not like unfamiliar cologne or sharp aftershave. He smelled like the Emmett she remembered. Memories of him flooded back to Morgan.

She smiled back then looked down before taking a deep breath and returning her gaze to Emmett's. "So. How's Bardstown?"

"Good. Real good. I'm in law."

"I know."

"Oh, you do?" He twisted, and somehow it brought him half a step closer to her. He looked up into the cavern of the hangar. She inhaled another breath of him and just about swooned. "What're you up to in here?" He returned his eyes to hers. "It's probably not safe."

"What, you a liability lawyer?" she teased.

"Naw." He kicked at a small heap of hay then his head snapped up. "I'm sorry." His foot worked the hay back in place, and Morgan laughed at the little-boy gentlemanliness that was Emmett Dawson.

"So, what kind of law do you practice, then?"

"Family law."

Morgan winced. "Like, divorce and stuff?"

"Actually, more like estates and trusts."

Morgan nodded. "Well, you should stick around, then. We might just need your help."

"Really? 'Cause I heard Miss Essie did a bang-up job."

"You heard that, did you?" Morgan didn't buy it. She hadn't seen the will or the trust or whatever yet. She'd only known what her mom said and what Amber threatened, but still, Morgan trusted that everything would work out in the end. Because ultimately, Morgan trusted Memaw, despite their ups and downs.

"What're you doing after this?" Emmett asked, almost shyly.

Morgan looked at him. "What am I doing after my grand-mother's funeral?" But it occurred to her that, actually, she didn't have plans. She'd done all the crying she needed to. A lot of the reminiscing, too. And since she'd been back in Bramble-berry, she hadn't yet even been out much. Not around town, at least. "I don't have any plans."

"Can I take you to dinner?" His face reddened and he shook his head and took a step back, holding his hands up in front of him. "That was crazy. I'm sorry. Your grandmother just passed. We're at her funeral, I just meant—I just wondered if—"

Morgan closed the gap between them and grabbed his hands. "If you're asking your high school sweetheart on a date, the answer is yes." Maybe it was the passage of time or simply the funeral itself, but Morgan was coming to a new under-standing of her life. Of any life, actually. It was short. Too short to spend chasing a dream that wasn't hers in a city with prickly cactus rather than supple bluegrass. Life was too short not to be with Emmett. Seeing him again had made her heart leap in a way that it hadn't in years. She knew in that very moment that *this* was what was always meant to be.

Emmett's face lit up and he held her hands back, their fingers slotting into place, laced together, like way back when. "Really?"

Morgan fell into him, their hands separating as they hugged one another. His familiar scent enveloped her. A farm boy fresh out of the bathtub. Whiskey and woods. And a little bluegrass. No fuss. No cologne. No pretenses.

But Emmett drew back, and worry shadowed his features. "So, you and Nick broke up for good?"

"You know about Nick, too?" she finished his question.

He nodded. "Word gets around the family."

The family. Like he was part of it. Butterflies tickled her insides.

"We broke up for good."

"Any particular reason?"

Morgan smirked. "Several of them."

"Sounds pretty final." The way he said this made Morgan realize then and there that no matter where she'd gone or where he'd gone, neither one of them had forgotten the other. Neither one of them had let their heart get lost in the distance or the time. Or in another person. At least, not *all* the way. His voice lower now, he added, "I guess he wasn't the one for you, then."

Morgan grinned, an ear-to-ear type of grin. "Nope, I guess not."

"Oh?" Emmett curled his hands back into hers and pulled her into him, their hips pressed together, him entirely comfortable with the lilt in her posture. Her, entirely comfortable with the icy burn that shot up her side when their bodies touched. Emmett ducked his face closer to hers. His eyes fell to her mouth. "You needed someone who could beat you in a cherry-pit spittin' contest."

"Yes," she whispered. "Someone who could pull me up out of the lake if I fell..." As the words curled over her tongue and out her mouth, Emmett dropped his lips to hers and before she could finish her sentence, they were kissing, and it was like old times, and Morgan wasn't falling into a lake or a job she didn't want. She wasn't falling for the idea that happiness was far, far away. She was falling in love with the same man she'd always loved. She'd just lost him for a while.

Morgan released Emmett's hands and ran hers up his chest, linking them behind his neck, as his lips brushed over hers and she slipped her tongue into his mouth and met his and her hip throbbed with a different sensation than pain. Thoughts of the funeral and Memaw whipped like wind into her brain, but she couldn't silence them. Morgan pushed Emmett away gently. "You know what I really need?"

He looked at her, his eyes lazy in love and his lips wet, parted. Hungry. "What?"

"I need someone who'll take me skinny-dipping."

CHAPTER FORTY-TWO

TWO MONTHS LATER

Morgan Jo

It was Saturday morning, and Emmett had come over for breakfast—biscuits and gravy, sausages, and coffee. He'd started coming for breakfast every Saturday at some point in October, when the weather cooled and they'd agreed that what they were doing—Morgan and Emmett—was more than a fling or a rebound. Plus, CarlaMay had said he ought to, and Emmett had never been one to disrespect somebody's mother.

This particular Saturday morning, Morgan suggested they cut through the fence out back, loop around the lake, and traverse through the orchards. Harvest season was over, but since he was around, maybe Emmett could help her check the apple trees and peach trees for any late bloomers. Also, Morgan had heard tell of a pecan tree that could do with a good shake to clear the last of its dregs, too.

Emmett was quick to agree to the walk, but they hadn't gotten as far as the fence before he stopped Morgan, tugging her back to him and pulling her so that she didn't have to face the crisp breeze.

He looked her in the eye, unsmiling, when he said, "I want to talk about something serious, Mo."

Morgan braced herself, but she nodded. "Okay."

"How are you feeling?"

"Feeling?"

"About Miss Essie's death? About your being home, and all? About everything."

Morgan considered this and looked away for a moment. "I'm still grieving, I think."

"That's natural, Mo. You might even carry that grief for a good, long while."

"But I'm feeling okay." She smiled. "I'm happy, in fact."

"Do you think you're getting back to normal? You and your family, I mean?" It was natural for Emmett to direct them to such a heavy topic as this. With his living in Bardstown, their conversations were limited to evening texts and phone calls, and much of that had been light and flirtatious, with only occasional exchanges about more grave matters, such as Morgan's sadness or even a challenging client Emmett was working with.

Morgan thought about the word he said. *Normal*. A saying came to mind. One that had been embroidered to her heart long ago. She pursed her lips then told Emmett, "As far as anyone knows, we're a nice, *normal* family, Emmett."

No explanation was necessary. Emmett knew the adage and the sign in Memaw's kitchen. The pair broke into peals of laughter. Morgan realized she didn't remember the last time she laughed so hard. He understood her, and that neither Morgan nor her family was normal.

And Morgan knew that Emmett wasn't either because what did normal mean, anyway? And who lived up to the idea of normalcy?

Did normal mean you had a grandmother who played checkers with you and baked cinnamon rolls and warned you off of dating?

"You know," Emmett said after giving her a quick peck and leading her off through the gap in the fence and toward the lake, "when I was growing up, before you and me met, I wanted to be a farmer."

"You did?" she scrunched up her features. It wasn't surprising to hear. In fact, if anything was surprising it was that Emmett had become a lawyer. He seemed more like an outdoors type.

"That's right. You know my mom and dad never quite fit into Bardstown that way, what with him a lawyer and her coming from money." It was no secret Emmett's mama was some rich lady from California. She'd met his daddy when they were in college, and that they settled in Bardstown was always a curiosity to Morgan. But he'd thwarted his parents' examples, instead following in the footsteps of his aunts and uncles and cousins, who were country bumpkins. That's probably why people loved Emmett. He was down-home and kind-hearted. A real salt-of-the-earth guy. Morgan's heart swelled just thinking about who he was inside of his good-looking exterior.

"You could still open a farm. Even up in Bardstown," she pointed out.

"Maybe I will. Did you know my Aunt Pepper raised cattle? She married someone who started a steakhouse. The steakhouse is still around, and Aunt Pepper still breeds."

"That'd be hard," Morgan replied. "I could never slaughter an animal."

"Yeah. I'd rather raise crops, I think." He slowed and gave her a wink. "But you won't find me giving up hamburgers any time soon."

"Me either."

They came to the backside of the orchard, and Emmett pointed. "Is that a *pear* tree?"

She followed his finger to a small tree with yellow fruit

hanging down low on it. "I didn't know they had pear trees. I don't remember this one."

Morgan marveled over the heavy, ripe green fruits. She picked one and took a bite. It was juicy and mildly sweet. She offered it to Emmett, who bit from the far side and hummed contentedly. "That's the most perfect pear I've ever tasted in my life." He stepped back and looked up at the tree. "These all look ripe. I bet it's pickin' time for these babies."

They ran back to the barn where Morgan found three metal pails and they headed back out to collect as many of the pears as they could. They only filled two of the buckets, which was still a great haul for a surprise discovery.

When she and Emmett returned to the big house, Morgan spotted Julia's car parked out around the side. Julia leaned up against the hood with a paperback in her hands, reading and oblivious to the nip in the air.

"Go on into to the washroom," she told Emmett and took the third pail with her to return to the barn. Emmett gave Julia a wave and headed in.

"What are you doing here?" Morgan called to her friend.

"We had lunch plans, remember?" Julia looked over her book at Morgan who strode her way. "I guess you've got other things on your mind these days."

Morgan checked her watch. "You're half an hour early. I bet you came to spy on me. You knew Emmett would be here."

Julia held up her book and laughed. "You got me. If I don't have my own person to make out with, it'd be nice to live vicariously, at least."

"That's disgusting," Morgan said, but she laughed. "You can head into the washroom. I'll be right there. I'm just going to put this back in the barn."

But Julia grabbed the pail and looked at her own wristwatch. "You two still have thirty minutes. I'll make myself busy in the barn."

Morgan rolled her eyes but secretly, she loved that Julia loved her and Emmett together. "In that case, can you dig around for a funnel while you're in there? Like, a big one? Something for us to use for this." Morgan held up her bucket of pears. Julia nodded and left for the barn.

When Morgan joined Emmett in the washroom, she grabbed up the first bucket and lifted it to the basin. "I'll set about rinsing these. Why don't you look up something we could turn them into."

"Like a dessert?" Emmett asked as he leaned against the door frame and scrolled his phone. "Or we could can them?" He was off to the races and Morgan brainstormed what she could use right about now. She wondered if Memaw had ever used pears for anything. *Surely she had, but what? Just for canning? Or what about Grandad? Maybe he'd made wine from pears?* "Do you make wine from pears?" she asked Emmett as she continued to rinse and stare out the window.

"Let me see." A few beats passed. "It's called perry, not wine. That's funny."

"Hm. Perry. Sounds *fancy*. We could do that?" Morgan took each fruit and ran it beneath the basin faucet. Then, someone outside caught her eye.

Amber was crossing the backyard, maybe on her way to talk to Travis. More often than not, Amber didn't come into the big house when she got home. Not right away, but that had nothing to do with Morgan. In fact, Morgan and Amber had found they had more in common than they'd previously realized. They were getting along well. It was probably more to do with Grant that Amber hid out in the bunkhouses half the time...

Ever since the weeks following Memaw's passing, Morgan and her mom were no longer the only ones who lived in the big house anymore.

Technically, the house itself was left to Morgan in the will. Her grandparents had made the change relatively recently, and it had apparently been a big to-do. The family lawyer had explained all of this with everyone present. Morgan's aunts, uncles, and cousins—everyone. They'd gathered for the reading of the will, like in some soap opera, and by the time it came to discuss who'd get the farm and all it included, ripples of anticipation had coursed through the small office.

Once the lawyer had said "Morgan Jo Coyle," a brief silence swelled then popped. Everyone cried, and—strangely—no one argued. They'd agreed that after what had happened—after the *incident*—it was okay for Morgan to have the house and grounds as reparations, of sorts. In fact, it hadn't even been a surprise. Well, it had to Morgan, who hadn't known about the big inheritance. Later, her mother would tell her Garold had pushed back privately. This had made Morgan uncomfortable until Geddy came to her and told her not to worry about his dad. Garold, just like everyone else, had something going for him somewhere else. Everyone else in the family agreed. Morgan had been searching for long enough.

It was time she found what she was looking for.

The sentiments and group support had been overwhelming, and at first, Morgan had actually asked about divvying up the property. But in fact, it came down to another matter. As much as anyone would love to own a hunk of history—and a valuable one, at that—no one wanted the responsibility of it. The bills and work were a lot, and Morgan had her work cut out for her.

But despite the fact that Morgan maybe deserved the farm in some twisted way, she couldn't stand to lord over her cousins like that. Besides, Morgan had made her peace with Memaw, and she was certain that Memaw knew that. Morgan felt it in her blood, deep down in her bones. In everything that Morgan was, her grandmother's presence was there, too. Sometimes, she wondered what might have happened had she read the letter sooner. Would she have had more time with Memaw? More good days? Maybe, maybe not. But there was no looking back.

Besides, Morgan had had plenty of good days with Memaw. Some of them, in fact, were the best days of her life. Going bra shopping. Talking about love and dating and Memaw's idea of a good match. Those good things, the good words and actions and all the love, it lived on through Morgan. She made sure of it.

CHAPTER FORTY-THREE

PRESENT DAY

Morgan Jo

While Barb and DanaSue had a hard time after Memaw's death, it was naturally CarlaMay who struggled the most. Morgan came upon her crying over little things at least once a day. A tub of homemade butter in the fridge—Memaw had churned it just a week before her stroke. A book of psalms that Essie had taken from the church's "Free Books" bin, complete with a crocheted bookmark. Morgan ended up crying, too. There were spells of time, too, that they'd both somehow forgotten that Memaw had died, like when they went to the Dewdrop and CarlaMay wondered aloud if she should take the leftovers home for her mother. Or when they got a phone call from someone who'd missed the memo, an old church friend who'd moved away. And the friend asked for Essie and Morgan said, "Just a moment, please," but then she had to come back on the line, shaking her head and furrowing her brows and telling the unsuspecting fool that Essie was long gone from this world.

But as they say, time can be a great healer, and as days turned to weeks and weeks to months, an acceptance fell over the household. With it, inspiration to do better. To bring the family back from the edge and to try and recapture the goodness that was at the very heart of the Nelson clan.

Eventually, this inspiration took the shape of natural changes, which set themselves into motion at the Moonshine Creek Farm. So much so, that it had made sense for new room and board assignments.

Seniority had it that CarlaMay got Memaw's old bedroom. At first, she'd balked. She couldn't sleep in the bed where her mother died. Could she?

It turned out she could, and it was a great comfort, even. Some mornings, CarlaMay would join Morgan in the kitchen for coffee and recount a dream she'd had about her mother and how everything was white and clean, and everybody was happy with one another. One day, she'd get a new bed and decorate. It was only sensible that she should, but for now, CarlaMay took great comfort, macabre though some may see it, in sleeping in that bed and living in that room.

Morgan kept her own room. She loved that it had always been her room, and she couldn't see herself out of it. Tiffany was offered CarlaMay's, and she took it. Travis and Geddy were also offered a room, but they declined, citing "Gentleman's Privacy," whatever that meant.

Amber and Grant were offered the basement, which came complete with a private bedroom and en suite bathroom. They agreed readily and lived down there together in occasional peace.

That left all the girls (and Grant) in the house, together, and the two boys at the bunkhouses still. Morgan took it upon herself to write up official rental agreements that stated the boys were free to live in the bunkhouses, so long as they kept the places in good working order. For eternity, or until Morgan died, at least.

As for the barn and the hangar, Morgan figured she'd better

think of something fast. The last position she wanted to be in was that of a mooch. Even Tiffany and Amber had jobs and pitched in for utilities and groceries, paying their fair shares. Morgan wasn't about to become the very thing she'd not too long ago scorned.

At first, her mom encouraged her to fix up the now-vacant bunkhouses and the barn and put them up as rental income. Morgan had the property-management experience. She could do some light renovations and add simple, pleasant decor. Initially, Morgan agreed it made sense. She'd pull in enough income to handle all the operations there on the farm without compromising its natural and long-held beauty. Rental income would mean repairs were a given. Paint, upgrades, the crops could even come back to life if they wanted to. She'd cover the utilities with rental income—and her mother and cousins wouldn't have to put out a dime, which was Morgan's long-term goal.

But it felt all wrong.

There had to be something more.

Most importantly, though, something had to be done about the infamous hangar.

* * *

"Here," Emmett said, stirring Morgan from her reverie. He joined her at the sink, showing her his phone screen, which had a simple recipe for perry. Simple for people who regularly made wine, maybe.

"Hang on," Morgan told Emmett. She pushed up on her toes to kiss him on the cheek, but he turned his face and her lips brushed his. Emmett held her up to him by wrapping his arms around her waist and pulling her close.

They kissed again, this time slower and longer, and butter-flies—always butterflies—fluttered inside of Morgan. Moments like this revealed to her how you could be excited to love someone and yet utterly comfortable with him all at once.

Morgan pulled back, smiled, and tapped her finger on Emmett's nose. "Love you," she said.

"Love you." He pecked her once more then released her.

Morgan swung past him to holler out the open door. "Amber! Come 'ere!"

"Hey, you all!" Amber greeted, bubbly as ever. She bounced up to the back door and looked around. "What're those for?" She pointed to the pears.

"We're gonna try to make something called perry. I guess it's like wine made out of pears," Morgan replied. "Do you know if Grandad ever made this? They had a pear tree."

She thought back on the past few months and all that she'd learned of her new, *old* world.

Once Morgan had settled back into the big house, she'd helped her mom nose through Memaw's things. They'd eventually made their way out to the barn, where Grandad had kept all his wine-making accessories. They were old and grimy and unusable, but just to see the miniature factory he was operating in there, years ago, had given Morgan a spark. She'd loved drinking Grandad's wine when she'd still had bottles of it. But returning home, she'd found that there were none left. The drink was so delicious that even Memaw hadn't thought to save one single bottle of the stuff.

Then again, could have been that Memaw had come across a hoard of the wine and dumped it all out. It wasn't only the old woman's letter that had finally cued Morgan into the reality of living with a man like Bill Coyle. Bit by bit, her mother and her aunts had emitted small revelations. Grandad had been tough on them growing up. He'd been tough on their mother. Cranky, mostly, but sometimes a little mean, too. Those emissions had reminded Morgan about how sometimes she'd felt that heat as a girl. Almost as though she'd stowed the memories away out of some way to protect who she was and where she'd come from. But they were there, down deep. The days he'd snap at her over touching one of his things or sitting in a chair that was meant for just looking at. Hollering at her to get her feet off the sofa since sofas were for sitting and not lying. Those little nuggets were a reminder that while Morgan *knew* her grandfather was a good man, he wasn't always an easy person. And that probably was felt the most by none other than his wife: Memaw.

Morgan was still sad, however, to find that not one of Grandad's recipes or set of directions existed. She couldn't replicate the tart blackberry wine or the warm, sweet cherry wine he'd crafted. Not exactly, at least.

And yet something pulled her to do just that. To connect with not only her grandfather, who'd made the stuff with the very berries he'd picked there on the farm, but to connect with the farm itself. With Memaw, who grew up eating those berries. With her great-grandparents who used the land to make a go of it. The original Brambleberry Bootleggers themselves.

Morgan chuckled at this thought and gave her head a shake. "I mean, they still have the pear trees here. On the property. Obviously." She held up a yellow fruit.

"Perry? Well, yeah." Amber looked like she'd forgotten she was headed anywhere else than the big house, and she sidled up at the sink with Morgan. "Now that you mention it, I think I saw him make some once. You were there, Morgan. We were kids. Remember? Travis hated pears, and so Grandad joked he'd like his special pear juice, and Travis knew it was alcoholic—we were like, thirteen or so. Anyway, Travis asked for a sip and Grandad offered him one, and Travis hated it something awful." She laughed. "Anyhow, don't you remember? Grandad made Travis drink the whole glass of it, and that boy was rolling out of the barn."

"You know how to make it?"

"No, but I bet we could figure it out," she replied.

Emmett waved his phone helpfully, but Morgan was a little unsatisfied. She'd love to know for real how Grandad had made it. She'd love to be able to transport back in time and *watch* him, even. Of course, that was a pipe dream. Maybe the internet would have to do.

"That'd be a great idea for your business," Amber said.

Amber was motivated by Morgan making a business of the farm, despite the fact that she did well for herself as a hairdresser on Main.

Morgan had a suspicion about Amber, though. Amber might be less satisfied with her life than she led on. Maybe, like Morgan, Amber was searching for something more, too.

"What business, Amber?" Morgan asked, crossing her arms and giving her cousin an impatient look. As if Morgan had anywhere else to be.

"Well, now, see, I've been thinking about it. And talking. And I have a client talking to me while I'm doing her perm, now, see."

"Perm?" Morgan cut in.

"This isn't the West Coast, Morgan Jo," Amber said on a sigh. "Anyhow, yes. A perm. And she's telling me that her daughter's comin' down to B-Town to get married, and at first I'm all sore about it, but then I asked her, well, where in the hell she gon' have the reception?"

"Okay." Morgan knew where this was going, and she wasn't that interested.

But Amber gave her a look. "The Bourbon Trail Bridal Hall, out off of Rolling Fork."

"Okay." Morgan's curiosity ratcheted up a notch. "So, they have a venue. So, what does that have to do with us?"

"Well, she said the shower's next week, and this woman with the perm, see, she was gon' host the shower, but her basement flooded with that storm we just had, see, and her husband's real aggravated about it all, and he says they can't have the shower anymore."

They were back at square one. "Amber," Morgan interjected, "I don't think I want to do that."

"What, you don't want host a bridal shower?"

"Right. I mean—"

"But that's what Memaw loved to do. I think she figured we'd carry it on, you know?"

"Memaw hosted events, not just bridal showers."

"I know, Morgan Jo. She hosted events. *Such as* bridal or even baby showers. People *pay* for that kind of a thing, ya know? You're leaving money on the table. Every day that barn sits empty, you're leaving money on the table. And the hangar, too. It's an opportunity."

Morgan swallowed this point down, and it hit the bottom of her stomach like a brick. Memaw hated waste, and it was true that she loved to host events. Was it up to Morgan Jo to carry on a legacy she had no interest in? Was it up to Morgan to make something of the barn or the hangar? Or should she just tear them both down, ultimately fulfilling her grandmother's greatest single wish?

Or was it up to Morgan Jo to follow her dream and somehow *incorporate* her grandmother's wish as well as her legacy?

But then, what about the waste? What about leaving money on the table month after month?

The back door whooshed open, and in through it fell Julia, who'd returned from the barn.

Julia had returned with something in her hands. A brass object—to the layman it might look like an urn. Morgan knew better, though. Julia probably didn't realize what she held in her hand was an antique spittoon.

"Julia, hey," Morgan greeted her. "Don't worry about the

funnel. I found one in the kitchen. Thanks anyway." Then, she frowned. "What took you so long?"

Amber interrupted. "Julia, don't you think Morgan Jo should open an events business here, on the farm? Picture it: *Moonshine Creek Farm Fun and Events*." Amber framed her invisible words in the air, but even Julia made a face.

"Mo would hate that." Then, Julia turned to Morgan and lifted the vessel. "Look what I found." She set it on the sideboard of the basin, and the three of them crowded around as Morgan assessed the thing.

It was definitely an old, rusty spittoon. No doubt one of Grandad's or Great Grandaddy Coyle's. The insignia was hard to make out, but Morgan managed. "*Moonshine Creek Farm Tobacco Growers*." Morgan gave a solemn nod. She knew that Memaw'd had dozens of these and other such relics from when the farm was in its heyday.

"Wow," Julia marveled. "Is it a vase?"

Morgan shook her head. "It's a spittoon. But they had a ton. These and canteens and everything else. Memaw and Grandad had 'em all made up back when they gifted stuff to distributors."

Amber looked confused.

Morgan asked, "Don't you remember? Grandad used one in the house when we were kids and he chewed tobacco back then. Memaw was always hollering at him to quit it. It was so gross."

Amber made a face. "Still is gross, I guess."

But Julia tipped the opening toward them. "No, it's got something in it. Look, Mo."

Morgan peered into the shallow darkness of the brass antique and saw what looked like a book. She reached in and pulled it out. She had to roll it to get it through the opening, but the book was thin, and bound in cheap leather, or maybe imitation stuff. No title or words on the front.

She opened it. The lettering on the pages within were

nothing short of chicken scratch, and every word seemed misspelled or badly formed.

Morgan looked at Amber, passing the book along. "What is this?"

Amber turned more serious. "It looks like Grandad's handwriting."

"You remember his handwriting, but you don't remember him spittin'?" Julia asked.

Amber shrugged and hooked a thumb at Morgan. "She didn't remember when Travis got drunk off of perry when we were kids."

"She's right," Morgan agreed. "It's his handwriting."

"What is it though? I can barely read it," Amber added. Morgan felt the same. They passed it to Julia who squinted and fell quiet. Her lips moved silently. At last, she looked up. "Mo, it's his wine recipes."

Morgan took the book back and looked again. Across the top of each page, though faded with time and the impermanence of pencil lead were labels, clear as day, even if they weren't quite spelled right.

"Look here," Amber pointed to the inside front cover. Just barely, they could make out a title for the book.

MOONSHINE WINE BY BILL COYLE

Morgan shook her head in disbelief, then she turned the pages, reading each and every last one.

REGALAR WINE MADE WITH GRAPE
PLUM WINE
WINE MADE OF PEECHS
PERRY WINE—PERR WINE (A.K.A.)
GOOSE BARY WINE
BOYS 'N' BARY WINE

STRAW BARY WINE
WINE MADE OFF THE BRAMBEL VINES –
BLACK OR RAZZ BARYS

Julia was right. She'd found them. Grandad's wine recipes.

Emmett leaned over her shoulder and said, "If I didn't know any better, I'd say this is a family artifact."

"It's a recipe book," Morgan whispered.

And just like *that*, Morgan knew what business she was going to open. She knew what was next for Moonshine Creek Farm. And it'd be a little bit of everything. A little bit of Grandad's wine. A little bit of Memaw's events. And a little bit of Morgan's love for history.

Especially, her love for the history of her very own family, there at the farm with the wild vines and the brass spittoons and the stained dish towels, south of the Bourbon Trail, in Brambleberry.

"Maybe Memaw did have a good idea," she murmured.

Amber said, "You mean about opening up a distillery?"

Morgan looked at her sharply. "She told you about that, too?"

"Yep. She said she thought maybe Grant could help tear down the old hangar and erect a real bourbon room there."

"I have no idea how to make bourbon," Morgan said, regretfully, but as she turned the brittle pages in her hand, Julia spoke.

"You know how to make wine, though."

Morgan smiled at Julia then at Amber. She thought about the wine recipes that Grandad had left behind like a hidden treasure. The old hangar that needed to come down and be home to something else. The future of her grandparents' legacy... Morgan couldn't do it all alone.

"You two will help me?" she asked Amber and Julia in turn.

Each nodded her head, and a small, quiet agreement formed

among the three of them. A new beginning, a shared business, and a chance to unravel, over time, the secrets that still remained at Moonshine Creek. But they'd do it together, all three of them.

Maybe four of them, in fact. Morgan sighed and looked up at Emmett.

"Mo Jo," Emmett said, "I think you've found what you were looking for."

She closed the book and swiveled into him, pressing the small volume against Emmett's chest and looking into his dreamy blue eyes. "Actually, I never lost it."

He slid his arms around her waist and lifted her up, twirling her in a circle before easing her back to the ground and kissing her, chastely, on the lips.

In fact, Morgan had found everything she'd ever searched for. She'd found love. She'd found the truth about her family. Forgiveness in her heart.

But mostly, Morgan Jo had found home, right there, in Brambleberry Creek.

A LETTER FROM ELIZABETH

Dear reader,

I'd like to thank you most sincerely for choosing to read *The House by the Creek*. If you did enjoy it and want to keep up to date with all my latest releases, just sign up at the following link. Your email address will never be shared and you can unsubscribe at any time.

www.bookouture.com/elizabeth-bromke

I hope you enjoyed *The House by the Creek*. If you did, I would be so grateful if you could write a review. I'd love to hear what you think, and it makes such a difference helping new readers to discover one of my books for the first time.

I love hearing from my readers! You can always get in touch with me on my Facebook, Twitter, or Instagram pages, or through my website.

Sincerely,

Elizabeth Bromke

KEEP IN TOUCH WITH ELIZABETH

www.elizabethbromke.com

 facebook.com/elizabethbromke

twitter.com/elizabethbromke

instagram.com/authorelizabethbromke

ACKNOWLEDGMENTS

Before this book, I never knew how many people could possibly make such a big mark on a story. First of all, I'd like to thank my incredible team at Bookouture. Natasha Harding—your faith in my capabilities and your enthusiasm for this book have been nothing short of inspiring. Thank you so much for all your hard work on this story—from sweeping structural ideas to the finer points of word choice. You are a master editor and are fast becoming a wonderful friend. I am ever grateful to you for bringing me into Bookouture and helping this book become what it is. Thank you!

Thank you most sincerely to Lucy Cowie for your masterful hand at copyediting this story. Your careful attention really makes Morgan and company shine. You are so lovely!

Lizzie Brien, for your hard work on producing and distributing the book, thank you! I'd also love to thank the following for their invaluable contributions to *Brambleberry*: Ruth Tross, Jenny Geras, Peta Nightingale, Kim Nash, and Natalie Butlin. Thank you each for helping bring my work to the world.

My wonderful readers, my ARC team, editors past and present, cover designers, and writerly friends: thank you for being my tribe!

Naturally, there is one special woman I can't go without mentioning. My very own Memaw, Rita Flanagan. Grandma, thank you for showing me that women must be strong. Thank you for teaching me that you only get somewhere in life if you take risks. Every risk I've taken is because of you. I love you, and I am so lucky to have experienced the world because of you.

On a similar note, I wish to thank Grandbob for being a mainstay of loyalty, honesty, and hard work. Thank you for being ever willing to talk to me and teach me about your life and times whenever I call. You drop what you're doing and take me on a tour through time and space, and I'm ever grateful. I love you.

Grandma Engelhard and Grandpa E. in heaven, you know your footprints are on my heart and on my work. Your gentleness and kindness, stability, and values are imprinted in everything I am and everything I do. I love you.

My parents, my brother, aunts, uncles, and cousins—thank you for giving me a full upbringing from which I can draw rich characters and anecdotes. The same goes for my fabulous in-laws in Philadelphia and Florida. I love you all.

Lastly and always most importantly, Ed and Eddie: always for you.

Made in the USA
Middletown, DE
14 January 2023

22132117R00161